ALSO BY AMULYA MALLADI

Song of the Cuckoo Bird

Serving Crazy with Curry

The Mango Season

A Breath of Fresh Air

THE SOUND OF LANGUAGE

THE SOUND OF
LANGUAGE

a novel

AMULYA MALLADI

BALLANTINE BOOKS / NEW YORK

A Ballantine Books Trade Paperback Original

Copyright © 2008 by Amulya Malladi
Reading group guide copyright © 2008 by Random House, Inc.

Published in the United States by Ballantine Books, an imprint of The Random House Publishing Group, a division of Random House, Inc., New York.

BALLANTINE and colophon are registered trademarks of Random House, Inc.
RANDOM HOUSE READER'S CIRCLE and colophon are trademarks of Random House, Inc.

LIBRARY OF CONGRESS CATALOGING-IN-PUBLICATION DATA
Malladi, Amulya.
The sound of language : a novel / Amulya Malladi.
p. cm.
ISBN 978-0-345-48316-4 (pbk.)
1. Afghans—Denmark—Fiction. I. Title.
PS3613.A453S65 2008   813'.6—dc22   2007028571

Printed in the United States of America

www.randomhousereaderscircle.com

2 4 6 8 9 7 5 3 1

Book design by Casey Hampton

For refugees everywhere — may you find home

THE SOUND OF LANGUAGE

ONE

15 MARCH 1980

When we first decided to become hobby beekeepers, it was because our friend Ole had been doing it for a very long time and seemed to find a lot of solace in the rituals and responsibility. But I had some doubts.

The wings of honeybees stroke about 11,400 times per minute—hence the distinctive buzz. I wondered about the buzzing of the bees. I was sure that constant hum would drive me crazy. But now, after a few seasons, the buzz of the bees is like a soothing rhythm, almost like a song, the song of spring.

Skive, Denmark—January 2002

Bzzzzzz, that was how she thought it sounded.

Bzzzzzz, like the buzzing of a thousand bees.

The same sound she used to hear when she visited her uncle Chacha Bashir in Baharak. He had been one of the wealthiest men in town with his silk and bee farm. Silk and honey, he would say, "The riches of the kings are mine." Then the Taliban killed him and no one knew what happened to his family.

That was how the Danish language sounded to Raihana, like the buzzing of Chacha Bashir's bees.

The Danes mumbled, she thought as she watched them in supermarkets, on television, and on the streets. She had never seen so many white people before, and this was the first time she was seeing white people at such close proximity. So she stared at them, she just couldn't help it.

They were different from what she had imagined. They were not all tall and fair and beautiful, some of them were short and ugly. And they mumbled when they spoke. The standing joke, Layla had told her, was that they spoke like they had hot potatoes in their mouths and Raihana agreed.

She had escaped a second brutally cold winter at the Jalozai refugee camp in North Western Pakistan when the Danish government offered her asylum. It was difficult for a single woman with no family, no husband, and no education to survive. Her choices had been limited. She could either die in a refugee camp where the cold wind from the mountains pierced its frozen fingers through the tents to all but peel the skin off the bones, or she could go to this country where her distant cousin and his wife had agreed to give her a home.

A part of her didn't want to leave the camp. She had to wait, she thought, wait for Aamir, or maybe go back and look for him? But even she wasn't foolish enough to go back to Kabul. Everyone knew that Osama bin Laden was responsible for the plane attacks in America and everyone knew that the Taliban were the same species as al-Qaeda. America would attack; that's what powerful countries did. The Taliban would fight back, they said, and though the Afghans in Denmark, like many others, didn't like the idea of American troops on

Afghan soil, it was better than the Taliban. Some thought the Taliban had been unjustly rousted out of power, that they were the good guys.

So Raihana joined the small number of refugees living in Denmark, all of whom watched the news with desperation, wondering when they could go back. Afghanistan, they knew, would be a war ruin for several decades to come, but there was still hope. They wished that, somehow, Afghanistan would no longer be synonymous with tortured men and women living in penury. Maybe things would change and Afghanistan would become a safe haven, a progressive country, a normal country.

"Have to go home someday, can't live here all our life can we?" Kabir would say almost every day. "Don't unpack everything, Raihana, we'll go back soon."

"Go back to what?" Layla would ask her husband, her hands on her hips as her son, Shahrukh, pulled at her *salwar*.

"*Mor, slik,*" he said, pleading with his mother to give him candy, which she had strict rules about not giving to him.

"Look at him, *hai*, Shahrukh, it is not *Mor*, it is *Ammi*, say *Ammi*," Kabir said as he always did, but Shahrukh never took him seriously. "*Mor* is some Danish woman, not Layla, she is *Ammi*. Now say *Ammi*."

"Leave him alone, he's just two," Layla said. "And he's calling me mother, not some evil name. All his friends call their mothers *Mor*, so he calls me *Mor*."

Raihana watched the young couple battle about going back, about staying. She had been scared when the people from the Danish immigration told her that Kabir wanted her to live with him. She remembered Kabir from her childhood, a long time ago. He was her mother's sister's husband's brother's son. The families had not been close, only meeting at weddings and celebrations. Kabir's family had lived in Kabul while hers settled in a village outside Kabul. But he was the only one who had offered her a chance to leave the refugee camp and she had taken it. She hadn't had much of a choice. The rumor was that Aamir had died in a Taliban prison, but a part of her never believed it. However, she knew she had to leave Pakistan because whether she liked it or not, there was a good chance the rumor about Aamir was true.

But she wished—wished until she went mad with it—that he was alive. She wished they had been able to leave together. She wished she wasn't alone and cold because even though Kabul had been hell, she'd had someone to share it with, someone to keep her warm. But in the refugee camp in Pakistan, there was emptiness, insecurity, threats from other men, and fear.

It had been a stroke of luck that when she rattled out the names of relatives and where she thought they lived, she had named Kabir. The others had not panned out, maybe they couldn't be found or maybe they hadn't wanted her, she didn't know. What she did know was that Kabir and Layla had welcomed her with open arms and that was a debt she would never be able to repay.

As she sat at the dining table chopping carrots for the Kabuli *pilau* she was making for dinner, Raihana was grateful for the turn her life had taken after she'd moved to Denmark. When she'd first come to Skive nine months before, she had been worried that Kabir would be a religious type. She didn't intend to wear a *hijab* or an *abaya*, not after having left Afghanistan and the rules of the Taliban so far behind.

Kabir hadn't asked her to wear a *hijab* and neither had Layla, who never went out without donning one herself, in addition to an *abaya*. Kabir, who drank merrily on Friday nights to celebrate the weekend, didn't ask his wife to get rid of her *hijab* and she didn't ask him to stop drinking.

"Islam says smoking and drinking is wrong," Layla told Raihana on one of the Friday nights when Kabir was out of the house. "What do you think?"

Raihana didn't know what to say about things like this. She believed that people should do what they wanted but knew that was not what Layla wanted to hear.

"I think it is wrong," Layla said before Raihana could answer. It wasn't like Raihana was talkative, and she didn't always respond to people. Layla had met women like her, men too, people who had scars so big hidden under their skin that they were really one big wound. She didn't know the details about Raihana's life in Afghanistan, but no one knew the details. Raihana wasn't talking and her past was not well known.

When Raihana had first arrived, Khala Soofia, who lived next door, had tried to get Raihana to talk about her past, about her life in Kabul, the dead husband, but Raihana didn't say anything. Khala Soofia had come to Denmark in the early 1990s. Her husband had been a doctor in Jalalabad. Her son had died of cancer, and her daughter had moved to America with her husband, also a doctor, and their children. Soofia talked about moving there all the time.

Soofia's husband, Dr. Sidiq Rehman, had spent several years when he first came to Denmark petitioning the Danish integration minister and the Danish Medical Association, and writing letters to EU Parliament members, that he should be allowed to work in Denmark without having to go to medical school again. He understood that he had to learn Danish, which he had done by diligently going to language school.

Now he'd stopped the petitions and the letters. He didn't come out of his house much. He was depressed, they said, because he couldn't practice medicine. Still everyone called him Doctor Chacha. While Doctor Chacha silently mourned the loss of his life's work, Soofia kept hoping that her daughter would send for her.

"Visa problems," she always said. "But it will happen soon. You know daughters, they need their mothers."

Everyone nodded patiently and no one pointed out that Soofia's daughter rarely wrote and when she did the letters were filled with excuses as to why she couldn't find the means to bring her parents to America. Soofia read out the letters to whoever would listen and would try to put a positive spin on her daughter's excuses.

"You are just like my daughter, my Deena," Soofia told Raihana when they met at a birthday party. Habib and Jameela were celebrating their son's first birthday and had invited all the Afghans in Skive for a party. It had been a tumultuous first year for the boy, who had been born with heart problems, but after two surgeries he seemed fine and the doctors predicted he would have no further problems.

Raihana was barely paying attention to Soofia, who talked constantly, either about her daughter or about local Afghan community gossip. But soon enough, Soofia got to Raihana.

"So, where is your husband?" she asked.

Raihana was not stupid. She knew people were curious.

"Dead," she said quietly and then tried to change the subject by asking Soofia about her gold bangles. Soofia was easily distracted, especially when someone talked about her jewelry or her clothes. She had brought along her things from Jalalabad. She'd had the time. She had not been rushed to save her life. She had not had to escape after seeing a bloodbath, running and hiding through plains and mountains to enter another hell in a refugee camp in Pakistan.

"Dead? How?" Soofia asked and Raihana just smiled and shrugged. "You have to talk, if you keep it bottled in . . . talk, tell us. We're your family now," Soofia insisted, but Raihana didn't have the words. She was considered strange by most, a little too quiet. She had obviously been through some unspeakable tragedy, they all sensed. When she talked about going back to Kabul, it just confirmed their suspicions.

"From Iran it is easier to get into Afghanistan," Walid Ali Khan told her as he sipped tea from Layla's prized teacups.

Walid Ali Khan and Zohra were Kabir and Layla's closest friends and they visited them often for lunch on the weekends and then stayed through dinner and past their children's bedtime.

Walid and Zohra had come to Denmark six years ago with one child. Between maternity leaves and giving birth to two children, Zohra still went to language school, while Walid worked at the supermarket Kvickly.

"But now is not a good time to go. You know how the Americans are bombing from Kabul to Kandahar and everything in between?" Walid said shaking his head.

"Killing Taliban they say, but they are also killing innocent Afghans, bastards," Kabir said. "Bastard Americans and bastard British people! All of them saying we Muslims are evil. Propaganda like that is not right. Yesterday in business school my marketing teacher asks me if I think my wife should wear a *burkha* and sit at home. And she asks me if I think it is okay to beat my wife. What kind of questions are those? What kind really? *Hai*, Layla, have I ever hit you?"

Layla sighed. "Kabir . . ."

"Have I?"

"Allah, you are stubborn!"

"Maybe I should," Kabir said angrily. "Apparently all Muslim men beat up their wives. What, Raihana, your husband beat you too?"

And then all eyes turned to Raihana in the hope that she'd drop another scrap of information about her past and her husband. The bits and pieces Kabir had garnered from friends and family who lived in Pakistan and told the others was not much. Apparently Raihana's husband had been a teacher and the Taliban had been after him for not following their new curriculum. His brother-in-law had also been anti-Taliban, a doctor who treated women when the Taliban had prohibited it. He had been killed, and so had his wife.

"Walid hit me once," Zohra said suddenly.

"I didn't hit her, a book slipped and fell on her head," Walid cried out and the conversation turned away from Raihana.

In the small city of Skive in northern Denmark, there were just fifteen Afghan families, and these Afghans had achieved what they never had in Afghanistan. For the first time in her life, Raihana saw a Pashtun eat at the same table as an Uzbek. The Pashtuns, the Hazara, the Tajik, and the Uzbeks had been fighting for as long as Raihana remembered and now in this strange country they huddled together, accepting one another and their differences because beyond the huddle was the white man, looking at all of them with equal suspicion.

To Raihana it was still unreal—that she was not in Afghanistan anymore, that she was in this cold and wet country. Sometimes she closed her eyes and pretended she was back home, surrounded by the smells and scents of Kabul. Sometimes she remembered the taste of sugarcane juice and felt her insides churn in thirst.

But life in Skive was not bad, she had to admit, especially for a family like Kabir's. She didn't understand why Kabir complained so much. They had rented a nice house with two floors, bought a twenty-year-old and functional car, and installed their son in a free day care, which was paid for by the county.

Kabir made frequent trips to Germany to buy spices and other things they needed, and had even been to Pakistan on vacation the year before to visit his uncle, who was dying of cancer. Since he hadn't died yet, Kabir was planning another trip to Lahore as soon as he had enough money saved.

Money was always tight in the house, but they still went to Legoland with Shahrukh, sometimes drove to the zoo in Ålborg, went to the movies, and entertained friends. Kabir and Layla had a full life with friends and family, most of their material needs fulfilled.

"But we have to learn Danish" was Layla's big complaint about living in Denmark. "And it is so hard, Raihana."

Raihana couldn't even comprehend how she would learn a language that sounded like buzzing bees. There didn't seem to be any substance to it, just froth lolling out of everyone's mouth.

"You'll start in module one because you're a beginner. There are five modules and I can't wait to be finished with this stupid language," Layla told her as Kabir drove them to the language school on Raihana's first day.

It had taken the Skive county over nine months to get Raihana signed up for language school, which had been just the right amount of time. She'd had the time to learn about her surroundings and get through the cruel Danish winter. With spring getting closer, the idea of bicycling early in the morning to go to school was not as frightening.

In the winter Layla seemed to have managed riding to school, the supermarket, and everywhere else with just minimal complaining, while Raihana had stayed at home. She had cooked and cleaned and had babysat Shahrukh, allowing Kabir and Layla to go to a Hindi movie in Århus or to visit friends in Copenhagen, which was too long a drive to make with a little boy.

By the time the Integration Centre had sent her a letter stating that she had been signed up for language school, she was ready to leave the house and do something beyond housework.

Layla was exceptionally proud of her language accomplishments. She had passed module 4, which meant that she could reasonably communicate in Danish and understand most Danish, spoken and written. She hoped to pass the final exam, *Prøve i Dansk 3*, in the summer, after which she could look for a job.

"Maybe I will go back before I have to pass all these modules," Raihana wondered aloud.

"Yes, yes," Kabir said and Layla snorted.

"We are here, Raihana, and we live here," she said. "If you keep one foot in Afghanistan, you will be neither here nor there."

"But we will go back," Kabir insisted. "Don't listen to Layla! Soon, very soon things will be—"

"Don't listen to him," Layla snapped. "He has passed the Danish exam and is going to business school. He doesn't have to pass any more Danish exams. He talks about going back but knows there is nothing to go back to. We now live in Denmark."

"Just until we get citizenship and then we leave," Kabir continued. "But soon, Raihana, soon, we will go back, you wait and see."

Layla snorted again. "You are here," she said. "Live here, not in the past in a country that you can't go back to."

The language school was small and was housed in the VUC, Voksen Udannelses Center, Adult Education Center. It was on the second floor and had six rooms dedicated to it. Four were classrooms, one a large computer room, and one an office with an adjoining copy room. Downstairs were the teachers' lounges, one smoking and one nonsmoking, and a small kitchen. Students were not allowed to use the kitchen. In the basement there was a large dining area and a vending machine, which Layla told Raihana not to use. It was cheaper to bring cola or water from home than to buy it from the vending machine.

The woman who ran the language center was tall and white. She wore her blond hair tied in a tight bun and dressed in a pair of black pants and a black jacket. She had silver-framed glasses perched on her nose and she looked very stern.

"Layla says that you understand English," Sylvia Hoffmann said in heavily accented English.

Unsure of herself and everything around her, Raihana nodded and looked at Layla. She had gone to English school in Pakistan at the refugee camp for almost a year and Aamir had tried to teach her English as well. She knew how to say "how are you" and "thank you" and understood some of what was said when people spoke in English, especially in movies, but regular conversations? She felt her palms go cold with fear.

Sylvia smiled. "Maybe we can talk in English then?"

Raihana shook her head violently.

"I not English well," she managed to say without stammering.

Sylvia said something to Layla in that bee-buzz language.

"She says that I can translate for you, okay," Layla told her in Dari and Raihana sighed with relief.

"You live with Layla and Kabir, and they have come a long way in the past three years they have been with us," Sylvia said in Danish. "You will pick up Danish better if you speak it at home with Layla."

After that Sylvia tested Raihana's Danish abilities. She showed her pictures and asked what they were. Some Raihana knew in Danish, most she didn't. But she knew the Danish words for the everyday things, like butter, milk, oil, and flour. She had seen them often enough on television and in the supermarket when she went shopping with Layla.

Sylvia Hoffmann didn't indulge in any small talk and Raihana wondered if it was even possible to chitchat when you had to talk through a person. Layla was merrily translating from Dari to Danish and Danish to Dari without stumbling on her words.

Layla was so competent, Raihana thought and panicked some more. She would never be as proficient as Layla, she thought, never be able to speak Danish like this. She would never finish her education and she would never find a job and then . . . then what? Would they send her back to Afghanistan? She felt fear race through her and she had to force herself to pay attention to Sylvia Hoffmann, calm her breathing, and quiet her racing heart.

"You can come to class tomorrow," Sylvia Hoffman said.

Raihana nodded. "*Tak*," she said.

"*Velbekomme*," Sylvia said.

"That means welcome," Layla whispered to Raihana in Dari.

Raihana said *velbekomme* under her breath and decided to use it the next time someone said thank you to her in Danish.

"*Hvad hedder du?*" Layla began Raihana's private Danish class as Kabir drove them back home. "That means, what is your name. *Hvad hedder du*, Raihana?"

"Are you starting the Danish lesson already?" Kabir asked.

"Sylvia said that if we speak Danish at home Layla will learn faster," Layla said. "It is hard in Denmark without Danish. You can't go to the supermarket, get a job, go anywhere, do anything."

"She will do fine," Kabir said. "Stop scaring her, Layla."

Raihana wasn't sure what to believe. On the one hand she understood that she had to learn Danish so that she could earn a living, on the other hand the Danish government did give her some money to survive on every month. It wasn't much but she didn't have many expenses. She gave money to Kabir and Layla for food, lodging, and other necessities, but she still managed to have some money left in the bank every month.

If only Aamir could find his way here. What if he showed up at Layla and Kabir's doorstep? Could that happen?

It was a sweet dream, like the fantasy of a child who wished to meet dinosaurs or fly to the moon. It was a futile hope. Aamir was probably dead as so many people had told her, but she was not ready to believe that.

TWO

---

3 APRIL 1980

Is anything sweeter than the sound of bees buzzing? I don't think so. The buzzing of bees announces the start of spring and bees are the harbingers of renewal. Maybe I romanticize bees because our relationship with them is still new, still fresh. We haven't dealt with the challenges of beekeeping, season after season; maybe once we do we'll change our minds and be more realistic about bees and beekeeping.

When Gunnar and I first started to talk about becoming beekeepers, we only thought about the honey. But after a year with bees, we think about the honey less and the bees more. Our lives have been enriched, remarkably, by the bees. I wait to see the waggle dance, I wait to hear the buzzing, I wait eagerly for spring to come and see how my bees did in the winter. Our lives have divided as the bee season does—we welcome spring with gusto, enjoy the bees and honey-making through summer and fall, and then in the winter we hibernate like the bees.

With the bees we have found the peace we have always looked for. Bee-keeping is more than a hobby, more than livelihood: it is a way of life.

Gunnar loved his wife, his children, and his bees and not always in that order. But the past year had been difficult and he had yet to start preparing for the bee season.

He knew everyone was worried about him: his children, his grand-children, his friends. If his parents were alive, they would have worried as well. He could see it on everyone's faces when they talked to him, slowly and patiently, patting his hand or nodding in sympathy. He was sick and tired of looking at their pitying faces. And because he was sick of their constant sympathy he had stopped looking at them. He had even stopped opening the door when someone knocked. A man had a right to mourn, had a right to smoke pipe after pipe and drink coffee all day and whiskey all night, if that was what he wanted. A man had that right and to hell with those who thought he needed to move on and start living again. He was living, wasn't he? He smoked his pipe, drank his coffee and his whiskey, and watched television. It wasn't the life he had lived a year ago but life had changed and he with it.

Anna had gotten satellite television despite him being against it be-cause she wanted to watch the DR2 channel and their damn theme nights. It had all begun when the Danish television channel was broadcasting an Elvis theme night and she had managed to get the satellite connection within a week. The expense had been the biggest problem for Gunnar, but it was hard to argue with Anna when she set her mouth in that way. She would purse her lips, with her nose jutting out—she looked ridiculous, but he gave her what she wanted. In any case, she didn't need his permission to do anything. Anna was a mod-ern woman, and she did things her way—and he'd had no choice but to let her.

Now he was glad for all the channels on the television because the images filled the emptiness at two in the morning, when the two Danish channels were quiet. There was a sense of peace in letting the pictures run in front of him. Sometimes he even muted the sound and read the subtitles.

The movie they were showing on the TV2 channel was an old one; they had shown it several times in the past few months. He watched it anyway and let the night slip away as the familiar images flashed on the screen.

His doctor, whom he had known for the past twenty years, had told him that he would sleep a lot. Sleep helped people deal with grief. But Gunnar wasn't that lucky.

He had always had trouble sleeping; even before Anna died, he couldn't sleep. He used to take advantage of his insomnia by reading books on bees they bought or borrowed from the library.

He had been dedicated to his bees. Now he wondered if his dedication came from wanting to please Anna. She was the true bee lover, he had just tagged along. Hadn't he?

"Your bees are dying," Peter had said when he barged in the previous day. He hadn't even knocked on the door, just came in.

"You're living like a pig," Peter added. "Anna would be ashamed of you."

"She must be turning in her grave," Gunnar said. "I live like this now. This is my life," he added petulantly.

Peter sighed and studied the mess around him. The coffee table was covered with dirty glasses and a few plates with unidentifiable food. Newspapers were strewn around the living room, along with clothing and balled-up used paper towels.

Peter rolled up his sleeves and started collecting the newspapers in one pile.

"You have to check on the colonies or your bees will die and the colonies that have become big will swarm. Do you want to lose your bees?"

It was a stupid question to ask a man who had just lost his Queen, his wife. Gunnar had done none of the things that had marked the start of spring with Anna and the bees. He had not wired frames; he had not set the foundation wax on the frames and had not waited impatiently to check on the bee colonies to see how they had grown, what had been lost over the winter. He had not checked his bees and he had not checked Anna's bees—if he had cared about his bees, he would've checked on them, maybe even fed them some sugar by now.

They had twenty-six colonies between them. All the even-numbered ones had been Anna's, and Gunnar and Anna had competed with each other every spring to see whose bees were doing better, whose colonies had grown and whose had died. They had mourned the loss of any colonies together.

It had been Anna's idea to make different kinds of honey so they could harvest from June through September. At first Gunnar had scoffed, saying it would be too difficult to transport the colonies. But Anna set her mouth and made Gunnar read pamphlets about heather honey.

Gunnar did more than read the pamphlets. He called and spoke to the consultant hired by the Danish Beekeepers Association about leaving their bees in the west coast where the heathers grew. The consultant suggested a couple of places where Gunnar and Anna could leave their bees.

So every July, Gunnar and Anna went to the west coast with some of their colonies, usually half Anna's and half his, so that their bees could suck the nectar of the wild heathers that grew there. They would rent a summer house, leave the colonies there, and check on them each weekend. Then after six to eight weeks, they would bring the colonies back home, laden with heather honey.

Now that Anna was dead, her bees were his, but without her, there just didn't seem to be any point.

"What about Anna's bees?" Peter asked as he scooped some trash into a big black bag. "Do you think this would make her happy?"

"She's dead, Peter, beyond joy and sorrow," Gunnar said. He was bitterly angry that she was dead and he alive, still alive, unable to just lie down in the grave with her.

Peter looked at his friend and sighed, reading Gunnar's grief on his face. "You need to start wiring frames," he said. "Maybe you and I should do it together. What do you think?"

"Not now," Gunnar said.

"You don't care if your bees die?" Peter demanded.

"No," Gunnar said.

"Have you eaten?" Peter asked.

"Get out," Gunnar said. "And take that trash out with you."

Gunnar and Peter had known each other too long for Peter to have taken him personally, but after two hours of getting nothing out of Gunnar, Peter finally left looking defeated. Friendship didn't die quickly, though, and Gunnar knew that Peter would be back, with something else under his sleeve, some other trick to drag him into the world.

Gunnar had stopped picking up the phone because his daughter, Julie, called from London every day and his son, Lars, from Odense. Both wanted to know how he was doing and if they could help. He had told them to stop calling. He had lost his wife, he needed to mourn.

The fact was that he was afraid. He tried not to admit it but he was afraid of living alone. He had never lived alone. He had lived with his parents and then moved in with Anna thirty-seven years ago. For thirty-seven years they lived in this house and raised their children. And for the last fifteen years their bees had lived there with them.

Julie and Lars joked about the time before the bees and after the bees.

"Before the bees, you spent some time with us, now . . . ," Julie would tease when she came to visit.

"After the bees, they behave like a newly married couple, ignoring everyone but themselves and their little honey-makers," Maria, Lars's wife, teased.

His grandchildren only knew them as beekeepers. With great joy, Gunnar had taught four-year-old Brian and six-year-old Johanna how to wire frames, spot the queen bee, and uncap the top layer of wax before running the honey-filled hives through the honey extractor.

Johanna and Brian had joined him and Anna in stirring the honey as it rested in various buckets in their windowless "honey room."

When Gunnar and Anna had been new to beekeeping, they had left their first harvest in the sewing room with an open window. By the next day the bees had found it and were working on sucking the honey back from the honey frames. So the honey room was constructed next to the garage with no windows that could be accidentally left open.

He and Anna had loved beekeeping, Gunnar thought. Sometimes he had wondered if they had loved beekeeping more than they had loved each other. He glanced at the worn copy of the Danish Beekeepers Association's manual, *Lærebog i Biavl*, which still sat on the end table next to Anna's favorite chair by the window. They bought that copy when they had first started talking about keeping bees and they never replaced it.

Every winter, Anna would sit in that rocking chair and read the manual time and again. The window faced the backyard and Anna would look out once in a while and say to Gunnar, "I hope they're doing well. Do you think they'll survive the winter?"

And Gunnar would always say, "Yes, they will."

There was a time when the buzzing of the bees was within him, a humming that accompanied his time with Anna, their grandchildren, their children, and friends. Now Gunnar wasn't sure he could stand the sound of the bees. He was sure it would drive him mad to hear the bees without Anna.

Some days were harder than others for Gunnar.

On the hard days, he woke up forgetting she was dead. During that fragile time when sleep mingled with reality and Gunnar's mind was still fuzzy, he forgot Anna was dead. And then like the quick sting of a bee, reality would sink its stinger inside his fuzzy brain. Anna was dead, he would remind himself. Then he'd lie in bed unable to get on with living through another day.

It was on such a day that Peter arrived to try once again to get his friend out of the house.

After much persistence, Peter managed to drag Gunnar to the apiary school that the Salling og Fjends BF, Salling and Surrounding Areas Beekeepers Club, rented for meeting and to hold classes about beekeeping. The school was housed in a small old farm in the outskirts of Skive. The old farm building was a large well-kept room with a bathroom and small kitchen.

Since the weather was good, the first day of apiary class was being conducted in a shed that used to be a barn. The beekeepers had set up chairs and tables for the apiary school. Colorful flyers lay on the tables alongside coffee and dream cake, a simple white cake covered with thick gooey coconut and brown sugar icing. A whiteboard with felt pens stood in a corner next to an old honey extraction machine.

People were milling around the cake and coffee, picking up flyers, chatting with beekeepers, discussing how the bee season was going.

Gunnar sat in the back, away from the crowd. He wasn't interested in the people or the cake. He wanted some coffee, but didn't want to walk through the maze of people between him and the coffee. He knew most of the people in the room. They'd talk to him. They'd ask him how he was doing. They'd annoy the hell out of him. No, he was better off sitting here smoking his pipe.

"Can't you get him to come here and talk to people," Birthe, Peter's wife, asked him. "Does he have to sit there looking like all his bees died?"

Peter looked at her in exasperation. "I got him here and it took a lot of work. I had to actually force him under the shower. And you're still not happy?"

Birthe frowned. "I can't stand to see him this way. Over Christmas, I understood. Anna had just died. But . . ."

"It's only been a few months," Peter said. "We should give him time. Would you want me to get on with my life if you died?"

Birthe smiled. "No, I'd want you to mourn for the rest of your life."

"Mourn about what?" asked Hans, another beekeeper and long-time friend of Peter's and Gunnar's.

"Birthe wants me to mourn her for the rest of my life when she dies," Peter said.

"I think Bettina would say the same thing about me," he said cheerfully and then sighed when he looked at Gunnar. "On the other hand, it'd be such a waste."

"It's the shock of it," Birthe said. "One minute she was talking about how great their September harvest was and the next minute, she was dead."

"I always thought that was a good way to die, you know, boom and you're gone. But now I wonder if it's better to have cancer or something like that. You at least have time to plan," Hans said.

"How is Gunnar going to get over this?" Birthe said sadly. "In a way I do understand the way he is. If Peter died, I don't know if I'd be able to look at those bees again."

Gunnar watched them and he was sure they were talking about him. It was the way that Birthe kept glancing at him that made him certain. He knew they were worried about him. A part of him was relieved that someone gave a damn. Another wanted them to leave him alone.

It was easy for them to talk. Easy for them to say move on, Gunnar. She's dead. What did they know? He'd like to see how well Peter would do if Birthe died, or Hans if Bettina died. Sure, they would sit and worry about their bees like they wanted him to. Like hell!

"*Hej*," a couple said as they sat down next to him.

They were almost his age, retired and bored probably, Gunnar thought. The woman was not very tall and her white hair was cut short. She wore steel-framed glasses and brown pants with a matching brown jacket. The man wore jeans, a bulky sweater, and thick-looking plastic-framed glasses.

"Are you here for the class too?" the man asked, rubbing his hands together.

Gunnar didn't say anything, but the woman didn't seem to care about his lack of response.

"We are so excited. Anders found out about the apiary school and we just had to come. My daughter is married to a beekeeper in America. Do you know much about beekeeping?" she asked.

Gunnar grunted noncommittally.

"Sonia is just crazy about honey," the man said proudly. "And I thought maybe we should make our own honey—it would be fun, now that we're retired."

"Making honey is a lot of work," Gunnar commented sourly. "A *whole lot of work*."

"But we'll do it together," Sonia said, grabbing her husband's hand. "We're retired; we have all the time in the world."

Bitterness and envy assailed Gunnar. He and Anna had retired too, he from teaching carpentry at the technical school and she from managing the kindergarten. They retired and were going to do the things they hadn't had the time to do when they were working. They would travel in the late fall and winter; go to the warm places, away from the long Danish cold. They would go south to France, Spain, and Italy, and learn new beekeeping techniques.

"Are you alone here?" the woman asked.

Gunnar stared at her for a moment and anger bubbled inside him. He wanted to snap at this woman who sat so happily beside her cheerful husband that, yes, he was alone. He was the most alone man he knew.

THREE

---

16 APRIL 1980

I read something in the paper today and felt that it should be part of this journal. I didn't know this, but bees have been producing honey for at least a
hundred million years. Bees produce honey as food storage for the long winter when flowers aren't blooming and no nectar is available to them.

Apis mellifera, the European honeybee, produces far more honey than the
hive can eat and we harvest this honey and sweeten our lives with it.

Praktik! The word set panic in Raihana.

"It's to help you integrate better into the Danish society,"
Sylvia Hoffmann had told Raihana. "And you're obligated by the Danish government to do a *praktik*. We'll find one suitable for you."

Layla worked at the grocery store cleaning the floors and picking up after everyone. This was her *praktik*, her apprenticeship. It was a part of the language school curriculum since Danish immigration law required refugees to work in a place where they could pick up day-to-day Danish as well as become familiar with Danish culture.

Layla didn't mind her *praktik* but she admitted that she wasn't learning any Danish at the supermarket. She worked with Shabana, another Afghan from Kabul who had come to Denmark two years ago. They talked in Dari about life back in Afghanistan, life in Denmark, the latest wedding, this festivity and that, and the Hindi movies they had recently seen.

Raihana thought she would be happy with a *praktik* like Layla's even if she didn't learn any Danish. The work was easy enough and she wouldn't feel stupid when she tried to speak that bee-buzz language. But when the time came to choose a *praktik*, Raihana surprised herself.

Raihana had been relieved on her first day in language school to find that Sylvia Hoffmann was not her language teacher. Raihana had been afraid that she would have to sit in class every day with the stern Sylvia Hoffmann and was happy to see a pleasant-looking woman step into her classroom.

Layla was in a module 4 class while Raihana was in a module 2 class, and for the first time since she had come to Denmark, Raihana had to manage outside of the home without the help of Layla or Kabir. It was daunting, but she was excited to do this all by herself. Sometimes, outside of class, she felt she didn't need Layla's help, especially in the supermarket, but it seemed rude to spurn Layla's protectiveness. Layla was only trying to help, to make things easier for Raihana than they had been when she first came to Denmark. So Raihana let Layla speak for them both. But here in class, Raihana was expected to speak for herself and she enjoyed it.

Just after a week of classes, Raihana decided she liked her teacher, Christina Møllehave, best among all the Danish people she had met.

Christina spoke Danish very slowly and very clearly. Raihana could actually understand some of what Christina said because she didn't mumble like so many other Danes did. And she took the time to explain what a Danish word meant each time a student asked.

Once she began school, Raihana's life fell into a routine. Everyone at home woke up early, got ready, ate breakfast, and battled with Shahrukh to eat his slice of bread with butter and jam and a boiled egg.

Kabir dropped Shahrukh at his day care on his way to school. Kabir went to *handelsskole*, a business school where Danes who didn't want to go to university went to after high school. Kabir had finished high school in Afghanistan, but that had been a long time ago. Most of his classmates were almost fifteen years younger than him. He felt awkward, not only because of their age, but also because they were all Danes. After going to language school where everyone was a foreigner, it was strange to go to a class where he was the only foreigner.

Layla and Raihana bicycled to the language school. Usually they went together, but sometimes Layla got a late start. She watched too many Hindi movies at night and couldn't always wake up on time.

It had taken Raihana awhile to get used to bicycling everywhere. She had been scared in the beginning, worried that a car would run her over, but with the passing months she gained confidence.

Language school was tough. The first week, Raihana felt like crying all the time because she felt as if she understood very, very little. She felt she spent as much time looking through the Danish-to-Dari dictionary as she did listening to Christina. She pieced her sentences together with her little knowledge of Danish and translated words from the dictionary.

The language was not easy. The way Danish was written was not how it was spoken. Danes swallowed half their words and letters when they spoke and there were no rules.

"You won't learn Danish by tomorrow," Christina had warned the class. "I know the pronunciation is difficult. But I promise, you'll learn the language."

Raihana thought she'd never be able to speak Danish fluently, not the way Layla could, and she said as much to her.

"It took me six months to get to where you are," Layla told Raihana, sounding a little annoyed. "You've picked up so much in a week, it's astonishing."

Raihana didn't really believe that, but felt a small surge of satisfaction at having impressed Layla.

"I learned so much from the television," she said. "And you," she added to please Layla.

Wahida, who came from Kandahar, sat next to Raihana. There was also a woman from Iran, two from Bosnia, and one from Malaysia.

"How come there are only women here?" Raihana asked Wahida on her first day. "Where do the men learn Danish?"

"There are men," Wahida said. "Just none in our class. My cousin Asslam is in module 2, but in a module 2 class for immigrants who have no education. He has class on Monday and Tuesday and his *praktik* is at the butcher."

"What does he do there?" Raihana asked.

"Cuts meat." Wahida said and then her voice dropped. "Even pig's meat. He hasn't said anything to anyone, but my husband told me. It's an evil world that makes a good Musalman soil his hands so."

"Why can't he find a *praktik* elsewhere?" Raihana asked.

"These Danes, they force us into such situations," Wahida said acidly. "They make us do these jobs so that we won't be Muslim anymore. You should wear a *hijab* and *abaya*, Raihana, walking around like this . . . it's not right. You have to show them that you are a good Muslim woman."

"I don't think a Muslim woman is good because she wears a *hijab* and *abaya*," Raihana said tightly.

Afghans like Wahida believed that wearing a *hijab* and *abaya* made them better Muslims and who was Raihana to argue with that? Everyone had their own ideas about religion and whatever Raihana's ideas were, it was between Allah and her. None of Wahida's business.

"You have to cover your hair here, cover your body," Wahida insisted. "You have to show these white people that you are a good Muslim," she repeated.

The first few days, Raihana just ignored Wahida's remarks. She didn't want to sit with strangers, people who didn't speak Dari, so she sat with Wahida even though the Muslim talk made her uncomfortable.

But by the end of the week, Raihana had had enough.

"If this is all you're going to talk about, I won't sit with you," Raihana said.

After Wahida stopped insisting Raihana wear a *hijab* or an *abaya*, they struck up a tentative friendship. They were the only two Afghans in the class and they stuck together, at least in the initial days when everyone else in the class spoke a different and stranger language than theirs.

Raihana was frightened of Sylvia Hoffmann and tried to avoid her. Sylvia Hoffmann would always stop and talk to the students *in Danish*. Sylvia didn't say much, just asked how she was doing, but Raihana was tongue-tied around her and could barely get the words out. She now knew what to say when someone said, *"Har du det godt?"* She only had to say *"Fint"* to respond, but she was too flustered to say anything. So Raihana just nodded, looking around nervously, feeling like a fool.

It was worse with her caseworker at the Integration Centre. Karina Hansen was young and prone to giggling on the mobile phone when Raihana sat down to talk with her. She used Layla to interpret, and Layla, Allah bless her, always came along to make sure Raihana was not lost.

"No one helped me, so I want to make sure you have help," Layla would say. "I had Kabir . . . you have me."

It was Karina who talked to Raihana about the *praktik*. They were looking for something appropriate, Karina told her, and then answered the singsong tone of her mobile phone, speaking rapidly in Danish.

"Her boyfriend," Layla whispered to Raihana in Dari. As if whispering made it less likely for Karina to understand Dari. "She is saying something about some dress and . . . some party."

Raihana felt embarrassed, as if she were listening into a private conversation, even though she needed Layla to translate what Karina was saying.

Sylvia was stern, Karina was irreverent, and Christina was absolutely wonderful. Raihana felt that Christina cared a lot about her students and worked very hard to teach them Danish.

For some reason, Christina had taken a special interest in Raihana. She came to her during breaks during the day and asked if she had any questions. In the beginning Raihana had been shy and just shook her head, but after a few weeks she had started asking questions.

Raihana thought the toughest part was grammar, which Christina assured her was hard for everyone. On Wednesday afternoons Raihana would meet with Christina for one-on-one class in the computer room. Raihana liked the computer room; it was a big room with many computers, all in black. The screens were large and sleek and the keyboards and mouses were wireless, so you could put the keyboard on your lap and type. Kabir had shown her how to access Afghan newspapers. In her breaks during class, Raihana, like all other students, would bring up newspapers from her homeland on the computer and read a familiar language again.

It was such a delight to find everything on the computer. You could just type a few letters and go back home, even if only for a short while.

Raihana still had to look for the right keys and envied Kabir, whose fingers moved so quickly and easily on the computer's keyboard. He used to use an English typewriter back in Kabul, he told her; that's why it was so easy for him.

All the computers came with headphones so that the students could listen to taped Danish conversations. During her lunch break, Raihana browsed an Afghan music website Kabir had shown her and a Hindi movie website to see pictures of newly released movies and listen to new Hindi movie songs. Everyone in Afghanistan watched Hindi movies, Pakistani teleplays, and television programs from Iran. Raihana especially loved old Hindi movies and the songs in them.

"It is the irregular verbs that are the most problematic," Christina told her whenever Raihana complained about them. They would have a one-on-one class every Wednesday for three hours, when Christina would go through Raihana's homework.

Uregelmæssig verbum. Raihana knew that term. These were verbs that didn't follow a set pattern and Raihana always made mistakes when using them.

"You will get used to the verbs," Christina said.

"*Jeg kan ikke,* I cannot," she said desperately. She didn't think she could ever get used to this language and its rule-less verbs.

Christina laughed. "You will. When you start speaking Danish fluently, you won't even think about the verbs."

"*Nej, nej,*" Raihana said, shaking her head.

Christina nodded. "You're learning Danish very fast, *meget hurtigt.*"

Raihana glowed at the praise. When she came home, Raihana felt even better because she realized that she had had a whole conversation with Christina in Danish and had understood almost all of it.

The class started every day with a different song that Christina played on the tape recorder. It was the day Christina played the song about *solskin,* sunshine, in Raihana's fourth week at the language school, that everything changed for Raihana.

The talk of spring, sunshine, the song of the birds, and the buzzing of bees changed everything for Raihana.

"My uncle make honey," she managed to tell Christina. The language, as difficult as it was, was sinking in, much to Raihana's surprise. "I help him."

Christina had seemed very interested and the next week, Christina pulled Raihana aside during lunch and asked if she would be interested in working at an apiary.

Raihana barely understood what Christina said, even though she spoke slowly. Finally, Christina got Layla to translate for her.

"There is a man, an old man, his wife has died and he might need help taking care of his bees," Layla translated with a frown. In Dari, she added, "I don't think you should say yes to this, working for some old man doesn't sound right. You come and work with us in the supermarket."

Raihana wanted to warn Christina that she really didn't know that much about bees but Layla's insistence that Raihana go to the supermarket with her for her *praktik* gave Raihana pause. She loved Layla, but she also needed to get away from her. And why not work with bees? Maybe she would learn something, maybe she would be able to practice her Danish more, something that wouldn't happen if she worked in the supermarket with Layla.

So with Layla's warning ringing in her ears, Raihana, with confidence that surprised her, said yes. Yes, she would work in a bee farm for some old Danish man. She had no idea what she was getting into but since she had left the refugee camp, it seemed like getting into things that she didn't know much about didn't always turn out badly.

Raihana came home with a somber Layla and told Kabir that she had been assigned a *praktik*. Raihana was nervous about his reaction. She knew Layla wasn't pleased about her decision and knew that Kabir wouldn't be pleased either.

"So you'll join Layla's cleaning army?" he joked as soon as they came home.

Layla sighed deeply and Raihana bit her upper lip nervously.

"What happened? You didn't get the supermarket job?" he asked.

When neither woman said anything, Kabir became impatient. "Is one of you going to say something or are you both going to stand there like statues?"

The words tumbled out of Raihana and with each word she could see the growing disapproval on Kabir's face.

"No," he said, shaking his head after she was finished, and then looked at Layla. "Didn't you tell her that she should say no?"

"She wants to do it," Layla said.

"Work alone for some Danish man?" Kabir demanded. "You've both gone mad."

"But I'll learn Danish more easily," Raihana protested. She didn't want to upset Layla and Kabir. She lived in their home and she knew they cared for her.

Raihana wondered if the *praktik* was worth going against Layla and Kabir for. She had said yes and she still thought it was a good idea, but she was also nervous.

She didn't speak Danish, she only knew a little about beekeeping, and she was shunning a job at the supermarket with her friends. But the appeal of working with bees was strong, partly because it reminded her of the smell of honey from her uncle's house and partly because Christina had suggested it. She didn't want to disappoint Christina and she didn't want to admit that she had exaggerated about her experience with her uncle's bees. She had worked only a little with the bees, a very long time ago, and most of it was a faint memory, except for the smell of honey.

Raihana kept trying to convince Kabir and Layla the entire evening. Layla kept sighing and Kabir kept saying no. If only Layla were on her side, Raihana thought, then she could help convince Kabir.

"Why do you want to work there?" Layla asked Raihana. They were alone in the living room, watching a Hindi movie Kabir had brought back from Hamburg. "Tell me the truth."

"I remember the smell of honey," Raihana told her. "The sweet and rich smell of it. Just thinking about it reminds me of Afghanistan."

"But we're not in Afghanistan," Layla said sadly. "Nothing is going to bring that time back, Raihana."

"I know but let me try the job for a week. If I'm uncomfortable there you can talk to your supervisor and see if they have room for one more at the supermarket. Okay?" Raihana pleaded.

"But why? It might be hard work with the bees; have you thought about that?" Layla asked.

Raihana smiled. "I'm not afraid of hard work. I want to do this. Let me do this."

"Okay," Layla said, finally giving in. "Okay. I'll talk to Kabir. But be careful. Old or young, you can't trust these white men."

Gunnar couldn't believe Ole's wife's audacity. Hiring someone for him?

They said they had just come to visit, the liars. They had brought cake along to soften him, Gunnar knew. The chocolate cake looked good, but Gunnar didn't want to bother with getting plates, knives, and forks. And he hoped that Christina would make coffee to go with the cake because he just couldn't muster the energy to do it.

"It's not set in stone, Gunnar," Christina said as Gunnar all but vibrated with anger when she told him about Raihana and how she could help him. "Gunnar, don't you want to help this woman? She's young and—"

"I'm not having some Muslim woman running around my house," Gunnar erupted. "These people are in Denmark to suck our money and I—"

"You don't even have to pay her," Christina said. "And Gunnar, don't talk nonsense. They're here to survive. Her husband was killed by the Taliban. It wasn't a picnic for her back there. And she has worked with bees before. It will be good for you to have someone around the house to maybe clean up a little and help with the bees— or do you not care if all the colonies die?"

"I can take care of my colonies," Gunnar said.

"Really?" Ole asked. "How? Have you prepared frames yet? Have you done anything, man?"

"I can take care of my bees," he said again.

"She can help you," Christina said. "And it will be a good way for her to learn some Danish."

"You want me to hire a woman who speaks no Danish? What does she speak?" Gunnar asked.

"Dari," Christina said. "And maybe a little English. She learned it in the refugee camp in Pakistan."

"And how will we communicate? I don't speak English and I don't know anything about Dari," Gunnar said. "This is a dumb idea, Christina."

"You can show her what to do," Christina said, "And she will do it. She doesn't speak much Danish, but she isn't stupid, Gunnar."

"I don't want her here," he declared finally. "This is my house and I don't want her here."

"Fine," Christina said. "Then I'll call Julie and tell her how you spend your day and suggest that she come and stay with you for a while."

Gunnar's eyes widened. Julie was worse than Anna when it came to nagging. Far away in London, she didn't interfere in his life, but if she came here she would sort the house out, she would make him go on walks, eat, stop drinking whiskey, and he would be unable to say no because she could persuade him to do anything, just like Anna could.

"I'm not scared of Julie; go ahead and call her," Gunnar said stubbornly.

Christina pulled her Palm Pilot from her purse and started to look for Julie's home number.

She had dialed the country code when Gunnar told her to stop.

"This . . . this . . . is blackmail," he protested, half stuttering.

"Yes, it is," Christina admitted. "But you won't get off your high horse, so what do you want me to do?"

"I just lost my wife," Gunnar said. "Don't you feel any pity for me? Is your heart made of stone?"

"Oh please, can the melodrama," Christina, said waving her hand at him.

"Ole, talk to your wife, tell her that this is wrong," Gunnar said.

Ole shook his head. He was staying out of this.

"But I don't know these Muslim people. They seem . . . what if she brings a bomb inside the house? What if she blows up my house like all those suicide bombers in Israel?" he demanded.

"Then we won't have to worry about you anymore," Ole said and ran a hand over his bald head.

"Come on, Gunnar, she's a good girl," Christina said. "She's in her early twenties and she has already been through horror. She seemed happy when she talked about those bees."

"You need to stop getting involved in the lives of your students," Gunnar said. "Remember that man from Iran?"

"I'm not getting involved; I'm just finding her a job I think she will like," she said defensively.

"You're getting *me* involved," Gunnar said in frustration.

"But she hardly speaks Danish and you speak no Dari. Just talk to her about the bees and you both will be fine," Christina said. "I am going to make some coffee." As she walked past her husband, she cleared her throat.

Ole watched his wife leave the living room.

"She's already involved with this Afghan girl," Ole said. "She tries, you know, to keep her distance from the students, but there's this one student she gets attached to and wants to help."

"I know," Gunnar said. "I think about that student of Christina's from Iran and my problems don't seem too bad. Anna died in a hospital bed; no one tortured her or me. But living after her is torture."

"I can believe that."

"I can't help anyone," Gunnar said. "Not some Afghan girl, not even myself."

"Why don't you try it for a week or so? It will make Christina happy and it may not work out anyway," Ole suggested.

Gunnar looked out into the backyard. His and Anna's colonies were there, still hibernating, but not for long. Spring was nearly here. The bees would die or swarm, he thought.

"For one week only," he said to Ole, who nodded.

"If it doesn't work, you handle Christina and no calling Julie," Gunnar said and started to clean his pipe.

"Deal," Ole promised.

"And if I am going to do this I want roulade, with chocolate cream," he said loudly.

"I will get you one tomorrow," Christina called out from the kitchen and Gunnar could hear her humming as she finished making coffee.

FOUR

20 APRIL 1980

I love to check on the bees. See how they're doing; make sure a rat hasn't found its way in. It's like checking on your children after they've gone to bed.

In April we do some very quiet checking. It's the look around in the cold, huddled inside a warm jacket kind of checking. We don't open the colonies or peek in, though we desperately want to. We just walk around the colonies and wish the bees luck and hope they have gotten through the long and cold winter, safe and sound.

Since she started working at the language school, Christina had made a sincere effort at maintaining some distance from her students. She had been instructed to do this in her training. There was no point in getting close, beyond the boundaries of teaching Danish. She couldn't help anyone, not the way some of the students in her class needed help. She was not a psychiatrist. She was not a priest. She was just a teacher and her job was to teach these students Danish so they could get on with the business of living and working in Denmark.

But it wasn't easy. Christina was not prepared for how many of the students worked their way into her heart and into her life.

It began with Maher and his wife, Ester, a couple from Iran. They had joined the language school the same day Christina started teaching and for some reason she had felt a connection with Maher. He was her age, in his early thirties then, a clean-shaven quiet man who didn't seem to be picking up the language as fast as his wife and classmates. When Christina told the class about her five years as a teacher in Mozambique, he had perked up, and spoke to Christina about his stay in the African country in halting Danish.

Maher and Ester lived in a small apartment in Skive. They both spoke fairly good English as they were students in Iran before they came to Denmark. Maher had been studying to be an engineer and Ester had been working toward a degree in mathematics. They both wanted to continue their education and they had to learn Danish to do that in Denmark.

It was during the first summer vacation when her relationship with them changed and she became friends with them. Right before the summer holidays, Maher complained to Christina that he and Ester now had two months with nowhere to go and nothing to do.

When Christina invited them to her home to help with Ole's bees and the garden, they had jumped at the idea. Every morning Maher and Ester arrived on their bicycles, armed with a lunch box and sunscreen. Over the course of the summer they learned a lot about beekeeping and by the end of August had become amateur beekeepers themselves, starting an apiary with four colonies Ole gave them. But as they grew closer, Christina and Ole found themselves dragged into Maher and Ester's past.

They were eating lunch one day when Christina and Ole found

out about the horrors of Maher's life in Iran. It was a warm summer, and they all complained about the heat and how thirsty everyone was. Christina filled up Maher's water glass and he stared at the glass for a while before drinking the water thirstily.

"You *were* thirsty," Christina said and Maher's eyes filled with tears when she added, "Want me to pour out another glass or should I just give you the jug?"

"They would tie us up in the heat," he said quietly. "And leave water in front of us. We would be nearly dying of thirst, not having drunk or eaten for days, and we would watch the water evaporate."

Ester looked away while Christina and Ole stared at Maher. He had never talked about his torture but Ester had alluded to it when she and Christina were alone. That afternoon while she and Christina washed up the dishes, Ester told her.

"He came back with sores all over his body, a thin rail of a man, his spirit beaten," she said, tears rolling down her eyes. "And since then we . . . we haven't been together in the same way . . . you know what I mean?"

Christina hugged Ester and held her as she cried.

After they left, Christina insisted to Ole that they had to do some-thing to help.

"You should talk to Maher," she said. "Talking man-to-man can sometimes . . ."

"No," Ole said firmly. "I can't talk to him. *You* can't talk to him. You think a little conversation is going to change anything? They need counseling, Christina, not us meddling."

And ultimately Ole was right. Ester continued to tell Christina about the atrocities they had faced in Iran and Christina continued to feel helpless. It seemed to Christina that Ester believed Christina could help if she only told her more and more—as though she had to convince Christina that they were worth helping. But there was really nothing Christina could do aside from listening.

The job that she had been so passionate about started to become a nightmare as Christina found herself increasingly wrapped up in Ester and Maher's troubles. It was not until Maher and Ester moved to Copenhagen the next year that Christina realized the impact they had had on her life. She had become deeply depressed. She and Ole finally decided it would be best if she quit.

Now Christina wondered about the past life of all her students. There was the young boy from Sri Lanka, the thin dark woman from Somalia—almost everyone in her class had left their countries to save their lives. Christina worried about them.

But Sylvia Hoffmann didn't accept Christina's resignation. Christina was not the first teacher at the language school who had gotten dragged into a student's life and felt helpless.

"Teach them Danish. That is the best you can do. Don't try to fix their lives, you can't," she said. "The best you can do is helping them get on their feet. Don't talk to them about their past; you can't help them put their past to rest. If they need help, they need to see a therapist."

"But I want to help them," Christina had pleaded.

"You can't," Sylvia said. "Give it another six months. If you're still not happy here, then you can leave."

It had seemed cold then, but now after almost fifteen years in the language school, it was advice that kept Christina sane. However, once in a while, she would meet a student who tugged at the heartstrings and she would find herself getting involved in his or her life.

Each time it happened, she would promise it was the last, and each time Ole would wait for it to happen again. He had stopped chastising her about getting involved with her students.

With Raihana it was different, Christina was sure. Raihana had told her nothing, burdened her with no details. Christina was just trying to help a young immigrant woman. This was the first time in her years at the language school that Christina had met a single woman from Afghanistan and she was impressed with how quickly Raihana was picking up Danish.

Christina thought she was ready to pass module 2 and go into module 3 and she had only been at the school for four months. Christina was convinced that working with Gunnar would teach Raihana more Danish than gossiping with other Afghans in Dari while cleaning a grocery store or office building. Granted, Gunnar wasn't the most talkative person she knew, but he and Raihana would have to converse with each other in Danish and that would be enough.

Christina took Raihana to meet her new employer on a bright spring day. Layla didn't come along with them and Raihana was nervous. Christina spoke Danish slowly and Raihana understood about a third of what she said; the rest went over her head. Christina had a black car that smelled of cigarettes on the inside and the ashtray was smudged with ash. Raihana knew Christina smoked, had seen her go in and out of the teachers' smoking lounge downstairs.

"His name is Gunnar Sandberg," Christina told Raihana again. She was repeating herself, which was a good thing, Raihana thought, because she understood just a little more each time.

"Gunnar Sandberg," Raihana repeated.

"*Nai*," Christina said. "Gunnar Sandberg."

Raihana thought she was saying it right but she never quite did. It was agonizing because she couldn't hear the difference. The words sounded the same to her.

"*Hvor gammel han*, how old is he?" Raihana asked.

"Hmm . . . he took early retirement two years ago, so he is about sixty-four years old," Christina said. "He lost his wife last year."

"How did she dead?"

"How did she die?" Christina corrected automatically. "She had a stroke and died immediately. One day she was fine and the next she was gone. It was last fall; he is still mourning."

Raihana looked out of the car window. She had not understood how the man's wife died, only that she died in the *efterår*, the autumn. Last autumn Raihana had been grasping at a new life, preparing to come to Denmark. A year before that she had left Kabul. It had been cold then, she remembered feeling so cold. Aamir had insisted she leave without him, and he had promised that he would follow. As she drove away with neighbors who were also escaping, she had seen a man on the street. He was dead in the street, his eyes still open, the contents of his body spilling out of his skin, his white *kurta* red . . . he looked almost like Aamir, young, wearing that hideous beard the Taliban forced all Afghan men to wear.

That man's body was imprinted in her memory and every time she thought about Aamir, the eyes in her mind looked at the dead man on the street, wanting to see if he had been Aamir. Is that how he died? Was he tortured in a Taliban prison? Had he been in pain? The questions reeled through her and she struggled to get away from that bloody street in Kabul and back to Denmark, to Christina's cigarette-smelling car.

"Here we are," Christina said as they pulled into a gravel driveway.

The house looked small and old. The garden was still lying dormant. But it was only the end of March and Raihana had been warned that in Denmark sometimes winter crept into a cold spring and then transformed into a cold autumn, completely skipping summer. Raihana was used to being cold, but she craved the sun and longed for the heat, the smell of sun-dried clothes and of being unbearably hot.

The door looked newer than the house. It was dark wood with a polished brass knocker on it. The house was painted white while the windows were dark brown and the roof was thatched, as was the norm with old farmhouses in Denmark.

There were flowerpots everywhere and perennials grew in them, defying the cold weather, and several rosebushes lined the front of the house.

A big sandbox lay in a corner of the front garden and a plastic shovel and bucket peeked out from the wet sand. A blue tricycle lay against the sandbox. He must have grandchildren, Raihana thought.

Christina knocked on the brass knocker and they waited a while before the door opened. Raihana didn't mind waiting as she had more time to digest everything she saw. On the other side of the house was a garage that was closed now. A dusty red car was parked outside the garage.

"You will work there," Christina said, pointing to the garage. "Next to the garage they have a room where they keep honey."

Raihana nodded even though she understood absolutely nothing Christina had said except work, there, and honey. So she deduced she would work in the garage to make honey. But Chacha Bashir's honeybees used to be outside; here they kept them inside the house. How did the bees get to the flowers then?

Next to the garage was a gate that led to the backyard. The garden had an erstwhile manicured feel about it. The winter had taken its toll on the garden and definitely needed some spring cleaning. The neighbor's garden looked better despite the dry lawn. There were no scattered leaves in the garden, the weeds had been dug out, and the soil had been freshly turned.

After Christina knocked for the fourth time the door finally opened. Raihana had started to feel uneasy and her uneasiness only grew when the door opened.

Her first glimpse of the man was not impressive. He was wearing a bedraggled shirt and pants. His hair, what was left of it, was white, and stood up in spikes. His face was gaunt and his clothes looked as if they had been made for a thicker man. He was thin and looked sickly. He smelled of whiskey and coffee and smoke.

Raihana was scared of him.

She didn't know what to expect from a Danish person's house but she had thought this one would smell like honey, like her Chacha Bashir's house had. But this house smelled of what the man smelled of and it was not pleasant.

Christina spoke in rapid Danish and all Raihana picked up was *beskidt* and *stinker*. Dirty and stinking.

The man grunted back in Danish and went inside.

Christina turned to Raihana apologetically. "He is depressed," she said.

Raihana didn't understand.

"*Han er trist*," Christina tried again.

This time Raihana nodded. *Trist* meant sad. So the man was sad! Of course, he was in mourning. He had just lost his wife, what—a few months ago? What a luxury, she thought enviously, that he could mourn his loss like this when her husband had disappeared. She would have liked to give up on life and cry until she was empty of tears; instead she had to brave a refugee camp, a new country, and now a whole new language.

"Maybe we coming later," Raihana said.

"Maybe we should come later," Christina corrected her. "No, it is fine. He needs to get up and around and you need to start your *praktik*."

But Raihana wasn't sure now if she wanted to do her *praktik* here. This man seemed strange, his house stranger. What if something bad happened here? What if he was a bad man?

When the old Danish man came back he had washed his face and changed into a clean-looking but wrinkled blue shirt and a pair of jeans. His eyes were so hollow they looked like dark circles; like something out of a horror movie, Raihana thought. Like he had been tortured.

Still, when Christina had said he was sixty-four years old, she had expected an old man who walked with a stoop and seemed all but ready to die. Sixty-four was old in Afghanistan, but this man, despite being too thin and worn, looked as if he were in his early fifties.

"Sorry," he said to Raihana. "I was sleeping."

Raihana understood that much Danish.

"How will she get here every day?" he asked Christina as he drank coffee. They were in the kitchen and both Raihana and Christina had refused Gunnar's offer of coffee.

Raihana answered instead. "Cycle. I can cycle," she said.

"Okay," Gunnar said.

They sat in silence for a while, and Raihana kept her head bowed and stared at her practical black shoes.

"She will start tomorrow," Christina said finally. "What do you want her to do? Why don't you show her around?"

"How much Danish does she understand?" Gunnar asked.

"A little," Raihana said sheepishly.

"Enough," Christina answered at the same time. "She is here to make her Danish better; let's go see your workshop so you can show her the frames."

What is a frame, Raihana wondered as they walked to the workshop.

The workshop was the garage, really a wooden shed that Gunnar and Anna had lovingly built. Even now when Gunnar stepped inside he felt Anna's presence envelop him. She had painted the walls a deep honey color. She had hung pictures of their bees, of them in their hoods and veils as they harvested honey over the workbenches.

He saw the two stainless-steel smokers on the workshop table, scarred with the knives and hammers used to make the frames. His throat closed. They had fought once because Anna said Gunnar kept using her smoker. He didn't plug his smoker with a cork to kill the flames, so his smoker always ran out of fuel, while Anna's didn't. Gunnar had insisted he couldn't tell which was his and which was hers and Anna had tied a ribbon on the handle of her smoker. It was still there, the red ribbon tied into a pretty bow. Gunnar suddenly wanted to get Christina and that Afghan girl out of there. And he wanted to get out himself. This was too much, he thought, his despair becoming overwhelming when he saw Anna's smiling face in one of the photographs on the wall. He had to get out.

"Ah," Raihana cried out then and picked up a frame that was only half wired. There was relief in her voice. "I know this," she said to Christina and then she looked at Gunnar. "See," she said and sat down to slide the wire through the frame and pull it out.

"My *chacha* had same," she said.

"Who is *chacha*?" Gunnar asked and Christina whispered, "An uncle."

"He has many honeybees," the Afghan girl said. "Many honeybees."

"How many?" Gunnar asked.

She gave him a baffled look and then laughed softly. "I count them not," she said. "I try but they sting me, and I run."

Gunnar stared at her and saw an image of a little dark-haired girl looking into a bee colony trying to count each bee. He smiled.

"I have twenty-six colonies," Gunnar said and she looked at him absently.

"I have about a hundred thousand bees," he said and her eyes widened. Regardless of what Christina thought, Gunnar could see that this girl knew nothing about beekeeping.

"How do you count so many?" the girl asked.

"One after another," Gunnar said somberly and then laughed at the shocked look on the girl's face.

FIVE

5 MAY 1980

The sun, the sun, the sun! We have been desperately waiting for the sun because when the sun comes out, the bees come to life. Yesterday, as clouds gathered and stood morosely over my hives, there was no sign of bee activity. But today the bright yellow sun has brought the bees to life—waggle dancing, foraging for pollen, it's time to feed, to live, to buzz.

We went out in the morning right after breakfast and I had to calm myself through the last dredges of coffee in my cup. I could hardly wait. Gunnar felt the same excitement. Our bees were ready.

Hello, bees. It is always such a pleasure to pull them out of the boxes, go through the frames, touch them, hear them, and see them. We spot the queen and see how the brood is doing. All our hives have thrived. We need to make more colonies. By the next bee season, we will have ten colonies, I am sure of it.

We see capped brood in some colonies and we are excited, it means the queen is laying and the hive will be replenished by her offspring as the older ones die off. The cycle of life. The life span of a honeybee is just six weeks, six weeks of gathering pollen and nectar, six weeks of giving and giving and giving. And then winter comes and they snuggle into their cells and sleep until spring.

In one of Gunnar's colonies the queen has laid eggs. We have two colonies each and we will have to move the bees around, make six colonies out of our four. We'll have seven or eight by the time spring is here in full force.

I used to think the protective suits made you look silly, like you were a scientist working in a top-secret lab, but now they feel professional. Wearing them makes me happy because when I put one on, I know I will be seeing my bees again.

"So is he any better now or is he still sitting around and drinking coffee all day?" Layla asked Raihana. Raihana had been working with Gunnar, called "the Danish man" in Raihana's Afghan circles, for a month now.

Raihana had had little to report during her first month. When Layla and Kabir asked what he was like, she told them he was quiet and minded his own business. Raihana had found a *praktik* that was easier than Layla's as she had absolutely no work to do.

"The same," Raihana said. "Very moody . . . but then his wife just died."

"And you're not scared of him?" Layla asked.

Raihana shook her head. No, she wasn't scared of him. The fear had disappeared when he had laughed. He had joked with her about counting one bee after another and somehow that had made her feel better about him and the bees. He had suddenly seemed like a normal man, a friendly man, and she wasn't nervous around him anymore.

"What is that you do every day?" Layla asked.

They were making dinner together, as they always did. Raihana did most of the cooking while Layla helped with the chopping and cleaning up. The division of labor had asserted itself as soon as Raihana arrived in Layla's house. Layla had been relieved. She had tried to learn how to cook but just like Raihana couldn't sew anything without it going completely wrong, Layla couldn't cook. She started out making *biriyani* and somehow it never tasted right and more often than not, something got burned at the bottom of the pot. Once she had tried to make *samboosas* and it had been a disaster of monumental proportions.

Raihana, on the other hand, could take potatoes and onions and make the perfect *sabzi* to go with rice or *rotis*. She made excellent desserts, even Danish ones, after she had gotten recipes from a Danish cookbook in the language school's library.

Layla, Kabir, and especially Shahrukh had been thrilled to find Danish layer cake one evening—made just as it was in the bakeries with layers of sponge, yellow custard, fresh strawberries, and whipped cream.

"I have been making frames. Next week we check on the bee colonies to see how many are alive and how many died," she said. "We are already late. He should have started looking at the bees two or three weeks ago. It is the end of April now . . . many bees will have died and some colonies might be getting ready to swarm."

"Swarm?"

Raihana nodded casually as if it were a word that she used often. The truth was that she'd had to look it up and it had taken her several days and help from Christina to understand what it meant.

"If there are too many bees in a hive then half the bees leave and go elsewhere looking for food," she told Layla.

Layla stared at her. "How do you know this?"

Raihana feigned nonchalance. But she was proud of what she had learned about bees in just a month. Gunnar hadn't helped much. In the garage workshop she had found a black leather diary in which someone had painstakingly recorded a year of beekeeping with a blue ink pen. The writing was so neat that it seemed as if it had been printed on a laser printer like the ones at the language school, instead of being written by hand.

It was in Danish, and Raihana could decipher about a third with her Danish-to-Dari dictionary. For the rest she went to Christina with questions.

Christina had looked puzzled at the black diary.

"It is okay to use?" she asked Christina, worried that maybe she shouldn't have the diary.

"Yes, yes," Christina said. "Gunnar gave this to you?"

Raihana nodded. Technically he had not given it to her. She had found it and asked him if she could take it with her and he had waved his hand. She wasn't sure he had understood what she had said and if what she had said in Danish was even understandable. But it was just a book; she didn't think anyone would mind. Obviously the Danish man didn't seem to care.

"Okay, let's see what your question is," Christina said, flipping to the page Raihana had marked with a piece of paper.

For the next few Wednesdays during their one-on-one study sessions, Raihana and Christina pored through the black diary. The technical terms were the hardest for Raihana as there was no way to translate them. But Christina's husband was a beekeeper too, so she drew diagrams to explain the various tools used for beekeeping.

"Anna was a very passionate woman," Christina said, smiling at a passage where Anna talked about how hard the bees worked.

Raihana had to consult her dictionary to find out the meaning of the word *passionate*. Reading the dictionary was like putting the pieces of a puzzle together and Raihana took pleasure in the game.

Raihana preferred going to school than to her *praktik*. It was boring to go and sit in the Danish man's garage. The Danish man didn't speak with her or teach her anything. He sat there like a lump of clay, ignoring her. However, Raihana felt she couldn't back out now, not after she had convinced Kabir and Layla that this was such a good idea.

But she was annoyed about being in this man's garage, in his house, in his presence when he would barely acknowledge her. The house was horribly untidy and filthy in many places. She wasn't supposed to go inside the house. She was supposed to stay in the garage or go to the beehives in the backyard, but she got tired of sitting in the garage and there was nothing to do in the garden but watch the bees race around.

The more she found out about bees, the more she was in awe of them. The bees left during the day, hunting for honey, and then found their way back at dusk. She had learned that from the diary. She had also learned that the longer the Danish man waited to check on his bees, the larger the chance they would swarm—because they couldn't all fit in their box—or die because they didn't have enough food.

The Danish man always opened the door on the second knock, never the first. She would smile at him and he would nod without smiling in return. Then he would point to the garage and close the door in her face. Raihana would go to the garage and sit down. She had peeked in the room used for storing honey and saw a big steel machine, stacked white buckets, and some other equipment. Most of the time Raihana sat at the workbench, staring at the road and the cars that went by.

When it was time for lunch, she would open her lunch box and eat the sandwich she had brought and drink some of the juice she had packed in a plastic bottle that once had Coca-Cola in it.

She would wire frames for part of the day and then when she got bored she'd read the black diary. And when that got boring too, she'd look at her wristwatch, waiting to get back home.

She came to Gunnar's house for fifteen hours a week. The hours were split into three days so that she had time for language classes as well.

The first few days she didn't leave the garage until the designated time. She came in at eight in the morning and left at one in the afternoon. But as the weeks passed she started leaving ten to fifteen minutes before one o'clock and then eventually almost an hour before she had to go.

One day she brought chicken curry and bread for lunch and needed to go inside the Danish man's house to heat the chicken curry.

"May I use microwave today?" she asked the Danish man when he opened the door in the morning for her.

He looked at her confused. "Okay," he said and opened the door wide.

"No, not now, for lunch," she said.

"Okay," he responded and slammed the door shut in her face again.

When she knocked at lunchtime, he opened the door and let her in. He sat and watched TV while he drank his coffee; at least she thought it was coffee. The man lay in a stupor all day; she wouldn't be surprised if he was drinking something a little stronger than coffee.

She found the microwave, but it was so filthy that she couldn't bring herself to put her food in it. Raihana knew it wasn't her job but she couldn't help it. She had been raised in a clean house and when she had kept her own household everything had been spick-and-span, even though she and Aamir had lived in a one-room flat where the windows had been shattered by bullets a long time before and had been replaced with thick plastic. Raihana cleaned the plastic the best she could so that they could look out the windows without opening them. They didn't have much, but what they had, Raihana took good care of. Aamir had given the flat to their neighbor's uncle in order to get Raihana safely across the border.

Without asking for permission Raihana started to clean the Danish man's kitchen. She found cleaning supplies under the kitchen sink and rolled up her sleeves. First, she put all the dirty dishes into the dishwasher.

How much work was it to put a cup inside the dishwasher? Why hadn't the man done anything? she thought irritably as she used the Ajax spray she'd found over the counters and cleaned with a paper towel.

When she left that day, the kitchen wasn't exactly gleaming, but it was clean.

The next day she decided she'd clean the living and dining rooms as well. The Danish man had gone right ahead and left coffee cups and dirty plates all over the counters and sink. How could he have made such a mess in one evening?

She got the mop and vacuum cleaner from the garage and started cleaning. She didn't say anything to the Danish man and he didn't say anything to her. When she came into the living room armed with the vacuum cleaner, he scuttled farther inside the house. Raihana didn't want to clean any more rooms than she was already cleaning; she especially didn't want to think about the bathroom. There was a small toilet attached to the honey room, which she used. That bathroom had been neat and tidy, pretty pink curtains on the small window and a bar of pink soap in the sink. The pink towel was dirty, so Raihana had brought her own. It was also pink and Raihana took it home with her every other day to wash.

The dining room was narrow with a red-and-black carpet on the wooden floor. The dining table was huge and seated twelve. There had been dust on the table, greasy and thick, when Raihana first walked in. Now it gleamed with the furniture oil she had found under the sink.

The living room had a big sofa, two comfortable leather chairs, and a coffee table. There were knickknacks on the mantelpiece and on a shelf next to the television. Raihana dusted and wiped off everything and then vacuumed.

The Danish man didn't say thank you and he didn't say stop, so Raihana continued to clean. After a week of cleaning part of the house, she itched to clean the rest, just so that she'd have something to do. But before she could, the Danish man opened the door one morning and told her they would be melting foundation wax on the frames that day.

"Does he teach you everything about bees?" Layla asked as Raihana put the last of the diced mutton into the big pot she was making *biriyani* in.

"Not really," Raihana said. "He just sits in his house and watches TV. I do everything myself."

"Do you go inside the house a lot?" Layla wanted to know.

Raihana knew she couldn't tell the truth about how she spent a good part of her day inside his house, cleaning it. Both Kabir and Layla were paranoid about white men and had made her promise that she would stay out in the open and not go into the house where she would be alone with him.

It amused Raihana that Kabir didn't worry about Layla spending time in a grocery store after hours, alone with other workers, some of them Danish men, but was afraid for Raihana because she was alone with a frail old man.

Layla looked around to make sure neither Kabir nor Shahrukh was around. "Has he . . . you know . . . tried anything?"

Raihana stared at Layla for a second, unable to understand what she was asking, and then sighed in exasperation. "I told you, his wife died recently and he's still mourning."

"Just because someone's wife died doesn't mean they don't try to you know . . . ," Layla said. "Be careful. If he tries anything, anything inappropriate, you should leave. Promise me, Raihana."

Raihana couldn't imagine that sad man would ever do anything improper with her. He barely noticed her, but she knew better than most that people changed and that without reason, those you trust could become enemies.

"I promise," she said.

.   .   .

Gunnar would not have mentioned anything about the Afghan girl if it weren't for Maria's nagging. Why didn't she nag her husband instead?

She called almost every day and finally, to end her incessant talk about how Gunnar should come live with them in Odense for a while, especially since he was not taking care of bees this season, he told her that he had hired someone to help him.

"Hired? From where? Who?" Maria asked.

Reluctant to say much about Raihana, he told her that Christina had recommended someone. He ignored Maria's further questions about the gender, age, and identity of the someone he had hired.

He felt guilty about having that Afghan girl in his house. She just sat there and wired and wired and cleaned and he did not talk to her at all. She was here to learn Danish and he said about three words to her every day. But then, he reminded himself, that was not his job. He was not a Danish teacher and he hadn't wanted her to come in the first place.

She came at eight in the morning sharp, wearing some frilly shirt over pants. She didn't wear any headgear like the other Muslim women he saw on the streets and neither did she wear an *abaya* to cover the rest of her body. She wore sensible shoes, not like the skimpy, high-heeled ones Maria wore. And she brought a cheap-looking black backpack.

She ate lunch in the kitchen, alone, because the first time she had asked if it was time for lunch, looking hopeful, Gunnar had said she could eat and went inside his bedroom. When he came out there was no trace of her or her food except for the faint smell of exotic spices and garlic. She had also started to pick up after him in the living room, which was now devoid of stained cups of coffee, dirty plates, and crumpled and soiled paper towels.

In the kitchen, the dishes that had been lying in the sink for days, well, since Peter had last come and cleaned up, had also been taken care of. She had stacked everything neatly in the dishwasher and had even started it.

He was pleased because it wasn't easy to live in a mess when you had lived most of your life with the ultra-neat Anna. But he was too lazy to clean. And this was quite a perk for having that Afghan girl here, he thought. Maybe she could clean the bedroom and bathroom as well, he would be happy to pay her.

It wasn't because he was grateful to her for keeping the kitchen, living room, and now dining room clean that he decided to spend some time teaching her how to lay foundation wax on the frames. He did it because he was bored and drinking another cup of coffee could, he feared, erode the last of his stomach lining. He knew he had to do something, so that morning, when Raihana knocked, he told her they'd melt wax today.

Having the Afghan girl around had certainly changed a few things for Gunnar. She always seemed happy. Content. Far removed from Gunnar's mourning.

Gunnar wondered if Christina had told him the truth about this girl losing her husband in Afghanistan. She didn't look like someone who had lost a spouse. She was just a girl, about twenty-two, twenty-three? How long could they have been married? Two or three years? Not like him and Anna. Maybe when you were married a short time the impact of a loss was not as great. She grinned at his suggestion that they work together on the frames, decidedly one of the most boring parts of beekeeping.

Gunnar started the motor of the electrodes and placed them on the wires that ran through the wooden frames. Raihana laid a sheet of foundation wax, which smelled sharply of honey. It was made of the wax from the hives when they were full of honey. These were commercially bought sheets, Gunnar told her, showing her the label on top of the plastic bag that held the sheets.

Raihana had held a sheet of foundation wax and smelled it eagerly. The sheet was segmented evenly into cells. It had amazed her to read in that black notebook that the bees built their cells exactly on top of the cells on the foundation sheet.

"Is it going to be melting full?" Raihana asked in distress as the electrodes heated the wires that melted the foundation wax so that it stuck to the wires and became part of the frame. She worried the wax would melt away from the wires and onto the table.

"It doesn't melt that much," Gunnar said, a little irritated. Couldn't she wait to see what happened instead of jumping in? She was just like Anna, interrupting instead of waiting and seeing what happened.

"How do bees know where cells are to building their honey on top?" she asked.

"They just know," Gunnar said.

The Afghan girl looked at him, confused. He simply said, "They are born knowing."

It wasn't as hard as he had thought it would be. She was not stupid, though he'd had the feeling that she would be. He had thought she would not understand anything he said. She never got a whole sentence right, but she managed to communicate. Christina had said she had come to Denmark a few months before and had started going to the Sprogcentre just three to four months ago. So Gunnar was surprised at how much Danish she spoke and understood. He had always heard that Danish was a very difficult language to learn—everyone said so—and he assumed a foreigner would have a hard time learning it.

Once Julie had dated a Scottish man and he had given up learning Danish after a year because it had been so difficult. They had been living in London then and he had tried to learn Danish by taking classes there. Maybe it was easier for this girl because she was in Denmark. Maybe it was easier because she had no choice.

Gunnar got used to the Afghan girl and he looked forward to the days she came into his house and took some of the loneliness away. He hadn't realized how empty the house had been and now with her forcing her way in three times a week, a part of him wanted to wake up in the morning, drink coffee, have breakfast, even take care of his bees.

As he cooked a rather luxurious breakfast of fried eggs, bacon, and toast for himself, he marveled at how young she looked—almost painfully young. There was a suppleness to her face, her eyes, and the way she carried herself. Beyond youth it spoke of innocence but he wondered how innocent she could be if she had witnessed any of the atrocities they said the Taliban had committed. He had watched enough TV to know what was happening in Afghanistan, how the United States Army was there, taking revenge for the attacks on their country.

Just the day before, he had seen a documentary on TV2 in which a British Muslim woman, a journalist, had taken a hidden camera into Afghanistan. He saw a woman being executed in a packed football stadium. For a moment he wondered what was happening and when they shot the woman he had stood up and stared at the television screen. This couldn't be, he thought, you can't just execute someone in public. The Afghan women in the documentary had no faces, no bodies, no feminine shapes, no visible identities as they hid behind black garments.

Had this Afghan girl also worn that black dress? Had she been scared that she might be executed in a football stadium?

A Danish journalist who had been to Afghanistan had been interviewed after the documentary was shown and he had, to Gunnar's shock, said that executions were big entertainment in Kabul when the Taliban ruled Afghanistan.

Gunnar would never have paid this much attention to someplace so far away except that someone from that place was now in his life.

He sat down and finished the breakfast he'd cooked for himself. Gunnar turned the radio up to keep him company and listened to Danish pop songs and English ones. Almost everyone was calling everyone "baby" these days, he thought as he enjoyed the succulent breakfast sausages he had taken from the freezer. Maria had made sure over Christmas that the freezer was as well stocked as it had been when Anna was alive.

Gunnar poured himself another cup of coffee after finishing his breakfast and felt content. The breakfast was flawless, he decided, just like it was when Anna cooked it.

. . .

"Will we saw bees today?" Raihana asked him.

He had come with her to the garage—because the idea of sitting inside his house after that fabulous breakfast seemed untenable.

The weather had been quite good this year, which meant that he should have checked on his colonies in February to see if they needed food after the long winter. He was sure some of his colonies had starved to death and those that had survived would have picked up enough pollen and nectar from the first flowers in bloom—the small white snowdrops, *vintergækker*, and the bright yellow *erantis*—that they would be getting ready to swarm. Anna had supersonic ears and she could hear the bees as they got ready to leave the colony and find a new home. Anna was their swarm radar and she and Gunnar had always managed to avoid swarming by adding more boxes in time.

But this year he had been sitting on his ass doing nothing. It was the end of April. If swarming had begun he hadn't heard it, though he hadn't been out enough to hear any bee activity. Before the bees swarmed, scout bees would start looking for a place for the colony to move. And if he had been watching his colonies he would have seen the bees starting to make a new queen so the colony could split in two.

A pang went through him: what Anna would think of him ignoring the bees? She would be disappointed.

"See a honeybees todays?" Raihana asked again because he hadn't really answered, just nodding vaguely while he looked around the garage. Gunnar realized she was trying to get through to him, trying her best to get something out of this *praktik*.

"Yes," Gunnar found himself saying. Christina had told him to correct the Afghan girl's Danish when she said something wrong but he felt self-conscious speaking to her. Let Christina deal with correcting mistakes, he would just . . . do what? What *was* he doing with this girl in his house?

"We shall go see the bees," he said to her finally and opened the old wooden wardrobe in the garage.

It had been his mother's and when she died he had inherited it along with other furniture. Maria had wanted some pieces, like the big wooden chest and Arne Jacobsen chairs, and the old rocking chair that had been his father's had gone to Julie. Anna had complained about the cost of shipping it all the way to London but Julie was determined to have the old chair.

So Gunnar had sanded it and put on a new coat of paint, while Anna had sewn new pillows. She had chosen dark colors so that when something spilled on the cushions they wouldn't stain, even though she knew that Julie would have preferred something light, maybe pale yellow. If there was one thing Gunnar didn't like about Anna, it was how she easily disregarded what others wanted if she felt what she was doing was better.

"But this is better for you," Anna would say calmly when Gunnar protested, and he would quietly agree.

The Afghan girl looked curiously at the white protective suit.

"Put it on, otherwise bees will sting," Gunnar said.

Her eyes wide, she put the suit on. It was a bulky white shirt paired with bulky white pants. The suit had belonged to Anna and Gunnar hadn't wanted to give it to the Afghan girl but he knew it was silly to be so sentimental about the suit. Anna wouldn't have minded.

Gunnar handed Raihana a hood and veil and blue gloves, which she also put on. She looked a little silly, but everyone did when they put on the protective suits.

He picked up a bottom board and started piling things on it: extra frames they had just wired, an empty box to add to the colony if it was getting ready to swarm, and packets of white sugar candy for the colonies that needed extra food. Then he got out his tool belt and checked for his knife in the enclosed leather pocket. It was all coming back to him, and the difference between how much he used to love all of this and how cumbersome it felt now didn't escape him.

"Let's go," he said.

She waited as he stuck one of the smokers into his tool belt. "No suit for you?"

"No," Gunnar said.

"Will not the bees be biting you?" she asked.

"No," he said. "They know me."

Did all the bees know him? Raihana wondered. How could they? What about the bees that were born while he was sitting in his dirty house drinking coffee and doing God knows what?

She had not mentioned to Kabir or Layla about the bottles of whiskey she saw in the trash. She had also not told them that she went inside the house and cleaned it. She knew that if she did Kabir would ask her to stop her *praktik*. Kabir had spoken with Christina and explained to her that he was not happy about Raihana being alone with a man all day in his house.

Christina assured him there was no cause for concern, which didn't do anything to quell Kabir's fear. He carried the prejudice most people from Afghanistan and the East did that white men were immoral and without honor. He had read somewhere that two out of three marriages in Denmark ended in divorce and usually adultery was involved. He had shaken his head at that statistic. White men and women had no sense of family, no sense of honor, and they dared look at him like he was scum?

Raihana had tried to convince Kabir that the Danish man was harmless, which he was. It was even harder to convince the other Afghans, who were not as open as Kabir and Layla.

"Good Afghan women do not go cavorting about with white men," Wahida said when she sat with her in class.

"I am not cavorting with him. I work for him and take care of his bees," Raihana had said.

"*Take care of his bees,*" Wahida repeated sarcastically. "You know, you should wear a *hijab,* an *abaya,* and be a good Muslim woman. My husband organizes prayer every evening, you should come and join us."

Raihana looked away from Wahida. Kabir had told her about Wahida's husband, Hamud, who worked with other imams and radical Muslims in Denmark to convert other Muslims into conservatism.

"I went for evening prayer at Hamud's house once, thought it was a social thing . . . and then Hamud starts to tell me I should stop smoking and talks about jihad. I didn't go back," Kabir said.

Kabir thought Hamud gave refugees a bad name. He had gone to language school as all refugees had to by law, but he had not learned Danish. He had not bothered to find a job and lived off welfare. Hamud only did what he had to in Denmark to not get deported.

"His brother is the same," Kabir said to Raihana. "This is a family that dishonors Afghans. They live off charity and never intend to work."

Wahida was the same. The slowest to learn Danish in the class, she seemed to not care whether she learned the language or not, despite Christina's best efforts. There were other refugees like Wahida. Kabir told her about a man he knew in Viborg who had brought his entire family to Denmark from Iran and none of them worked. They all lived off welfare. Kabir was baffled that it didn't hurt their pride to not earn a living.

But for people like Wahida, pride was connected to how religious they believed they were.

"Raihana, this will end badly," Wahida warned her.

"Then that is my problem," Raihana said, not looking at Wahida, staring at her notebook.

"How you behave reflects on the entire Afghan community," Wahida said. "All of us are affected by this. Would you behave like this in Kabul?"

"Wahida, why did you leave Afghanistan? Why did you leave the perfect world that the Taliban was building there for people like you?" Raihana asked pointedly, turning to face Wahida.

"My husband's brother was here and he brought us here," she said defensively. "We were happy in Afghanistan . . . we just wanted to live someplace else."

"Wahida, we are Afghans, the only reason we leave our home is to survive. And—"

Christina clapped her hands and interrupted. "Raihana, Wahida, *vi taler Dansk. Hvad snakker om i?*"

Christina always interrupted conversations in languages other than Danish by saying "We speak Danish in class" and then asking the errant students to tell the class what they had been talking about.

"Nothing," Raihana said, picking up her books, and moved away from Wahida. She didn't sit with Wahida again.

SIX

17 MAY 1980

Last year Gunnar got stung all over the face by bees and since then we have a bee suit rule. But now Gunnar is ignoring the rule. He feels more confident than I without the suit. "But they know me," he says when I scold him, and they do. Our bees know us.

This morning we found more brood, more pollen, more nectar, and more bees. The queen has worked hard in the past month; our colonies have become thicker, richer, and stronger.

Sometimes I sit and watch the bees on the frames and every time there is precision. The cells are always one shape and the same size. I am amazed at their precision. So many bees working together in beautiful harmony makes me a little melancholy. Do they all want to be doing what they are doing? Are there bees that don't want to work so hard? I wonder about the personalities of the bees and I wonder if there is a rebel bee, one that wants to run away and find a new life.

After so many years of nothing to look forward to, the excitement Raihana felt about the bees was new, and fresh, and scary.

Even Layla had remarked that Raihana seemed happier. "What's going on?" she asked.

They were shopping in Kvickly while Kabir was with Shahrukh at home. It was a beautiful day and neither of them complained about having to bicycle to the supermarket and then ride back with all the groceries.

"Nothing," Raihana said.

"Something is," Layla said, picking up two cartons of Arla *letmælk*, skim milk.

"We need cream too," Raihana said and Layla grabbed a half-liter carton of thick cream, which they ate with sugar and strawberries in the warm evenings.

Layla looked at Raihana suspiciously. Raihana was thrilled about her *praktik* but she couldn't share it with Layla, who might misunderstand. Every Monday, Tuesday, and Wednesday, Raihana felt she was on an adventure when she went to the Danish man's house—she never knew what new thing she would learn about the bees.

There were twenty-six boxes in the Danish man's backyard, neatly arranged in rows of three. Raihana assumed that the Danish man's dead wife had been responsible for this because he did not seem the neat kind.

According to the black diary Raihana had found in the garage, as the colonies grew, they would place more boxes on top of the existing ones to give the colonies more room to grow. More boxes meant more honey and she couldn't wait to look into the boxes and see what was happening.

. . .

The Danish man seemed confused when they reached the bees, as if unsure of what to do. He pulled out a lighter from his tool belt and lit the fuel in the smoker and shut it, shaking the smoker to kill the flames so that only smoke poured out. Raihana had looked inside the smokers in the garage and had found small pieces of sackcloth inside. She noticed that the smoke coming out of the smoker was cold.

"Always use a smoker," he told Raihana as he pumped the handle. "Smoke makes the bees think there is a fire, so they eat as much honey as they can and then they don't sting."

"Because the bee stomach is full with honey?" Raihana asked.

"Yes, they don't sting when their stomachs are full," said Gunnar.

He put everything he had brought from the garage on an old wooden table that stood for this purpose in the backyard. The table was worn, the wood weathered from harsh winters and steady Danish rain.

He had brought a wooden base with a mesh-like frame and put that on the ground. He picked up the first brown box full of bees and set it on the wooden base.

"Never put the box with the bees on the ground," he said but didn't explain why. Below the box was another board, a wooden base, in which lay several dead bees.

Bees were everywhere, Raihana noticed. They were crawling out of holes in the boxes and going back in. The sound of the bees was almost overwhelming, like being in the middle of a busy supermarket where everyone was speaking Danish in loud whispers.

The man bent down and looked at the dead bees and sighed.

"Many have died," he said. "I am too late in feeding them. I should've given them sugar."

Raihana was not sure if he was talking to her. She didn't understand why they had died but she could see he blamed himself.

He upended the base and let the dead bees fall on the ground. Then he turned to the first box, which was clamped shut with a metallic bolt, and lifted open the lid. Immediately he pumped the smoker onto the mesh top and Raihana stepped back. There were a billion bees in there and they were all buzzing angrily.

It had been a sport while Raihana was growing up to throw a stone at wild beehives on tall trees. The hives would be in a semicircle, totally covered with bees, and Raihana used to feel an impulse to run all the bees off. The way they were packed next to one another always made her want to separate them.

Every time a stone hit the hive, the bees would rush in furious swirls and Raihana and her friends would run as fast as they could to get inside a house before the bees could catch up to them.

The Danish man was moving the bees around with his bare hands and looking into their hive. Raihana felt secure in her white protective suit, but the Danish man wore nothing and seemed quite comfortable, not afraid of getting stung.

He pulled a frame from the box, just like the ones she had been wiring. The cells in the frame were dark, seemed full, and were raised from the base. The bees had built their cells right on top of the foundation.

He ran his finger gently over the cells and looked the frame up and down. He picked up one frame and then another.

"Not enough bees in this colony now," he said.

He opened the second box and that one didn't have many bees either. He took the frames with the bees from the second box and added them to the first.

"They will grow together and become a better colony," he said. Raihana didn't understand so she didn't respond, and he didn't try to make it clear.

Then he picked out a frame and showed her a bee. It didn't look different from the other bees except that it had a small yellow mark on its back. "That is a queen bee."

Raihana nodded. She knew about queen bees.

"She lays eggs and makes more bees," he said, putting the frame back.

He pulled out another frame and showed her yet another bee, this one with a blue mark on its back. "This is also a queen bee but she is younger than the other one," he said. "The yellow one was made in 1997 and the blue one in 2000."

He had to repeat himself twice before she understood him.

"How bee know to be yellow in 1997 and blue in 2000?" Raihana asked. Gunnar seemed amused.

"I paint the bee," he said. "The bee doesn't change color."

"You paint bee? Why?" she asked, bewildered.

He explained something about coloring bees every year, or was it coloring queen bees every year in a different color?

"There can only be one queen in a colony," he said. "If there are two, they will fight and only one will live."

"How do you know what is queen bee?" she asked.

He tried again, slowly, but she didn't understand him completely. She had figured out that they looked different but she couldn't really see the difference and the buzzing, added to him speaking in Danish, was driving her crazy.

"You understand?" he asked after he finished speaking.

Raihana wanted to nod as she did when Christina talked too fast for Raihana to comprehend her, but she didn't want to lie to Gunnar.

"*Jeg kan ikke forstår*," she said honestly.

Gunnar said that it was okay that she couldn't understand, because she would soon. "*Du vil snart.*"

Raihana smiled at his confidence in her. She didn't believe she would ever learn Danish, not like Kabir had. It was one of the hardest things about being in this country, not being able to speak the language, to understand what people said. She couldn't get a real job until she spoke Danish. It grated on her that she got money from the Danish government. She was helpless here with no language, no education, no husband, nothing. That was why this *praktik* had come to mean so much to her. Even if she and the Danish man weren't talking, she was learning Danish from the little black book. She labored with the book in the evenings and wrote the sentences she didn't comprehend in her notebook. The next day she'd ask Christina for help. She hoped Aamir would be proud of her, proud that she was working this hard at learning a new language.

Aamir had insisted on her learning English for the day they would get out of Afghanistan and build a new life. That was why she had taken English classes at the refugee camp. Aamir couldn't have guessed that she would end up in a country where they spoke yet another language, a language that she thought was even harder than English.

He had been such an idealist, just like his sister and brother-in-law. Raihana was still surprised that Aamir had agreed to marry her, his poor and uneducated relative. But Aamir had confessed that he had fallen love with her at first sight. One look and he knew she would be his wife.

Everyone told her that she was lucky to get a young, handsome, and educated husband. And she had been fortunate to have a husband who loved her so much and so well.

Gunnar carefully arranged the new colony he made from his two failed ones in the brown box. He shifted them to make sure there was enough room between the frames and checked to make sure these two colonies could thrive as one.

They had lost colonies before. It happened. One winter three of Anna's colonies had been attacked by mice. By the time they had found out in early spring, the mice had been stung to death but not before they had eaten a good part of the honey and the brood.

They had also lost a few colonies, mostly Gunnar's, to swarming when they went on vacation to Italy. It had been Lars's fault because he hadn't checked on the bees as often as he'd promised. By the time they got back, the colony had grown so much that there just wasn't enough room. Half the bees had gone off to find a new home. Anna and Gunnar never went on vacation outside Denmark after that.

He opened another colony and was relieved to see it thriving.

There were larvae in several of the frames. This colony would need more room, he knew, as he pulled out another frame filled with larvae. Larvae became pupae, which became adult bees. Large number of larvae meant a thriving colony and more honey at the end of the season.

"Larvae," he said to Raihana and showed her the wriggly worms lying inside translucent shells. "Baby bees," he added when she seemed unsure.

Her eyes lit up when she saw the larvae. When one broke free from its shell and started to crawl out, she gasped.

Gunnar couldn't help but smile. It had been a long time since he had taken pleasure in the simple aspects of beekeeping. He and Anna had gotten so caught up in their hives doing well and the honey production that they often forgot to enjoy the process as they had in the early years.

Gunnar added a few empty frames in the box with the thriving colony to give the bees more room to grow. He knew the next time he was here he would have to add a new box to the colony so they could grow more, beyond their one box.

Gunnar put the plastic queen bee excluder on top of the frames. There was a debate among beekeepers in Denmark about using queen bee excluders. Since the queen bee was bigger than all other bees, she couldn't get past the separator, but the other bees could. This ensured that the queen stayed in the lower boxes of the colony and didn't contaminate the top boxes with larvae. Anna and Gunnar wanted to keep the larvae out of the honey in the top boxes.

Other Danish beekeepers felt it was wrong to restrict the motion of the queen and it was important to let her wander and lay her eggs wherever she wished. Anna had done research and talked to people and had decided they would use queen bee excluders.

Gunnar went to his supplies on the table and found a packet of white sugar candy. Yes, this colony needed more food and more room to thrive. He was relieved because this was one of Anna's colonies and he wanted to take better care of them than his own. As long as her colonies were not the ones dying, maybe she wouldn't come back to haunt him.

Gunnar cut a small piece of the plastic cover holding the white sugar candy and then put the packet of sugar, cut-side down, on top of the queen bee excluder. The worker bees could now wiggle through the spaces in the plastic mesh to get food.

The Danish man cut open a rectangular piece of the sugar bag and lay it on the frames so the bees could get to the sugar through the hole in the bag. He then put the wire mesh frame on top and closed the box.

"Food for the bees," he said.

Raihana wanted to ask if the bees couldn't get enough food from flowers but she didn't know the right words. She was also worried that he would get upset with all her questions, especially when she often didn't understand his answers. So she remained silent.

As Gunnar opened more boxes, he became more and more cheerful. The bee colonies in the next boxes were healthy and growing, so much so that they might swarm soon.

As he opened more boxes, he showed her the baby bees and the white waxy substance on top of the hives, beeswax. "It is used to make candles," he told her.

Whenever he put in a frame she had wired, Raihana felt proud that she had been of some use.

Gunnar stuck his finger into the hives, turned and twisted the frames, scraped things off. He sometimes smiled and sometimes sighed. Raihana stood in her encumbering white suit and watched. As he went from frame to frame and box to box, her excitement abated and she was actually getting a little bored wondering when she could go home.

Kabir had been to Hamburg over the weekend and bought four Hindi movies and one Iranian TV show on DVD. She and Layla were looking forward to seeing the new Akshay Kumar movie as they had heard the songs from the movie on the Internet and liked them very much. Neither of them spoke much Hindi but they understood just fine and in the cold foreign world they lived in, entertainment from back home was like a thick blanket they wrapped around themselves to keep warm.

Raihana was trying to glance at her watch when he suddenly pulled up a frame and then looked at her.

"Take your hood off," he said, pointing at it.

Raihana looked around at the bees. She didn't want to get stung but he seemed to think it was okay. He asked her again to take her hood off. Despite being scared, she finally took the hood off. The Danish man stuck his finger into the lush hive, breaking the intricate cells the bees had made, and pulled out some honey. He held it up to her mouth and Raihana looked wide-eyed at his finger covered with the golden and sticky liquid around it. Did he think she would lick his finger?

As if suddenly realizing what he had done, he pulled his finger back and stuck it in his mouth. He held up the frame toward her and she gingerly took a glove off, now wary of both the hive and the bees buzzing around them. What if they saw her take their food and destroy their home, wouldn't they get upset and sting her?

"Try, come on," the Danish man encouraged.

Raihana put a finger into the hive as he had and the warmth inside shot through her finger. It was wonderful. Her finger was floating in richness and as she pulled out a sticky glob of honey, she smelled its rich and unique perfume. She put her finger in her mouth and the flavor exploded. It was like waking up, she thought giddily.

Greedy for more, she dipped her finger in again, and as she pulled it out a bee stung her on the cheek.

SEVEN

1 JUNE 1980

We have been keeping bees for two years now and I have never been stung. Bees sting because we are not careful, not because they are aggressive— that is beekeeper fact. Today we had record temperatures. The weather was beautiful and in the afternoon I lay down on the terrace to soak up some sun. The kids were with Gunnar's parents for the weekend and it was just us and the bees.

Gunnar came home after dropping off the kids and started to talk about the weeds and the way the hedge was growing outrageously. We had had constant arguments with our neighbors about not cutting the hedge properly. Their side was always too high and I like it trim and proper.

It happened right outside the garage. A bee was resting on one of my Karen Blixen roses. I was trying to wrench out a hoe from its hook to start work in the garden, and I don't how the bee got hit, but it spun around and stung me on my hand, right below my thumb. It hurt, but not as much as I always feared it would. And I had no allergic reaction, which was a relief. It wouldn't do for a beekeeper to have a serious reaction to a bee sting.

It was all in all quite an eventful day. My first bee sting and the neighbors actually cut their hedge properly for the first time in ten years.

For days after, he remembered how the Afghan girl had winced and tears had filled her eyes when the bee stung her. But it could have been worse: she could have been allergic to the sting. As it was there was only a little pain, some irritation, and some inconvenience.

The rest of her face had looked so pale compared with the harsh redness of the sting. She said nothing when he grabbed her cheek to force out the venom. She looked suspiciously at the onion Gunnar raced to get from the kitchen and then held to her cheek.

"It's good for the sting," he said, letting go of the onion so she could hold on to it. After a while she put the onion away and told him uneasily that her cheek was feeling better.

He suggested that he drive her home instead of her riding back on her bicycle but she had refused, saying that she was fine.

He felt horrible because he was the one who made her take off her hood and veil. But he'd wanted to share that first taste of honey in the spring with her. It was a taste he used to crave in the cold winter, the warmth of it, the freshness of the honey. There was nothing quite like it, he and Anna had agreed. But now the Afghan girl had a big bee sting and a swollen, red right cheek.

By the next week, the swelling had gone down and only a small brown mark was left behind. She said she was fine but didn't suggest they go out to the bees. Instead she cleaned the house like she used to in the early days of her *praktik*.

He didn't press her. The Afghan girl cleaned up the kitchen, living room, and dining room. She even folded the clothes that lay in the washroom. She did some basic gardening—pulling weeds and sweeping out the leaves—but she didn't go to the backyard where the bees were.

Gunnar had not gone back since she had been stung either. There was no joy in going back alone. He wanted to go with her and show her everything, teach her about harvesting honey and making heather honey. She was so interested in everything he had to say; it made him feel good to have someone hang on to his words so carefully.

But the house was sparkling clean, which even Peter noticed when he came for a visit on the weekend. He also remarked that it was a pleasure to see Gunnar sober after so long.

"It's that girl Christina hired through the *praktik* program. She cleans. She isn't supposed to but she does anyway," he told Peter.

"What girl?" Peter asked.

Gunnar had been sure that either Ole or Christina would have mentioned something to Peter and their other beekeeping friends. So he explained about the Afghan girl and her *praktik*.

"You have some Afghan girl here all day? Are you mad?"

"She comes just three times a week and she's not here all day," Gunnar said, feeling a little defensive and surprised that Peter was reacting this way. First there was Christina, who had made him feel guilty for not helping the girl, and now Peter was making him feel guilty for having her here.

"Don't you know anything about these refugee types? All they want is EU citizenship and to gouge money out of our welfare system," Peter said vehemently. "What will you do if she says that you treated her improperly?"

"Why would she do that?" Gunnar asked.

"To get money out of you, to blackmail you," Peter said in exasperation. "These people are depraved. See what they are capable of? They fly airplanes into buildings. They kill people in the name of religion."

Gunnar looked at Peter as if he had gone mad. "Are you saying this Afghan girl is a terrorist?"

"She could be," Peter said. "You can't trust them. The coalition government of Radikale Venstre and Socialdemokratiet allowed too many immigrants into Denmark—now, with the new government, things are getting better. Immigrants don't get jobs, they don't learn Danish, they wear their stupid clothes . . . what? Why are you looking at me like that?"

Gunnar was shaking his head. He used to think the same way. Hell, he had voted for the Danish People's Party, commonly known as the anti-immigrant party. He had supported the party for their policies regarding care for the retired people. The fact that they passed laws to stop immigration into Denmark hadn't concerned him.

"You feel the same way," Peter said. "Admit it: every time you see one of those women dressed up like that you think it is strange too."

He used to, maybe still did, but this Afghan girl didn't wear those strange clothes. And did clothes change the person beneath?

"She seems like a nice girl," Gunnar said quietly.

"What was Christina thinking? This is crazy," Peter said.

"I don't think so," Gunnar said quietly.

He enjoyed having the Afghan girl in his house. He liked her silent company and he was enjoying teaching her about the bees. She was full of questions and even though she didn't seem to understand what he was saying half the time, it was a pleasure to have someone to talk to about bees. With Anna it was different because she knew as much as he did and he wasn't the teacher. They were more like competitors. With the Afghan girl there was no competition. But he couldn't tell this to Peter, he would laugh at Gunnar.

"If people like you and me won't help these immigrants then they will never learn Danish and never be able to get jobs," Gunnar said.

"They should not be here in the first place," Peter said. "Denmark is for Danes—"

"Your grandmother was German," Gunnar interrupted.

"She was from Flensburg, she was almost Danish," Peter said.

"No, she was German. She didn't even speak Danish until after your father was born," Gunnar said with satisfaction.

"That was different," Peter said. "She was European. You should think again about letting her come into your house. What if she steals something?"

"So now she is not just a terrorist, she is also a thief?" Gunnar asked.

"Anna would not have liked this," Peter said.

"Anna would have been happy to help this Afghan girl," Gunnar said firmly. "You don't know anything about Anna if you think she would have begrudged someone the opportunity to make a new life."

Peter was taken aback. "I don't understand why you're being so difficult about this," he said wearily.

Gunnar realized that neither did he.

"She is just some dark-skinned girl looking for a handout," Peter continued. "Get her out of your house before she does any permanent damage. That refugee girl is nothing but trouble; I can tell you that now. That girl—"

"Her name is Raihana," Gunnar cut him off, suddenly aware that he knew her name but never thought of her as Raihana. He always thought of her as the Afghan girl.

"What?" Peter asked, confused.

"You keep saying Afghan girl and refugee, but she has a name, Peter. It's Raihana," Gunnar said.

Raihana wanted to go back to the bees but she was scared of them and worried that the Danish man was angry with her about being bitten. Layla and Kabir had been frantic when they saw the sting and had even taken her to the doctor in Skive. The doctor had examined her, given her some antihistamine tablets, and had assured her there was nothing to worry about. Raihana never took the medication and watched the swelling on her cheek with fascination.

"At least now you must quit this nonsense," Khala Soofia said when the women were preparing dinner two nights after the incident. "Good girls do not go about getting stung by bees like this."

Both Layla and Raihana looked at Khala Soofia in bewilderment. What nonsense was the old bat spouting?

"My Deena never got stung by bees," she continued.

"Your Deena never worked with bees," Raihana said, annoyed by the woman's constant showing off about her daughter who lived all the way in America. Layla and Kabir and her Afghan friends took care of Khala Soofia, went shopping for her, cooked for her and her husband when she was sick, but Deena was so much better than them. If Deena was so great why on earth had she not visited her mother in five years?

"My Deena is too smart to have to—"

"Your Deena, your Deena," Layla said in irritation. "You know, Khala, all we hear is how wonderful she is but she doesn't even write often to her own parents and doesn't care that they live alone in some foreign country. If my children treated me like that I wouldn't think they were so wonderful."

Raihana wanted to hug Layla in gratitude. Finally someone had spoken up against the old lady. No one had ever said anything of this nature to Khala Soofia. But Layla had had enough. Raihana was struggling to do something with her life and instead of encouraging her everyone seemed to want to pull her down.

"My daughter is not disrespectful like you," Khala Soofia said, enraged.

"Then you should be with her at her home," Layla said.

"But she doesn't want you either," Raihana said and immediately regretted it. Why couldn't she allow this poor old woman to have her fantasies? She knew what Khala was doing. Raihana was doing the same in many ways, pretending everything was fine and getting on with life, always expecting that everything would work out when she had ample proof that nothing worked out, not the way you hoped.

"I am leaving." Khala rose from the chair in the kitchen. Her large frame seemed suddenly weary. Layla and Raihana stood up as well, abandoning the vegetables they were chopping at the dining table. "This is a dishonorable house and you are shameful women," Khala added with tears in her eyes.

They didn't make a move to stop her, but they both felt ashamed as soon as they heard the front door close behind Khala.

"We were not right to insult to her like that," Raihana said. "She's our elder."

"She is," Layla said with a sigh. "But enough is enough. How can we respect her when she doesn't respect us?"

"I know," Raihana said. But knowing that Khala was in the wrong didn't make what they had done right either. "I'll make *badam kheer* for her."

"With lots of saffron," Layla said.

"And we'll go there tomorrow and apologize."

"Yes," Layla said unhappily. "I'm just tired of everyone going on and on about your *praktik*. And I'm not *really* sorry about what I said. It was all true anyway. But I didn't like hurting her."

Raihana grinned mischievously. "Did you see her face when you said *your Deena, your Deena?*"

"Yes," Layla said, grinning back.

"Maybe now she'll stop telling us how wonderful Deena is and how terrible we are in comparison," Raihana said.

"And maybe now she'll stop complaining about your *praktik*," Layla said.

If Khala Soofia had been critical about the bee sting, Christina assured Raihana that it was a badge of honor. Sylvia Hoffmann also asked questions about the sting and said that she was very impressed with how quickly Raihana was learning Danish and believed it was because of her *praktik*.

Wahida wasn't so generous.

"This is what happens to whores," she said loudly in Danish. Later she had explained to the class that she hadn't meant to say *whore* but fallen woman. But the explanation came too late, as many of the students in the class were upset by what Wahida said.

Marika, the girl from Bosnia who sat with Raihana, and Suzi, a dark girl from Mozambique, told Wahida it was insulting to call Raihana a *luder*.

"It is my wish," Wahida responded.

"Then you are stupid," Suzi said, rubbing her seven-month-pregnant belly.

"What shit you talk," Marika said. "She got stung by a bee and you say she is a *luder*? You're mad."

"She must have done bad thing, that is why bee stung her," Wahida responded.

Raihana felt a surge of gratitude for Marika and Suzi. They had always supported her *praktik*, which they thought was much better than theirs, bottling marinated herrings in the nearby factory in Glyngøre.

Afghans like Khala Soofia and Wahida made Raihana even more adamant about continuing to work for the Danish man. This stubbornness was new to her. In the past she had easily molded, not caring so much about what was right, only what was easy. Aamir hadn't been like that. He had fought the Taliban the best he could.

In the early 1990s, at the beginning of the Taliban regime, there had been a sort of relief that there was some law and order in the country, but that quickly turned bitter when the *shariah* was enforced.

As bad as life became for many Afghans, Raihana's life, which had revolved around home and family, didn't change much. She had to wear a *burkha* and Raihana accepted it without protest. There were worse things, she decided. But Aamir had been furious, and he'd started going to underground meetings with his friends who were preparing to fight for democracy and equal rights for women. He had continued to teach science and math against the Taliban laws even after he was arrested for it. He was let out from prison after being beaten and threatened. Raihana had raised bail money by selling his old truck.

Going to prison had made Aamir angrier, while Raihana grew afraid. She didn't want to fight anyone, she told Aamir. She just wanted to live a quiet life without getting into trouble. She and Aamir argued about his continued underground meetings—and now he was dead for what he had believed in. If she now wore a *hijab* and *abaya* and behaved like a good Afghan girl as the Afghans like Khala Soofia and Wahida wanted her to, Aamir's death would become meaningless.

When she looked through the eyes of her mind into her heart, she saw hope that Aamir was still alive. She cradled the hope that suddenly he'd be here in Denmark.

In the evenings when she, Layla, and Kabir watched Hindi movies her eyes filled with tears.

"Aamir and I saw this on video at a friend's house, with the volume low so that no one would know," she whispered once.

She never talked about Aamir, let alone discussed such a trivial part of their lives together. Layla and Kabir waited for her to say more but she didn't.

"It's a good movie," Kabir said finally. "So, was Aamir a Raj Kapoor fan too?"

Raihana nodded. "His favorite movie was *Mera Naam Joker*." She didn't say anything after that and Layla and Kabir didn't press her.

"Peter called us and we just had to come," Maria said, her eyes darting around the house, searching for evidence of that Afghan girl her father-in-law had hired. "This is a stupid idea, you know that don't you?"

Brian, who was six, sternly said, "Don't call *Bedstefar* stupid."

"This has nothing to do with you, go out and play with Johanna," Maria said.

"Stop sending them away from me all the time," Gunnar said, grabbing his grandson in a fireman's lift, which made Brian laugh out loud. "I want to spend time with my grandchildren."

"First we have to talk," Maria called out after Gunnar, but he was already running outside with a hysterically laughing Brian. "Lars, why don't you say something?" Maria asked her husband.

"What do you want me to say?" Lars asked, walking toward the television to catch a game of soccer, any game of soccer. Lars's way of dealing with his wife and her problems with his father was to watch soccer. It was easier when his mother was alive because she had been the perfect buffer between Maria and his father; but now, as bad as he felt for Gunnar, he couldn't help him. His *far* would just have to learn to tune Maria out.

That night after the kids were asleep, Maria started the discussion again while the three of them sat in the living room drinking coffee. The television was turned on but Maria had muted the sound when it became obvious that Gunnar was not going to listen to her unless she made him.

"You know if you really need help, I can take some vacation for maybe one or two weeks and stay here with you," Maria suggested. "Brian and Johanna love being here."

"Not that you're not welcome, but I'd rather just have the kids here and . . ." Gunnar fell silent midsentence. He didn't know if he could take care of the kids all by himself. He and Anna always had the kids over for a week in the summer, for long weekends in May, during the potato break in the fall, and any other time that Maria and Lars needed babysitters.

Brian and Johanna came with them and the bees to the west coast where Gunnar and Anna left colonies every year to make heather honey. Anna would pack a picnic basket and after lunch Gunnar would drive the children to the vast sandy beaches.

Gunnar loved playing with the kids and reading them stories but he didn't bathe them or brush their teeth or change their diapers or take them to the bathroom or put them to sleep. Anna did that. Now with Anna gone . . . could he manage the kids on his own? He knew he couldn't. He was barely taking care of himself. And that realization filled him with self-revulsion. He couldn't take care of his grandchildren without her; could anything be more pathetic?

"Yes, leave Brian and Johanna with me," he said. He would take care of his grandchildren; he would take care of his grandchildren without Anna.

Maria ignored Gunnar and looked at Lars sternly, nudging him. "*Far*, Maria is worried and . . . ," Lars began, but his heart wasn't in it. He really was not interested in discussing some Afghan woman and what she was doing in his father's house. His father was a grown man and Lars, unlike Maria, didn't believe in interfering in his life.

"Your friend . . . what's his name, Jonas, he's married to a foreigner, you don't have a problem with that," Gunnar said.

"She's Norwegian, Gunnar," Maria cried out.

"Still a foreigner," Gunnar said. "And I'm not married to this girl. She just comes for a few hours, cleans the garage, helps with the bees. She wired frames for me. And last week she helped while I checked on the bees."

"How old is she?" Maria asked, her arms folded across her chest, her tone that of schoolteacher to belligerent student.

"I don't know," Gunnar said and then added, "about twenty-two or twenty-three, I really don't know and I don't care."

"You know what people think, don't you?" Maria said.

Gunnar looked at her blankly.

"The rumor is that something is going on between you two," Maria said with satisfaction.

"Maria," Lars protested. "Nothing is going on between *Far* and that Afghan girl and no one in their right mind would think that. It's pure nonsense."

Gunnar agreed; the notion that he and Raihana were having a relationship was pure nonsense. But Skive *was* a small city where everyone knew everyone and everyone's business. It had been endearing to Anna, though Gunnar could have done without people finding out the exact day on which they ran out of beer, bought new furniture, installed their satellite, mowed their lawn . . .

"Look, Maria, this is not such a big deal, so don't make it one. It is nothing. She barely speaks Danish and can't understand what I say half the time. There is no chance of a relationship," Gunnar said.

"Gunnar . . . ," Maria began and then fell silent when Lars started to talk about the upcoming wedding of Troels, one of Gunnar's nephews.

And as they talked about Troels and his wedding in Esbjerg, the coastal city in southern Jylland, Gunnar wondered how people could even imagine that he, an old dried-up man, could have anything remotely sexual to do with a girl as young as Raihana. It was disgusting.

EIGHT

---

10 JUNE 1980

Today I saw some bees kick out another bee that was trying to enter their hive. I was quite impressed. If a bee doesn't smell like the queen bee, guard bees will not let the bee into the hive. They do this because robber bees are everywhere.

Robber bees rob. If you are trying to feed a new or weak colony that has other strong colonies nearby, there is a good chance the weak colony will get killed by robber bees that come to loot and pillage if there are no strong guard bees to stop them.

"*Smager godt?*" Raihana asked nervously.

Gunnar dipped the *naan* in the spicy lamb curry again and chewed slowly. "It's excellent," he said with a smile.

Raihana smiled too. She had been nervous as she packed her lunch with the leftover curry and *naan* from the night before. She did it in secret so that Layla would not know. Layla left at six in the morning for the supermarket on Tuesdays. It was the only day she worked the morning shift and Raihana had chosen that day to bring food for Gunnar.

The previous week Raihana had brought the leftover lamb curry with pita bread for lunch to the Danish man's house on a whim. In a rare moment of conversation not about bees, the Danish man had said that he could smell garlic in the kitchen and asked her what she'd had for lunch. Raihana told him it was a lamb dish and he replied that it smelled very interesting. Raihana then decided to bring some Afghan food for him, so that he could taste the interesting smell.

Usually Raihana made herself a white bread sandwich as she could not eat the popular Danish rye bread, *rugbrød*. Layla bought chicken and roast beef cold cuts from the supermarket and they made sandwiches for their *madpakke*, lunch pack. Sometimes they made pita sandwiches with leftover lamb or chicken curry, but only if they didn't have bread and cold cuts in the fridge. The pita sandwiches were messy and Layla thought they should eat like Danes because that would help them integrate into the Danish society faster.

They went through ten of the colonies on the morning that Raihana packed lunch for herself and Gunnar. They added new frames and new boxes for colonies to grow. They cleaned up the dead bees from the base of the colonies. And they checked all the colonies for new larvae and diseases. All the colonies were doing well, except one where the bees were not producing much brood.

When they decided to break for lunch, Raihana asked the Danish man if he would like to eat some Afghan food. He seemed surprised, but he agreed. Raihana was surprised herself that she'd had the courage to ask. Layla had told her that Danes weren't interested in the Afghan culture, their food, or their lives. Danes just wanted the foreigners to learn Danish, find jobs, and stop taking money from their government. But the Danish man had taught her so much and Raihana wanted to give something back.

"We have drink with honey," she said and opened her Thermos. "It is called *shumlay*."

"*Shumlay*," Gunnar said, rolling the word around his mouth.

Shumlay was a traditional drink Pashtuns made. Raihana hadn't drunk it in a long time. But it seemed like the perfect drink for the Danish man because it was made with honey.

Raihana mixed a glass for him with the yogurt mixture she got from home, some ice cubes, and the liquid acacia honey.

"Try," she said, excited.

He didn't seem so sure. He sniffed and then looked uncomfortable. "What's in it?" he asked.

"Green chiles, coriander, cumin, and . . . ," Raihana said nervously.

He looked even more nervous than she.

"And honey," Raihana added hopefully.

He sniffed the *shumlay* again and took a tentative sip. He nodded appreciatively and then drank some more.

"Excellent," he said and poured a second glass.

"We will make it with our honey after the first harvest," Gunnar said.

In the four months since she started Danish classes, Raihana's Danish had gotten better. She comprehended more and more, and the language didn't seem as distant now.

Layla said she was envious of how quickly Raihana was picking up Danish. Raihana wasn't sure what there was to envy. She had passed her module 2 exam just the week before. The exam hadn't been hard, but she had spent all her evenings poring through grammar books, checking and rechecking words with her Danish-to-Dari dictionary. She hadn't told the Danish man about the exam. But she told him after she passed. He congratulated her but Raihana could see that he didn't understand the achievement, not really.

Christina was full of praise and so was Sylvia Hoffmann. They were both convinced that it was Raihana's unorthodox *praktik* that had taught her Danish so quickly. For Raihana, passing the exam meant she was more comfortable with the language.

Still, she wasn't comfortable speaking in Danish beyond the confines of the language school and the *praktik*. In the supermarket she still stuttered, stammered, and sometimes ended up gesticulating to explain.

As her fear of Danish subsided, so did her fear of bees. Getting stung had made her less afraid instead of more. It had hurt but not too much and not for that long.

She continued to wear a protective suit as she and Gunnar worked with the bees. But now there was a new fear, the anxiety of being watched. Every time she and the Danish man worked in the backyard Raihana could feel the eyes of the neighborhood on them. Cars slowed down on the street when she sat in the garage and people peered into the Danish man's garden to catch a glimpse of her.

Some of the neighbors came to visit the Danish man while she was there. She usually stayed in the garage then, away from their curiosity. But sometimes she got caught and her heart all but leaped out of her chest. She felt she was on display, as if she were doing something wrong. A part of her wondered if the other Afghans were right, if it was somehow wrong for her to be here with a strange man in his house. But she was having fun; for the first time in a very long time she was excited about something and despite the doubts she found herself willing to take the risk, to come to the Danish man and his bees.

"Gunnar, how are you doing?" one of the neighbors, a portly woman who wore unflattering black shorts and a red tank top, called out while Raihana and Gunnar worked in the backyard one day.

It was unusually hot for late April. For Raihana, the sun and summer held another promise, the promise of honey. The Danish man had said that soon they would harvest and Raihana could hardly wait. She loved to read about harvesting in the black leather notebook, of which she understood more and more now.

"Good, good, Ulla," he said, looking up at her, but Raihana could see he was irritated.

"So, we should reserve our jars of honey now," Ulla said.

"Sure, sure, always honey for you," the Danish man said casually. He looked uncomfortable when she crossed her yard into his.

She stood by the table they used to place supplies, both her hands behind her back as if she were doing an inspection.

Raihana didn't like her. She looked mean. The skin on her face wobbled while she talked and she stared at Raihana even when she spoke to the Danish man. Raihana hated the perusal of her face and clothes. She hated that this woman could just openly watch Raihana, accusations written on her face.

"So, do you know everything about bees now?" Ulla asked.

Raihana took a deep breath, not wanting to panic. What if she couldn't answer? Could this woman file a report at the Integration Centre saying that Raihana had not learned any Danish or anything about bees? Would they throw her out of the country and send her back to Afghanistan because she couldn't answer this woman?

Her mind raced with images of being told by Sylvia Hoffmann that she wouldn't be allowed to attend class anymore, of being told that she had to leave Denmark and . . .

"She knows," Gunnar said.

The woman kept waiting for Raihana to speak but Raihana's throat was closed up and the Danish words refused to come out.

"*Jeg ved nok*," she finally managed to say. "I know enough," she repeated and added, "enough to help."

"Ah," the woman said, clearly not impressed, and then started talking to Gunnar again. She spoke fast and even if she hadn't Raihana would have had trouble understanding. She couldn't hear past the anxiety pulsing inside her.

Propelled by a need to prove her knowledge of beekeeping, Raihana did something she had never done by herself. She walked over to one of the boxes and started checking the frames. She wanted to ask the Danish man if the colony needed more room, but she didn't want to stop and ask and maybe even sound foolish to the woman. So she looked through the frames again.

Three were full of brood, which was good. It meant the colony was growing. She walked up purposefully to the table where the woman and the Danish man were standing to get three empty frames.

She added the frames to the box and then looked for the queen bee as he had taught her to do. She placed the queen bee excluder on top of the frames, closed the box, and secured the lid with a metal clip.

Then she stepped away from the colony to admire her handiwork. Just for a moment she was so caught up in what she was doing she had forgotten about the woman and the Danish man. They were both watching her. The woman was looking at her and the Danish man was smiling.

He didn't say that she had done a good job until the woman left. He understood, Raihana thought, he understood that she needed that woman to think that she worked like this with the bees all the time, that she knew what she was doing.

Christina had never liked Maria. She hadn't understood how Anna could stand her, this woman Lars had made the mistake of marrying. She reeked of gossip and malicious curiosity.

Lars had been such a wonderful boy and then *she* had sunk her claws in and he would never been the same again. He seemed more distant than ever and spent all his time in front of the television or with the kids.

But Anna had seemed to love Maria. She told Christina that she loved Maria because Lars loved her and that was enough for Anna. She then confessed that she had never felt that Julie was *her* daughter—Julie had always been more Gunnar's than hers—but Lars, he had been hers. And even if he'd married the fattest, ugliest, and rudest woman in the world, Anna would love Lars's wife. To push Lars's wife away was the same as pushing him away and that she wouldn't do.

Christina knew why Maria had shown up at Christina and Ole's house on Sunday afternoon with a frail-looking Shell gas station flowerpot. Christina and Maria sat in the garden by the greenhouse while Ole worked on their vast herb garden.

How Maria felt about immigrants was not a secret. During various parties she and Maria had carried on heated discussions about foreigners, especially refugees, in Denmark. Maria thought they should all be thrown out, while Christina believed that the homogeneous Danish society needed foreigners and their knowledge, skills, and perspective to grow as a culture. The time for holding on to one people, one nation was long past. The world was becoming smaller and in a country the size of Denmark where interaction with other countries was vital to sustain the economy, there simply was no choice.

But Maria was one of those people who had voted against Denmark even joining the EU and was adamant about not joining the euro countries either. She thought that if Denmark started using the euro it would allow stronger countries like France and Germany to dictate Denmark's economic policy. And Danes would lose their excellent social welfare system.

Maria didn't like Christina or her job, so it wasn't surprising to Christina that Maria definitely did not like the fact that Christina had convinced Gunnar to hire an Afghan refugee.

The conversation started out innocuously enough, with both of them drinking coffee and snacking on homemade butter cookies. But soon enough Maria told Christina that she didn't approve of the Afghan girl working in Gunnar's house.

"We don't know anything about their kind of people," Maria said sweetly enough as Christina lit a cigarette. "I mean, I won't feel comfortable leaving my children there if she's there."

"She's there for only a few hours three days a week," Christina said blowing out tiny smoke rings. "She's helping Gunnar and he's helping her. She's learning Danish very quickly."

"But why should Gunnar help her learn Danish? Isn't that your job?" Maria asked, the sweetness leaving her voice.

"It's the society's job," Christina said. "Look, Maria, until she came he was just sitting at home drinking and smoking and living in filth. Now he's working with the bees. He's not mourning Anna the same way as he was."

"So now that she's there he's not going to miss Anna?" Maria asked. "Why, what is she doing for him? Or should I ask what is she doing with him?"

Christina crushed her half-smoked cigarette. "She's a young and innocent woman who has been through hell worse than you and I can imagine. She deserves our compassion and our help, not innuendo like this."

"It's not me, it's everyone who is talking," Maria said, undaunted. "I spoke to fat Ulla who lives next door and she thinks something is going on. The Afghan girl spends a lot of time inside the house with Gunnar."

"So what?" Christina said, though she was nervous about Raihana spending time inside Gunnar's house. This could cause problems, not just for Gunnar but for Raihana. If the Afghan community found out they would be furious. Christina knew from the whispers at school that there was already pressure for Raihana to wear a *hijab* and *abaya* and find another *praktik*. But whenever Christina asked Raihana how it was going, she always replied it was good and asked for more help in reading Anna's bee journal. Christina was amazed that Gunnar had let her keep it, but also pleased that he had.

"So what? What does she do inside? Gunnar says that she cleans but . . . I don't like it," Maria said.

"You don't have to like it," Christina said. "As long as Gunnar and Raihana have no problem with their arrangement, it's none of your business or mine."

"If Anna was there she would never allow it," Maria said bitterly.

"Anna would be happy to help someone in need," Christina said. For all her flaws, Anna had not been spiteful. She had a big heart.

"Anna always thought you were a little crazy to help these people,"

Maria said. "She told me she thought you were being foolish letting immigrants inside your home."

Christina felt a chill run through her. "Anna respected my work."

Maria laughed scornfully. "No, she didn't. She thought that only Danes should live in Denmark. I knew her better than you did."

Christina sighed. It could be true, couldn't it? But how could Anna have hidden that for the past fifteen years? No, Christina thought, she would not let Maria poison her memories of Anna.

"It doesn't matter what Anna would have thought, Maria. Anna is dead," Christina said.

NINE

16 JUNE 1980

The bees know when they need a new queen. The old queen gets ready to die and a new queen takes her place.

A new queen bee is being made in one of my colonies. It is remarkable to watch. The worker bees feed a batch of larvae royal jelly, and then they pick the larva that will become queen bee and continue to feed that one royal jelly. The one that gets royal jelly becomes the queen bee. It seems almost democratic.

Royal jelly is secreted by the heads of young workers and used to feed the baby bees until they develop to the desired rank. If a queen is needed, the larva receives only royal jelly as its food source, so that she becomes sexually mature and has the fully developed ovaries needed to lay more eggs for the hive.

We have a new queen in one of Gunnar's colonies. Usually queens are easy to spot, but this time we couldn't find her easily. After smoking the bees and frantic searching, we found her. Gunnar pulled her out and put her in a small container. I painted the bee's back yellow as this is a queen from 1980 while Gunnar added a new frame to the colony.

Some beekeepers name their queen bees; Gunnar and I decided not to. You get too attached and then when they die you feel bad. I am averse to getting too attached, especially to animals. A long time ago we had a dog and after the dog died we never got another one. With bees it is easier as there are so many of them and they usually live just six weeks. The queens are special though and live longer, so I do my best to keep an emotional distance from them.

Raihana didn't want to go to the party. She was worried there would be Afghans who knew about her *praktik*, who disapproved of it and would be rude to her. Layla thought she was being foolish and self-conscious.

Layla and Kabir had done nothing but talk about the wedding in the city of Viborg for days. One of the Afghan families there was spending a lot of money to marry off their son.

Kabir knew the father of the groom, Elias, because they drove together to Hamburg to buy Afghan spices, Indian movies, and CDs. Layla didn't like Elias's wife, Najeeba, much because she acted too high and mighty.

"Her husband has his own kiosk and she behaves as if he owns the world. Makes hot dogs for people, touches all that pig's meat and we are supposed to think he is so great," Layla said as she cleaned Shahrukh's nose for the fifteenth time since they had gotten into the car. She and Shahrukh were sitting in the back while Raihana sat in the front with Kabir, half turned so that she could talk to Layla.

"You behave yourself there, Shahrukh," Layla said to her son and then turned to Raihana. "One engagement party last year Najeeba tells me that Shahrukh seems too badly behaved. He was ten months old; he cried a little. What, her children didn't cry when they were little?"

"Elias is a good chap," Kabir said. "Just like me, eats and drinks and makes merry."

"Just like you he's not a good Musalman," Layla said, but there was no heat in her words.

For the occasion Layla wore her prettiest *hijab*. The scarf and *abaya* were midnight blue embroidered with golden thread. Underneath the abaya she wore a red- and-yellow *salwar-kameez*. She had insisted that Raihana dress up as well.

"Widow or not you have to dress well. Our reputation is at stake," Layla had said when Raihana told her she was worried what people would think if she wore something flashy. Finally she had relented and borrowed Layla's maroon-and-silver *salwar-kameez* with a shiny silver *dupatta* that had maroon tassels.

"A good friend of mine will be there too," Kabir said.

"Who is he?" Raihana asked as Layla hummed, something she did when she was nervous.

"A friend," Kabir said. "He is this close to getting citizenship . . . any day now," he added, putting his thumb and forefinger together.

"He works in a factory on Mors," Layla said.

"Mors is close to Skive, just twenty minutes," Kabir said. "It's an island. But you don't need to take a ferry because there is a bridge."

"He works for a factory that manufactures stoves, cast-iron stoves," Layla continued. "He earns good money."

"Almost twenty thousand kroner a month," Kabir said. "He has a wife in Pakistan, in Karachi. She lives there with her parents. He has two children and they live with their mother."

Raihana nodded as understanding dawned. They were trying to find her a husband. "How old is he?" she asked quietly.

"Just thirty-eight," Kabir said. "A little older than me."

"And he wants to marry again?" Raihana asked.

Layla cleared her throat. "It would be a good match."

Raihana stared out the window at the Danish countryside pass by. She slowly turned back to face her hosts. "I can't marry anyone," she told them. "I . . . I am not sure if Aamir is dead and . . . I . . ."

"What do you mean you're not sure?" Layla asked.

"I . . . I . . . ," Raihana stammered. "I can't marry anyone," she finally said. "Please, I just can't."

"I can find out if he's still alive in Afghanistan," Kabir said, his tone clear that he didn't think Aamir was alive.

Raihana wanted to say that she didn't want to know, that as long as she didn't know she could pretend he was still alive.

"If he's still alive why did you come here alone?" Layla asked. "Why did you think he was dead?"

"I don't know," Raihana said. "Look . . . I can't marry anyone."

Layla sighed. "Raihana, you need to find out. Is Aamir alive?"

"I don't know," Raihana said.

"But you told us he was dead," Layla said.

Raihana shook her head. "The refugee camp people decided he was dead, that he died in a Taliban prison. And he . . . why can't we leave it? I don't want to talk about this." She had tears in her eyes and she was just about ready to open the door of the moving car and jump out.

"Okay, okay, we will leave it," Kabir said. "It's up to you, Raihana. You don't even have to think about it if you don't want to. Just forget what we said, okay. Right, Layla?"

Layla ignored her husband. "What exactly happened to Aamir?" she asked Raihana. "Why can't you tell us? You can't live like this anymore. Half in Afghanistan . . . is that why you keep talking about going back? Because you think he might be alive?"

Why wouldn't they leave it alone? Raihana wondered. She didn't want to talk about Aamir, didn't they understand?

"Layla, let it go," Kabir said.

"Oh, Raihana, what are we going to do with you?" Layla said softly and patted Raihana's shoulder. "Okay, forget about this, but let me tell you about this woman you will meet there. Shafiqa has six children and is pregnant with a seventh. She has been pregnant so long that she has never gone to Danish class. Her husband just sits at home doing nothing . . . with six children they get so much welfare money that they can sit at home."

Kabir grunted. "These types of refugees give us all a bad name. Sons of bitches should get jobs."

"Hush, no bad language," Layla said, watching Shahrukh to see if he had picked up the bad word. "And what about that guy who used to have a shop in Århus, at Bazaar Vest?"

"That fellow is completely useless," Kabir said. "His wife now, she's something else. She runs the shop. Got a divorce, kicked him out of the house."

"What else could she do?" Layla said. "He used to beat her. She ended up in the hospital, once with a broken wrist. There are just too many men out there who think women are punching bags."

And so they left the matter of Raihana, her marriage, and her possibly dead husband alone. But they would eventually ask again, she knew, and she still didn't know what to say.

The wedding was taking place in a *forsamlinghus*, community center, in Viborg, where Elias lived and had a kiosk that sold magazines, hot dogs, beverages, and household supplies. It was not his only kiosk; he had two others in neighboring Ørum and one right outside Viborg. He ran the one close to Viborg while his two sons manned the others. Business was very good and Elias was one of the few well-off Afghans in the area.

Layla started to find fault as soon as they stepped into the wedding hall.

"Look at that," Layla said. "Father of the groom, you would think he would dress in traditional Afghan clothes, but no, he's wearing a suit."

Raihana smiled. "But so is Kabir, Layla."

"Kabir is younger than Elias, different generation," Layla said and gasped. "See that? Allah, what has the world come to?"

One of the Afghan men had his arm around a Danish woman dressed in a knee-length black skirt and white blouse.

"That is Walid Chacha's son, Uzra," Kabir whispered. "He broke Walid Chacha's heart by getting engaged to that Danish girl."

Raihana had never heard of an Afghan engaged to a white person. It just wasn't done. In Kabul this would've been unthinkable, here, the white girl was invited to a wedding. Poor Walid Chacha, this was probably not easy for him.

"But they have been here for almost fifteen years now. Uzra is more Danish than Afghan," Layla said, then grabbed her son close. "I will never let things get so out of hand that Shahrukh runs around with a white woman. We'll find him a nice Afghan girl, a nice Pashtun girl."

Raihana didn't say anything but as she looked around it was obvious there were two main groups of guests. One was the older generation and the new refugees. The others were the younger generation who were born and raised in Denmark, those who spoke Danish more fluently than they did Dari, those who didn't mind having Danish girlfriends and spoke to one another in Danish.

Shahrukh would be like one of the young Afghans here, Raihana thought. He would be more Danish than Afghan and Layla would not be able to control him. Raihana wasn't sure if that was a bad thing or not. A part of her wanted to hold on to their culture and traditions, but another wanted to claim the world they were living in now. Denmark was not Afghanistan. Wouldn't an Afghan wearing Danish clothes and speaking fluent Danish fit in better than someone like Layla, who struggled with the Danish language and wore a *hijab* and *abaya*?

"*As'salam alaikum, Kabir Miya*." Elias came up to them and hugged Kabir tightly.

"The wedding hall looks excellent," Kabir said.

Elias grinned. "My oldest son, Kabir *Miya*, have to get him married right."

"*As'salam alaikum*, where is Najeeba?" Layla asked.

"Out there with the other women doing God knows what," Elias said proudly. "Wedding rush you know, mother of the groom stays busy."

"Maybe we can help," Layla offered.

"You must be Raihana," Elias said, turning to Raihana. "*As'salam alaikum.*"

"*Walaikum as'salam*," Raihana said, "everything looks very beautiful."

Elias thanked her and as she and Layla walked away, Raihana heard Elias say, "She is perfect for Rafeeq."

So, Raihana thought, the man's name was Rafeeq.

This was very different from how marriages were set up back home. She and Aamir had gotten married in Kabul and that day everything had changed for her. She had moved from a small village to a big city—from being a daughter to a wife. But it had been remarkably easy in many ways because Aamir's father was her mother's cousin and she had grown up seeing Aamir, his parents, and his sister, Assia. His parents had died by the time they married, but Assia accepted Raihana with open arms.

Ismat, Assia's much older husband, was a doctor and he was horrified when the Taliban demanded he stop treating women. His nurses were not allowed to work and were sent home to live behind the *purdah*. His female colleagues were not allowed to work. Ismat had told Raihana how one of his colleagues, a widow and single mother, now had to beg on the streets to support her three children because she no longer had any income.

That last month had been chaotic, what with Aamir and Ismat trying to find a way out for all of them. But in the end Aamir had scrounged enough money for Raihana only. She was to go first as they had all decided that her need was the greatest.

Ismat and Assia were not in the refugee camp; Raihana had looked. It would have been easy to find an Afghan doctor in a refugee camp. The only doctor there was a retired old gentleman from Ghazni whose son-in-law had been executed in a football stadium. They had shot him in the head, the old doctor told Raihana. His daughter had committed suicide and his wife died of cancer shortly thereafter. He was the only one left and though he could get asylum in America or Canada he stayed at the refugee camp.

Ismat had been married before Assia, but his first wife had died. He had grown sons who lived in Pakistan and were not in close touch with him. Assia had told Raihana that she had always thought Ismat was special and when his parents proposed marriage, Aamir jumped at the idea. Ismat was respectable and came from an honorable family and Assia seemed to be happy about the marriage.

Assia and Ismat had dreams of renting a moving hospital to help the people living in villages where medical help was not available. Raihana thought their ideas were up in the skies. She was a girl from a small town and all she wanted was a home and family. But Ismat believed he could save the world, that he could save Afghanistan.

Then a few months after she arrived in Pakistan, Raihana found out that both Assia and Ismat had been shot in their home. Just like that. It had happened a few days after she had left. They never made it to Pakistan or to their dreams in the sky. Raihana knew she was lucky to be here. Lucky to be able to sit here at a wedding and pretend that the past didn't exist.

"My daughter-in-law, Farida," Najeeba announced loudly, gesturing to the girl dressed in a green-and-gold *salwar-kameez*. Her hair was tied stylishly with ringlets falling around her made-up face. Her lipstick was bright red and jewelry bright gold.

"Isn't she just a piece of the moon?"

"Absolutely beautiful," Layla said, peering at the girl's face. "Isn't she, Raihana?"

"Very beautiful," Raihana said in agreement.

For the wedding ceremony, they all congregated in one of the side rooms where the food was going to be served. Flowers adorned the room with garlands of marigolds hanging alongside shiny gold cur-

tains, tulips and azaleas in big vases, and rose petals strewn across the
floor. Colorful pillows, *toshaks*, were thrown on thick Afghan carpets
and suddenly it didn't feel as if they were in Denmark; this could just
as well have been Kabul.

A Farhad Darya song was playing on the CD player and women
were drinking tall glasses of cool *sherbet*, tasting the way it should, of
almonds, milk, sugar, and rosewater.

"*Sherbet*, straight from Hamburg," Najeeba said and offered a glass
to Layla.

"Straight from Afghanistan, that's what you should say," a heavily
pregnant woman suggested. "Layla, is that Raihana? Allah *hafiz*, I am
Shafiqa."

Raihana bowed her head a little. She remembered Layla telling
her about the woman who had six children and was pregnant again.

"The *nikah* ceremony was at home," Najeeba told Raihana as they
sat down, snacking on dried apricots, sugarcoated almonds, and salted
peanuts. The *nikah* ceremony was the religious and solemn part,
where the marriage contract was signed. The *arusi*, the fun and cele-
bration, followed the *nikah*.

"I told Elias that we will pull out all the stops for the *arusi*. Nothing left to chance," Najeeba said, smiling broadly. For an *arusi*, this
was more than adequate, Raihana thought. It was grand, in fact, nothing like she had seen in Afghanistan.

"Have you met Hadi?" Najeeba asked. "Such a good boy. Most
boys here, they don't want to marry who their parents choose. Look at
Uzra, going around with some white girl. Allah, what has the world
come to? I'd rather die than have that happen to me. But my Hadi, we
said marry this girl and he said yes, and Farida . . . like I said is a piece
of the moon."

"So, Najeeba, they will live with you," Layla asked as she arranged
her *dupatta* over her shoulder.

Raihana smiled to herself. Layla had told her that Hadi and Farida
were not going to be living with Najeeba and Elias. The couple had
rented an apartment in Viborg and planned to live there. If it were up

to Hadi, he would've preferred to live with his parents, or so Najeeba said. It was Farida who wanted to live alone. Not that Najeeba was blaming anyone.

"They are a young couple, they need their privacy," Najeeba said. "We understand; times have changed. Young couples don't live with their parents anymore. It is the way it is when you live in a foreign country."

"These are bad times," a woman wearing a pink-and-white *salwar-kameez* said. "Did you read the news report in *Jyllands Posten* the other day? My husband showed it to me. They are saying that immigrants working in Denmark take more sick holidays than Danes because they have exotic diseases. What nonsense is that, I ask?"

"Exotic diseases?" another woman said. She was wearing a dress similar to Raihana's and her hair had been dyed with henna. "What, they think we have some special diseases in Afghanistan? Like what?"

"God knows," Najeeba said. "You should see how these Danes talk to us at the kiosk, like we have stolen something from them. We are citizens too, have EU passports and everything. But they behave like we are taking something from them."

"How long have you been here, Raihana?" the woman with the henna-dyed hair asked. Though Najeeba had rattled out everyone's name when they first sat down, Raihana couldn't remember them all.

"Just ten months," Raihana said.

"And she already speaks great Danish," Layla said proudly. "Passed module two in four months' time."

"I heard that you are doing a strange *praktik* for some Danish man, going to his house alone and whatnot," a woman in a white-and-blue *salwar-kameez* in the corner put in.

"Madiha," Najeeba cried out.

"I help him with his honeybees," Raihana said calmly. "I have experience, you see. I used to help my *chacha* who made honey and silk."

"So what do you do to help?" Madiha asked, undeterred by Najeeba's shushing.

"I check the beehives; help make frames so that the bees will have more room to make honey. I help him add more boxes to increase the size of the colonies and when it is time to harvest, I will help him make honey," Raihana said. "What do you do for *praktik*?"

Madiha snorted. "I work in a factory."

"What kind of—" Layla began when Najeeba clapped her hands. "Enough, enough, the wedding singers have arrived."

As Raihana got up to leave, Farida, the bride, touched her shoulder. "She works in a meatpacking factory and hates it," she said. "They are just envious that you don't have to clean supermarkets and pack meat like them."

Raihana smiled at her new ally. "She is my mother's cousin," Farida said. "I can't stand her either."

Usually the bride went and got ready while food and tea were served. However, since they were in Denmark things were being done a little differently. Farida was already dressed and mingling with the other female guests.

When Raihana married Aamir, she didn't see Aamir until after the *nikah* ceremony, during which she signed her marriage contract by proxy. Here, the bride and groom went together to city hall and signed their marriage contract before the *nikah*.

If they'd had the choice, she knew Aamir would've preferred this Western-style wedding. He would have liked the idea of her standing next to him as they were married. She would have liked that too.

The groom was seated on a *takht*, throne, raised up on a platform, and was dressed in plush red velvet and gold. Farida's veil was pulled over her face and her mother, Khusboo, held the Koran over her daughter's head. As soon as Farida sat down next to Hadi, the mirror ceremony began. The *Takhtee Khina* was brought out and put on the table in front of Farida and Hadi. The silver tray had a beautifully embroidered brown shawl on it and a bowl with henna.

Najeeba slid the Koran under the shawl and Hadi leaned over and whispered something to the veiled Farida, who giggled.

Layla shook her head at the blatant disregard for tradition. The groom and bride were just too free with each other before the ceremony was even complete. Raihana watched with a shaft of longing going through her. Had she ever been that young? That playful? Had she and Aamir giggled and been happy?

Farida removed the shawl from the tray and opened the Koran. Both Farida and Hadi read the lines expected of them. There was no accent to their voice, nothing Danish about what they said and how they said it. Raihana thought that no matter where they lived, Afghans would always be Afghans.

Farida's father, who was dressed in traditional Afghan clothes, put henna in Hadi's hand and wrapped it with a piece of white cloth, and then Elias did the same for Farida.

The ceremonies that followed were less formal and more gregarious than the mirror ceremony. Farida removed her veil and laughed openly while talking to Hadi.

"They knew each other before the wedding," Madiha, whom Raihana didn't like at all, said to Layla. "Look at them cavorting."

Layla's eyebrows went up. "Not arranged, you think?"

Madiha leaned closer, conspiratorially. "Lucky for Najeeba that Hadi went and fell in love with an Afghan, an Uzbek at that. Look at Walid; he keeps threatening to kill Uzra. And that Danish girl, couldn't she wear our clothes when she comes to one of our weddings?"

Raihana looked at the Danish woman who was watching the proceedings with her eyes wide. She kept asking Uzra questions. She had probably watched the ceremonies more keenly than anyone. Everyone else was busy chatting, drinking *sherbet* and *molina*.

After the ceremonies ended the bride and the groom were seated on a velvet sofa in the main room of the community center while the wedding singer—hired from Århus for an insane five thousand kroner according to Madiha—started singing "Khinna-ba-karha," the traditional wedding song, followed by other popular wedding songs like "Aros-e jan-e madar."

"Ask him to sing something by Larmal Wasiq next, *Ammi*," Farida said to her mother, who sat on the sofa next to her. "Have you listened to his *Qeel-o-qal* album, Raihana?"

Raihana looked up, uncomfortable at being singled out by the bride. She hadn't listened to the album and said as much.

Farida grinned. "We just love his music, don't we, Hadi?" she asked her husband who smiled, his thin mustache wiggling as he spoke softly to his wife.

"What you love, I love," he said, making his bride laugh.

"I will listen to a Farhad Darya *ghazal* any day," Layla said. "And we also have to listen to songs from all Shahrukh Khan's movies. You know Kabir—to be his wife I had to love everything about another man, Shahrukh Khan."

Everyone laughed and the conversation turned to Indian movies and songs.

"Aishwarya Rai, she is just forty-five kilograms," one of the men said. "And she is so tall. They say almost five feet eight inches. Ah, now that is beauty."

"Hakim knows her weight, height, and everything else in between," another man joked.

It had been a long time since music had been a part of Raihana's life. When she first came to Pakistan, it had been a shock to listen to music being played out loud in the open. During the Taliban regime, she and Assia would turn on the tape recorder very low and listen to songs. Assia had been the brave one, wanting to put the volume a little higher while Raihana was so scared that she wanted to turn the music off. They never knew when someone might be listening outside the flat, by the window. They could be arrested, killed for doing this.

She was so scared then, so insistent that they do as they were told. But neither Assia, nor Ismat, nor Aamir had listened to her. And then the Taliban looted her father's village fifty kilometers outside Kabul. Her father's house was burned down and he was killed. Raihana's mother had died before and it had been just been Raihana's father and thirteen-year-old brother living there, keeping their cows in the yard of their small house.

Raihana's brother managed to escape, Raihana learned later, but he was killed anyway. A stray bullet some said; others said it was intentional. He was just a boy.

Now in the wedding hall surrounded by music and happiness, the past seemed far away, like a bad dream, like something that never happened. As she celebrated this wedding of strangers, it was more meaningful than ever that she could listen to music, that it could be played as loud as they liked.

Raihana met Rafeeq after dinner. She had hoped she wouldn't have to, but Najeeba dragged him along and introduced them. Things were different here, Raihana thought. Back home her family would have settled the marriage and told her about it later. She remembered Salma, whom she met in Pakistan. Salma had been fifteen years old and had escaped from a prison in Kandahar. The Taliban had thrown her in prison for refusing to marry the man her father chose for her. Pretending to accept the marriage, Salma had gotten out of prison and then, with the help of a foreign aid worker, escaped to Pakistan with her aunts and cousins.

Salma was brave. Raihana had been in awe of her bravery.

Here in Denmark, Raihana didn't have to be extraordinarily brave to make a choice; she didn't have to fight for it. In Denmark, it was her right to choose the man she married. The freedom she had was not unlimited, but it was more than she'd ever had before.

"Layla tells me that you speak very good Danish," Rafeeq said.

Raihana saw Layla and Najeeba watching them.

"She exaggerates," Raihana said.

"She is very proud of you. And so is Kabir," Rafeeq said.

Raihana didn't know what to say to a man who was not her husband or relative. How could Kabir and Layla ask her to speak to this stranger? What did they want out of her? And then it struck her that he wasn't the first strange man she had interacted with. There was the Danish man.

Maybe it was not that Rafeeq was a stranger that was the problem; maybe it was his interest in her that made her uncomfortable.

They talked some more. He told her about his job and about the island he lived on. He told her that he rented an apartment in the city and alluded that he would buy a house once he had a family in Denmark and his Danish citizenship. He wasn't struggling in Denmark, Raihana thought. He was settled in Denmark and comfortable living here.

Once the conversation hit a lull, partly because she wasn't telling him anything about herself, Raihana made her excuses and all but ran to Layla.

"What did you think of him?" Layla asked that night after they came home.

"I can't marry him, Layla," Raihana said and then added a little harshly, "Please don't put me in such a situation again. If you want me to leave your house, let me know, but—"

"How can you even think that?" Layla cried out. "You're family. You can stay here forever."

But Raihana started to wonder if she could. As she lay in bed in her small room, the converted attic where the roof sloped above her, she knew she had to do something. She would have to get married, because that was what Afghan girls did. They got married and left the refuge of their parents' home, in this case her guardians' home. But she didn't want to get married. So what was it she wanted to do?

TEN

28 JUNE 1980

I read a beautiful beekeeping journal last week. It was a poignant passage through the bee season. I was touched and now I worry that my journal pales in comparison.

I wonder if my children's children will use the journal. I know that my children think beekeeping is a boring occupation; it is also to blame for stealing their parents away. But I do hope that someone will use my journal and learn something from it.

Maria didn't leave with Lars on Sunday but stayed back with Brian and Johanna. Gunnar knew she wanted to wait for Raihana and he wasn't happy about it. He didn't like that she thought she could pry into his life. He needed help in getting her out of his house, he decided, and he called the person he thought could help him.

He called Julie, who said what she thought without worrying about the consequences.

"What do you mean she thinks it's a bad idea? What business is it of hers?" Julie demanded just as Gunnar knew she would. Julie didn't like Maria any more than he did and since Julie was an immigrant herself, she was not closed-minded about immigrants in Denmark.

"She's here now. She wants to stay the week. That poor girl will come here today and I don't want her harassed," Gunnar said. "What should I do?"

"What can I do, Far? You kick her out, tell her to leave," Julie said and then sighed. "I'm going to talk to Lars . . . actually, give the phone to Maria. I will sort her out."

Gunnar smiled to himself. He found Maria in the kitchen and handed her the phone. He waited a moment to hear Maria sputter in rage and then sneaked outside to play with his grandchildren.

It worked like a charm. Within the hour, Maria was packing up the car and the kids. Gunnar was sorry to see Brian and Johanna go, but Maria looked so angry that he was a little afraid to ask her to leave the children with him for a couple of days.

Raihana was coming late today as she had to first go to the language school. And that was a saving grace; it gave him time to get Maria out of the house. He hadn't liked it when fat Ulla—not to be confused with thin Ulla, who lived across the street—had all but interrogated the poor girl the other day in the backyard. He was determined to avoid another interrogation session with Maria.

"I don't understand your behavior," Maria said as she finished packing up the car. "You are such a stubborn old fool."

Gunnar was taken aback. She was not always pleasant but Maria had never been downright insulting. Though he wasn't completely surprised for he had seen Lars get a dose of her sharp tongue several times.

"How could you leave Brian's bottle at home? What were you thinking?"

"How could you forget to fill up the gas tank? Did your brain take a walk?"

And so on and so forth.

Gunnar wanted to defend himself but wasn't quite sure what to say. He wished Lars was still here. Lars would know how to handle his wife in a temper.

"If you don't care what happens to you, why should I?" Maria said, throwing a pair of Brian's shoes inside the trunk. "If this is your decision then we won't come and visit again."

Gunnar sighed. Maria could be so melodramatic.

"What is your problem with this girl?" Gunnar asked as Johanna and Brian watched the drama from inside the house.

"She is a Muslim."

"So what?" Gunnar asked. "So what? She is a young girl who helps me and I hope I am helping her learn Danish. She is not some femme fatale out to blow up the world and trap your old father-in-law."

Maria stared at him. "Then why don't you want us to meet her? Why are you kicking us out of the house?" She was yelling now.

"Because I am worried you will talk to her the way you talk to me," Gunnar snapped back.

Maria calmed for a moment and Gunnar tried to smile at Brian and Johanna, who were enjoying the show with their eyes wide open. Gunnar never lost his temper. Never yelled. Never made a scene.

"What if I promise not to be rude to her?" Maria asked.

Gunnar took a deep breath. "I want you to stay. I want the kids to stay. But I don't want that girl harassed."

"Okay, okay, we'll treat the Muslim girl like a queen," Maria said in exasperation.

"Her name isn't Muslim girl, it is Raihana," Gunnar said. "And she seems very fragile. A little lost at times. She understands some Danish but not a lot. Don't talk too fast, but not too slowly either . . . she isn't stupid. Okay?"

"Okay," Maria said. "Anything else?"

"Sometimes she brings food from home. If she gives you some, eat it, don't make a face," Gunnar said and walked away, glad to have had the last word.

Since Maria was going to be there, he planned the day a little, not wanting Raihana to clean the house like a servant. He decided they would check the hives again. He couldn't hear the early signs of swarming the way Anna could, so he had to do it the hard way, looking through the colonies one by one and making sure they had enough room.

He was suspicious that colony numbers eight and ten were getting ready to swarm but he didn't want to go into the backyard alone, without Raihana. So far he had only worked with the bees when she was there. The rest of the week he waited for her to come back so they could go back to the bees together.

Maria was determined to get rid of the Afghan girl. It was unconscionable that her own father-in-law was allowing one of those people into his home. She didn't have anything against Muslims or foreigners, she really didn't, she just didn't think they should be living in Denmark.

Now, if Maria went to Saudi Arabia or one of those other Muslim countries, she would be expected to wear a scarf and whatnot, but Danes were just supposed to accept that these women would wear their strange clothes in Denmark. Not only that, what was really frustrating was that Danes had to pay for the education of these people, their lives here, and then they didn't even go out and find jobs. She had recently read an article in *Børsen* that half of the immigrants in Denmark didn't work. How could they not work? Didn't they have any pride?

And she didn't trust people like this Muslim girl. What if she was stealing things? Gunnar wouldn't care; he didn't even know what was in the house.

In all honesty, Maria didn't like Gunnar much. He had always been passive, following Anna like a little puppy. Anna decided how the children would be raised, what they would buy for Christmas, where they would go on vacation, and how they would take care of their bees. Maria had fully believed that after Anna's death, Gunnar would get rid of the bees; that he would sell them. His and Anna's bee colonies were worth fifty or sixty thousand kroner, according to a friend of Maria's who knew of such things.

Gunnar was not that interested in the bees. Anna had decided they needed a new hobby; she had read about bees and Christina's husband, a beekeeper himself, had encouraged her. Anna had told Gunnar they would keep bees and he had wagged his tail and said, "Yes, dear."

Maria remembered the Christmas when Gunnar was keen on duck but Anna had decided they would have ham and the Danish sausage, *medister*. Gunnar really liked duck but when Anna firmly said that she would only make ham and *medister*, he had not argued. Maria had felt sorry for him and wondered why Anna couldn't just make duck for Christmas.

"I already said ham and now he wants duck? He always wants something else, like this is a restaurant," Anna had said.

"But he likes duck," Maria pointed out.

"So what? I decide what we have for Christmas dinner. If he wants to decide, he should learn how to cook."

Then Anna roasted a duck for New Year's Eve and Maria marveled at her mother-in-law's ability to come out looking like a shiny øre coin because she had finally relented and made her husband's favorite dish.

Maria hated to admit it but she herself could be a lot like Anna—at times. Maria wasn't as manipulative as Anna but they had similar beliefs about raising their children and handling their husbands. Maria was less dominating than Anna, but she felt it was her job to keep Lars on the straight and narrow.

There were rules and Lars had to live accordingly. Sure he could go out on Friday night with the boys and come home drunk at four in the morning. Certainly he was allowed his weeklong ski vacation in Austria with his friends while she took care of the children at home. But then she decided who their friends were, what clothes everyone wore, what they ate, what kind of house they bought, and what kind of house paint they used. He had some freedom but she was the queen of her house.

Maria had harbored no doubts that after Anna's death she would take over that role for Gunnar, caring for him and helping him manage his life. But he was becoming more and more belligerent. He was getting out of control.

By the time the Afghan girl arrived at Gunnar's house, the children had already eaten lunch and were napping in Lars's old room. Maria had kissed their warm, flushed cheeks and held them as they fell asleep still talking about their soccer game in the yard.

Raihana was surprised to see a woman in the house when she arrived. She suddenly felt unsure about coming in as she was not really supposed to go into the house. She quickly retraced her steps and went into the garage, sitting down on one of the two wooden chairs at the worktable with the black leather notebook.

The Danish man followed her, almost immediately, and sat down on a chair across from her. The woman came inside the garage and stood behind him.

"This is Maria," the Danish man said after a long silence. "My *svigerdatter*."

Raihana didn't understand the word *svigerdatter* and for a moment wondered if it meant stepdaughter. The Danish man saw the confusion on her face and explained that Maria was his son's wife.

The woman was wearing blue shorts and a white T-shirt. Her hair was blond and short, like a man's, and she looked at Raihana with suspicion.

"I think colony number eight and ten might start swarming," Gunnar said to Raihana, like they always spoke about the bees at the start of the day.

Raihana nodded, uncertain of what was going on. Was Maria checking up on them? Is that why he wanted to start working on the bees right away? Not that she minded because she liked the bees better than cleaning his house or sitting there doing nothing.

"You check colony eight and I will check colony ten, okay?" Gunnar asked.

"*Jeg vil*," Raihana said.

As she stood up to put on her protective suit she heard Maria clear her throat and whisper something to Gunnar. He didn't lower his voice enough when he whispered back because Raihana could hear him say, "But she's dead and has no need for it," and then something else.

Raihana stared at the protective suit and swallowed uneasily. This was his dead wife's suit. Of course it was. Why hadn't she realized it before? And then she looked at the black leather notebook. It was his wife's too.

His wife was not real to her. She had seen pictures in the house of a regular Danish woman. Not too fat, not too thin. She had short hair, like Maria's, and wore dangling earrings in all the pictures she had seen.

Maria came farther inside the garage and looked around. Her hands were locked behind her back and she was peering at the things on the table.

"This is Anna's," the woman said to Gunnar, picking up the black leather notebook.

Gunnar looked at the notebook and smiled. He had forgotten about it. Anna wrote it in their second year with the bees. She wanted to get it published but it never happened. She had written in those pages, painstakingly, reading out to him what she wrote from time to time. She would first write in a regular notebook and would then write the same thing in the leather notebook, once she was happy with it.

"What is she doing with it?" Maria demanded.

Gunnar had no answer. What was Raihana doing with it?

Raihana felt as if a bullet had ripped through her.

"This is my mother-in-law's book," Maria said, speaking in Danish, loudly and slowly as if Raihana was stupid. "Where did you get it?"

Raihana's hands were clammy. "In . . . in brown closet," she said, pointing to the cupboard in the garage.

"And you just took it?"

Raihana was going to tell her that she had asked Gunnar and he had given her permission, but before she could, Gunnar spoke.

"I gave it to her," he lied.

"No, I found it and I . . . I . . . you say okay." Her voice was shaking.

"It is okay," Gunnar said, glaring at Maria. "She's reading it to learn about beekeeping and to learn Danish."

Maria's eyes blazed. "This is my children's legacy and you are giving it to a stranger," she cried.

"No," Gunnar said. "This was my wife's and I choose to do what I want with it."

Raihana was so nervous that she hardly understood what they were saying. Her eyes filled up with tears. She was not a thief, she wanted to say. But just like before, she couldn't get the words out. It had happened at the bazaar one afternoon; she never knew why the storekeeper screamed at her that she had stolen food as she walked away from his shop. Two Taliban soldiers were on her almost immediately, ripping her bag from her shoulder, shoving her onto the ground. They searched her bag and shouted at her, asking her what she had stolen, where she had hidden it.

"Don't you know what we do to those who steal?" one of the men demanded. Raihana's body went cold, her breath choked her, and her tears blinded her.

A Taliban soldier pulled her from the ground, his fingers a vise around her arm. Small moans escaped her mouth but she didn't have the courage to proclaim her innocence. They were big men, she could barely see them through the opening in her *burkha*.

"No, no, it's okay," the shopkeeper said then. "The apple is right here."

The man let her arm go. "Don't ever steal, okay," he warned and then shoved her away.

She cried for hours that day after she got home—out of relief and fear and frustration. She wiped the tears before Aamir came home and never told him about that incident. She had been ashamed.

But this time, Raihana thought as she lifted her chin, she wasn't going to be ashamed. She had survived mad gun-wielding men, this woman wasn't going to scare her.

"This is my children's," Maria said, hugging the notebook to her chest. "You can't keep it."

The words that eluded her came out her like warm honey. *"Det ok, jeg er færdig med det."*

Maria stared at her and Raihana knew that whatever this woman had expected she had not expected her to speak proper, if accented, Danish and say, "It is okay, I am finished with the book."

"Nej," Gunnar said. He gently took the book from Maria and held it out to Raihana. "You can give this book back when you speak Danish as fluently as I do."

Raihana's heart was beating so hard that she only heard a part of what he said, the part about her needing the notebook. She nodded, took the notebook, and placed it back on the worktable.

After this scene in the garage, Raihana thought Maria would leave them alone, but she didn't. She came with them to the backyard.

"Late, we're late," Gunnar said, holding up a frame to Raihana and explaining, "When bees start making a new queen, it means they are ready to swarm."

"Bees do dance now?" Raihana asked.

Maria was standing close to them and Raihana wanted to show off what she had learned from the notebook and from Gunnar. Raihana was ready to put on the same performance for Maria as she had for Ulla, the fat neighbor.

Gunnar's wife had written in detail about bee dancing and once Raihana understood what it was, she had been fascinated and wanted to see a bee dance.

Bees communicate by dancing. When scout bees find a nectar source, they do a special waggle dance to show where the nectar is. When the bees are ready to swarm, scout bees look for a new home and when they find one, they do the figure-eight dance. The center of the eight formed by the dance, in relation to the sun, points the bees to their new home.

The entire paragraph made little sense to Raihana; not only was the Danish difficult, but the whole bee dancing business was confusing. Christina had explained with diagrams the previous week and now Raihana felt she knew all there was to know about the subject.

"What does she mean about dancing bees?" Maria asked.

Gunnar grinned, obviously proud of his pupil. "Bees talk to one another by dancing," he told Maria. "Anna wrote quite a lot about it in her book. Maybe when Raihana is done with it, you can read it."

It was the first time he had said Raihana's name aloud and Raihana's eyes shot up. For the longest time she thought he didn't know her name and the fact was she still thought of him as the Danish man, not Gunnar.

Maria didn't answer her father-in-law and watched Raihana with curiosity as Raihana looked for the second queen bee in the tenth colony.

Raihana was startled at how much she had learned in the past few weeks. Maybe she could get a job as a beekeeper? Could she find such a job? She would ask Christina the next time she saw her in school.

It was almost time for her to leave when Johanna and Brian woke up. Raihana couldn't imagine how these two little angels had come out of that suspicious, angry woman.

"*Jeg hedder* Brian," the blond, blue-eyed boy said. "*Hvad hedder du?*"

"Raihana," she said and kneeled down in front of him.

"You are the Muslim girl, you are darker than us," Johanna said and cleared her throat because her mother shushed her. "I wish I had skin like yours," she added and then giggled.

At the end of the day, right before Raihana was about to go home, Maria stopped her. They were alone outside, and Raihana was holding on to her bicycle for dear life.

"I am sorry about Anna's book," she said.

Raihana didn't say anything.

"I miss my mother-in-law and that's why I was so angry," she added. "You can keep the book."

Raihana didn't thank her. She knew the book wasn't Maria's to give.

"Why don't you wear a scarf like other Muslim women?" Maria asked.

This question Raihana did understand. Many people had asked her that. Some of them had been curious; others, like Maria, were suspicious.

"Why you ask?"

"Because I want to know," Maria said.

"How matter it? I same woman under scarf or hair," Raihana said.

Maria seemed staggered by that response. The two women looked at each other for a moment and then Raihana left, smiling at her victory.

"So what did you think?" Gunnar asked Maria as she packed the car for the second time that day. They had stayed for dinner, which Maria cooked. She had made pork roast with baked potatoes, so that Gunnar would have food for the next day as well.

"She's not a thief. I don't think so," Maria said.

"Well, I'm glad your mind is at rest," Gunnar said.

"She wasn't like I thought she would be," Maria said.

"What do you mean?"

"I thought she wouldn't be able to speak Danish at all, would be lazy and useless . . . I thought she would be dumb," Maria admitted.

"Why did you think that?" Gunnar asked.

"I don't know," Maria said. "I just did."

ELEVEN

4 JULY 1980

The weather has been ugly. Last summer was beautiful, sunshine all the time and no rain; but this summer, the sun has hardly made an appearance. We had some good days in May, but that was pretty much it.

But this morning the sun was shining, even if it started raining by nightfall. During the day, however, we had fabulous weather. The temperature rose to almost twenty-four degrees.

We spent the day with our bees. When Gunnar pulled out the frames they were laden with nectar and wax. The bees have plenty of food despite the bad weather and without any help from us.

I smoked away the bees from a frame full of honey, brushed the remaining ones, and dipped my finger in. I had my first taste of raw honey this year. It was warm, smooth, like liquid gold.

Yesterday, while it rained, I read that thousands of years ago, ancient man knew about bees. Several cave paintings show man drawing honey from natural beehives. I'm fascinated by this. What techniques did they use? How did they discover the first load of honey? It must have been quite a thrill to find honey, a source of sweetness in a world where there is so little sweetness. Did ancient man eat honey like dessert? Or was it sacred, only eaten on special occasions?

I like to think that honey was sacred to them, something special, because to me this whole process of making honey, harvesting it, and then putting it in jars is a spiritual experience. For beekeepers, bees and honey are a religion.

From the end of April through the middle of May is confirmation season. Fourteen-year-old Danes around the country are confirmed in the Lutheran faith. The church ceremony is followed by lavish parties for friends and families.

Anna had pulled out all the stops for Lars's confirmation. Lars patiently went to church for religion classes leading up to the confirmation and was actually fairly enthusiastic about it. But Julie had rebelled; she wasn't going through the farce of confirmation.

According to Julie, it was just an excuse to get gifts, and Gunnar agreed that was the big part of it. Lars got almost five thousand kroner in cash and a hoard of gifts, including a color television for his room, Nike running shoes, and a bicycle from Anna's parents.

Anna had been furious that Julie wouldn't be confirmed. Gunnar supported Julie but halfheartedly. He believed that sometimes you just went with the flow. They celebrated Christmas even though no one went to church for mass? They roasted a leg of lamb for Easter without paying any attention to Christ?

Confirmation was similar. You went to church, got confirmed, wore white, and had a big party. You invited all your friends and family to your backyard, had a big tent, good Danish food, and plenty of beer and wine.

It was a reason to celebrate, to meet friends and family, eat good food and get drunk. It was about having fun. But Julie would not have any part of it. For her fourteenth birthday she asked Gunnar and Anna to send her to Israel, which they didn't.

Instead they gave her enough money for her trip and the practical Julie saved it, added to it with summer jobs, and used the money to get out of Denmark and their lives.

It still hurt that she lived far away in London. It still hurt that she spoke English flawlessly and sometimes grasped for Danish words. She'd had a string of English boyfriends. There was even a French guy who had been a total snob. Both Anna and Gunnar were relieved when they broke up.

Julie had only dated two Danish boys. One she broke up with because he believed that Denmark should have the death penalty. She was fifteen. The second she broke up with because he'd had a confirmation for the presents.

Anna had longed for one of Julie's relationships to become serious—so that they could have another wedding in the house. Anna loved confirmations, weddings, and baptisms, and in the years they had been married, Gunnar had learned to tolerate these occasions.

Now he had to go to a confirmation without Anna. Marianne and Mogens had lived on the next lane for twenty years, almost as long as Gunnar and Anna had lived in their house. They had always been good friends. Mostly Anna and Marianne had been good friends. Gunnar and Mogens got along well but they weren't friends; Mogens was an engineer working for a pipe factory in Viborg and Gunnar had the impression that Mogens felt he was superior to Gunnar, who only taught carpentry at the technical school.

Julie had babysat for both of Marianne and Mogens's children, Anders and Anker, who were now sixteen and fourteen. How time had passed! It was Anker's confirmation and Gunnar had no idea what to buy for him. Marianne had given him Anker's wish list and Gunnar could see the boy wanted white Nike Air Jordans, a portable DVD player, a leather jacket from Royal Skin, and some other expensive items. Gunnar had no inclination to go down to *gågade*, the walking street, to buy a gift from the list. When he hinted as much to Marianne, she said, "You can just give him money."

That sounded good to Gunnar. Of course, Anna would not approve, but he was starting to come to terms with the fact that he couldn't live his life according to her wishes and rules. But he missed her. God he missed her.

He was sixty-four years old. He had another ten years left, maybe fifteen; how was he going to live for so many years without her?

"Buy one of those pretty envelopes," Maria suggested on the phone. "Or why don't I put your name on our gift?"

Maria, Lars, and the kids were coming for the confirmation. Since she had met Raihana, Maria had not said anything about her. In contrast, Julie asked about Raihana whenever she called and kept saying that she was so proud of her father. He wasn't really sure what she was proud of.

Now that two months had passed, he and Raihana had fallen into a rhythm and it didn't seem that strange anymore to have her in his house. She arrived in the morning; she went to the backyard with him, they checked on the bees and then she cleaned the house, had lunch, and then she left.

The previous day, while he and Raihana worked together, Gunnar had noticed that she was getting bolder about asking questions and expressing opinions.

"I like bees," she told him. "I like the sound. I like the work."

"Good," Gunnar said, and then asked her a question that he had been wondering about. "Do you like living in Denmark?"

"Much better than Kabul," she said after a pause. "Much better."

Gunnar almost invited her to the confirmation then. Wouldn't it be good for her to meet more Danes? He hadn't asked, though. He had felt uncomfortable. In any case, he didn't think she'd say yes.

"You could at least have had it dry-cleaned, Gunnar," Maria complained when she pulled out his dark blue suit from the closet in

Julie's room. Anna had used Julie's old closet to store clothes that Gunnar and she didn't wear often. Her clothes still hung there. Her maroon pantsuit that he liked so much. The white frock that made her look twenty years younger. The golden vest that he disliked immensely. The closet smelled of Anna's perfume. He felt a punch in his gut. He had erased most of Anna's presence from their bedroom. Julie had packed Anna's clothes, shoes, makeup, everything away and put it all into the attic. But they had forgotten about these clothes for special occasions.

"I am not wearing a suit," Gunnar said grumpily. "I am wearing pants and a shirt. No suit, no tie."

"Gunnar, this is—"

"No," Gunnar said. Anna had made him wear that suit for Lars's confirmation and every other confirmation they had been to even though Gunnar was not a suit kind of man. Now he was on his own and he wouldn't be coerced into a wearing a suit.

"Okay," Maria said and sighed. "I will iron your white shirt."

Gunnar grinned, pleased that he was besting his daughter-in-law.

"You look handsome," Gunnar said to Brian. His grandson stood tall in corduroy black pants, a white shirt, and a red tie with teddy bears.

"And me, me?" Johanna asked as she twirled in her frothy pink dress. There were frills and flounces everywhere and her blond hair was tied in some fancy way with pink ribbons. She looked like a princess and Gunnar told her so.

"You didn't get a nice envelope?" Maria asked when Gunnar put three hundred kroner inside a plain white envelope.

"You have a good hand, write it to Anker from me," Gunnar said, handing a blue pen to Maria.

"If you had told me you were going to be stubborn about this, I would have bought one for you," Maria said.

"Just write it pretty like you did on your wedding invitations," Gunnar said and patted her cheek. "Anker won't care about the envelope. He won't even care who gave him the money."

"Have you heard how Anders is doing?" she asked as she wrote.

"Fine, I think," Gunnar said. He had no clue how Anders was doing. Was something wrong with the boy? Anna would have known.

"You think?" Maria asked. "Haven't you talked to Mogens and Marianne lately?"

After Anna died, it was hard enough for Gunnar to just do the basics. Shopping, cooking, making coffee, picking up clothes from the floor, doing laundry. He just hadn't had the time or inclination to keep up with the neighborhood gossip.

"You know he has been hanging around with the wrong kind of boys," Maria said as she painstakingly wrote Anker's name on the white envelope. "Two boys moved to the area recently and he shaved his hair off last month, just like them. Haven't you noticed?"

"No," Gunnar said.

"*Gunnar.*" Maria sighed in exasperation, "He's talking a lot about Hitler and Nazis, Marianne said. She and Mogens are worried out of their minds."

"He's a boy, he'll come around," Gunnar said. "I don't understand why these boys have this fascination for Hitler. He lost the war."

"Marianne said she found some white supremacist brochures in his room. They tried to talk to him but he doesn't listen," Maria replied. "Anyway, you know how they are, letting their children run around doing what they want. They never disciplined Anders and they never say anything to Anker. There are consequences if you don't teach children right from wrong."

Gunnar was only half listening to Maria. He wasn't that interested in the lives of these children. That was Anna's job, to stay on top of gossip; he only listened when she ranted on about it. Into one ear and out through the other.

Ole and Gunnar often commiserated about their respective wives' penchant for talking about things that no one in their right mind would be interested in.

"As long as I have a beer in my hand I have no problem with Christina's chatter," Ole once said.

Gunnar nodded. "A beer definitely helps, but how about a glass of whiskey."

"That would be even better," Ole said.

The church was packed. About ten thirteen-year-olds were being confirmed, so the family and friends of all the ten boys and girls were squeezed into the church. Vor Frue Kirke, Our Lady's Church, was small, high up on a hill with a brilliant view of Skive. The church had almost been torn down in the early nineteenth century because it was considered too small. But then murals from the sixteenth century were discovered underneath the modern plaster and the church was saved.

Gunnar didn't care for the religious sentiment portrayed in the murals, said to be the largest presentation of all known medieval saints in Denmark, but he did think they were beautiful. The church was built around the year 1200 and rebuilt several times, with the latest renovation in 1992. Gunnar had taken his students for a tour of the construction to show how the workmen were restoring the windows and doors.

Three years ago a new junior minister had been hired by the church. A woman. A young woman. A beautiful and young woman. Annette was a sweet girl, Gunnar thought, though she didn't look like a minister. She wore knee-length skirts with high boots when she wasn't in church and Anna had reported that Annette had been seen on a date at the bar Crazy Daisy. A minister going to Crazy Daisy had certainly raised eyebrows but she was twenty-five years old, and she was a good minister—Gunnar didn't see the problem. He sort of liked having a young woman for a minister. It was better than seeing some ugly old stodgy fellow spout scripture.

"Those are the boys I was talking about." Maria nudged Gunnar as soon as they were settled in their pew. "Look," she urged Gunnar.

They were hard to miss: three boys with shaved heads shining under the lights of the old church. They stood in the pew right in front of Gunnar. Two of the boys wore jeans and T-shirts. Gunnar recognized the third as Anders. He seemed to have grudgingly put on a suit, but without a tie.

During the ceremony Anders took his jacket off and underneath was a short-sleeved white shirt. Anders stroked his bald head often and each time he did, his sleeve slid up. Gunnar tilted his head a little and was surprised at the shape of the tattoo on Anders's arm. A swastika? Had the boy really gone and gotten a swastika tattooed on his arm?

"He used to be such a nice boy," Maria continued. "And now . . . what a shame for Marianne and Mogens."

"You can't always blame the parents for the children," Gunnar replied as quietly as he could.

"Of course you can," Maria shot back. "If Brian or Johanna behaves poorly it's my fault. I will be to blame."

"You and Lars," Gunnar said.

"Of course Lars will be to blame as well."

"Sometimes I think you think the children are only yours," Gunnar teased.

"Sometimes I do," she replied.

Anders and his friends were whispering and laughing. People shushed them, but they continued. Finally, when Gunnar could barely hear the ceremony over the noise from the boys, Annette turned to them.

"Anders, you and your friends can either keep silent or take your show outside the church," she said. Her voice immediately silenced the boys. "I personally would prefer if you left the church, though I know your parents and your brother will be disappointed. But it's up to you."

The boys snickered a little but kept quiet. Marianne and Mogens looked thoroughly embarrassed, as did Anker.

Once the ceremony ended, Lars drove Maria, Gunnar, and the kids to the reception in a function hall a little way outside Skive.

There must have been a hundred people there, children, parents, couples with no children, babies, friends, family, and three boys with shaved heads. The boys were drinking a lot of beer. They sat at a table with others but they seemed isolated, talking in loud whispers.

"That boy needs to be talked to," Lars said angrily. "Have you seen his tattoo?"

Søren Gade, a neighbor who was also sitting at Gunnar's table, was disgusted as well. "I don't know when Anders went from being a decent boy to this. How could his parents allow it?"

"What can Mogens and Marianne do?" Søren's wife, Pernille, said. "Anders got the tattoo last week in Århus. Marianne didn't notice it until yesterday."

"Thomas says that no one talks to these boys in school. Thomas and Anders used to be friends, they went to *børnehave* together, but the kindergarten days are behind us," Søren said. "These boys are out of control."

Marianne came by their table then, her rail-thin body in a white pantsuit and her lips set in a plastic smile. "We will eat soon," she said. "How are you, Gunnar?" She took Gunnar's right hand into both of hers. "I miss Anna so much."

Gunnar nodded. "So do I, every day."

The topic at the table turned to bees once Marianne left. The hot topic was a recent and unprecedented theft.

"How are the bees this season? Did you hear about the bees that were stolen in Esbjerg?" Pernille asked.

It was the worst kind of scandal. Someone had stolen forty bee colonies over the Easter weekend. It had never happened before. No one stole colonies.

"Maybe it was just a onetime thing," Gunnar said.

But Gunnar knew the beekeeping community was concerned. Only those who were comfortable with bees would be able to steal them, which meant that there was a thief among them.

Pernille patted Gunnar's hand. "Yes, let's hope it doesn't happen again."

. . .

The party officially began with a speech from Mogens, who thanked everyone for being there. Then, as was tradition, the band started to play. The lyrics of all the songs that would be sung during the party were placed next to the place cards on the tables. The first was a traditional Danish song and everyone held hands and swayed to the music as they sang.

Anker's aunt had written a song for him, which Maria confided had actually been bought from an experienced songwriter.

"They paid an insane amount of money for this and the gifts they got Anker . . . ," Maria said.

Annette came by and shook hands with Gunnar and Maria. Annette always found some time to spend with Gunnar during such events.

"Good you put those boys in their place," Maria said.

Annette just smiled.

Maria waved to an acquaintance, made her excuses, and walked off to speak with a large woman in a gray dress.

"It breaks my heart that he's behaving like this," Annette said. "I have seen teenagers do crazy things and move on. I did crazy stuff too, but they seem malicious."

"He's just a boy, he'll get over it," Gunnar said.

"I have met neo-Nazis," Annette told him. "Anders is going in the wrong direction."

"Nah," Gunnar said. "It's just a fashion, saying that Hitler was cool . . ."

"Maybe," Annette said. "I have heard a rumor that you have a young Afghan girl helping you with your bees."

Gunnar was surprised Annette knew so much. But Skive was a small town and news traveled quickly.

"Raihana. She has to do a *praktik* while she goes to the language school and Christina thought it would help her learn Danish faster," Gunnar explained.

"That's wonderful," Annette said.

"You really think so?"

"Yes, absolutely," Annette said.

"I'm glad, because not everyone has been this supportive," Gunnar said.

"People take time to adjust to new situations," Annette said.

The first course was Danish soup, beef or chicken bouillon with small meatballs, dumplings, and bits of carrots, celery, and leeks.

The main course was pork roast, leg of lamb, roasted potatoes, a green bean dish, a mixed green salad, mint jelly, caramelized new potatoes, pickled cucumbers, and brown sauce. Fresh bread was laid out fancifully on the buffet table.

As the reception progressed, Gunnar felt bereft without Anna by his side. He hadn't been to a party like this since Anna died. Maria and Lars were mingling with friends and even though people stopped by and spoke to him, he felt lonely.

He saw Mogens stand by the bar, looking slightly drunk, and Gunnar decided to join him instead of sitting on his own sulking. He got himself a beer at the bar and nodded to Mogens.

Mogens gestured toward the boys with his half-filled beer bottle. "Did Lars ever run wild?" he asked.

Gunnar nodded. "There were times when he didn't come home until the next morning. Anna and I would sit up scared shitless."

"Now they all have cell phones," Mogens said. "Still, I can't get in touch with Anders. He got a tattoo. A swastika."

Gunnar didn't say anything.

"He's reading books about Hitler and getting these strange magazines from America," Mogens said. "German newsletters come in the mail all the time. The boy barely talks to us," he continued. "Anker asked me if we are the superior race and I asked what nonsense was that and he said Anders told him."

Gunnar continued to nurse his beer.

"I talked to Anders and told him he was wrong and he said 'fuck

off' to me," Mogens said, his eyes filling with tears. "To have your children talk to you like that . . . what should we do?"

Gunnar had no idea. Anna would know, he thought. She would be
able to give advice. Gunnar almost started to look for her among the
guests, but Anna wasn't there.

"What the hell should I do, Gunnar?" Mogens asked again, staring
at his son.

"You should get him away from those boys," Gunnar found himself saying. He never had an opinion, never shared his thoughts, but
here he was handing out parental advice. Anna raised the kids; he had
just been a spectator. What the hell did he know?

"Where will he go?" Mogens demanded.

"Anywhere. Don't you have a brother in Canada? Send him there
for a while," Gunnar said.

"Maybe for the summer that would be best. If he's here with them
all day every day, he is going to end up wasting his life," Mogens said,
appearing to really like the idea.

"Sounds good," Gunnar said.

"I'll talk to my brother," Mogens said. "Yeah, that's what we'll do.
That's a good idea, Gunnar."

Gunnar was relieved that Mogens hadn't laughed at his suggestion.

Once dessert was served—rhubarb and apple pies with fresh
cream as well as chocolate cakes and petits fours—the party started to
get livelier. The band was playing traditional Danish party music and
the dance floor was full. But the three bald boys sat with beers in their
hands, their sneaker-shod feet on the table, staining the white table-
cloth.

Still feeling triumphant, Gunnar decided to talk to the boys. It was
really none of his business and he wasn't the type to get involved but
maybe he could help these boys. They were just sixteen; they just
needed some firm conversation.

"Hello, Anders," Gunnar said and Anders looked up at Gunnar.

He nodded at him before remembering his friends and rolling his eyes to show that he wasn't really acknowledging this grown-up.

"How are you?" Gunnar asked.

"Fine," Anders said.

"Looking forward to summer holidays?"

"Sure, whatever," Anders said, turning away.

Gunnar felt foolish trying to talk to these boys. It was humiliating that he had thought he somehow could make a difference, change the boys, like he was some hotshot.

Gunnar, slowly, went back to his table.

"What were you talking to them about?" Maria asked as he sat down.

Brian was sleeping on her lap while Johanna had curled up on a bench next to them, covered with a blanket.

"Nothing," Gunnar said sheepishly. He shouldn't have gone and talked to them. What was he thinking?

"Marianne regrets making Anders come," Maria whispered. "The boys have done nothing but make noise and drink."

Gunnar zoned her out. He was tired of talking about Anders and his friends. Anders was Mogens and Marianne's problem, not his, and he didn't want to be dragged into it anymore.

He sat quietly and wished he could curl up on the bench like Johanna and go to sleep.

TWELVE

ENTRY FROM ANNA'S DIARY
A Year of Keeping Bees

10 JULY 1980

Honeybees have been known to fly over fourteen kilometers from their nests in search of pollen and nectar. It's amazing how much territory they must cover to fill our jars with honey. The work of a bee is physically strenuous and dangerous. Leaving the safety of the honeybee nest is risky for the forager bees that collect nectar and pollen. Wind currents and raindrops can blow the little bees off course. Birds, lizards, robber flies, and spiders can prey on the hapless forager bee. Most forager bees leave their nest four to eight times a day. What brave little bees!

They didn't bother her, not much, but Raihana knew they were there. They spoke loudly whenever Raihana bicycled by them and she felt they were yelling at her.

There were three boys, all with their heads shaved, probably fifteen or sixteen years old. They lived on the street before Gunnar's and sat on the cement bench on the curb smoking cigarettes and drinking beer.

They never came near her but the boys made her uncomfortable. She knew boys like these, had seen their cockiness, the hard glint in their eyes. Just because these boys were white didn't mean they were any different from the many young men she had seen in Afghanistan wearing bandoliers across their chests, carrying Kalashnikovs in their hands and hatred in their hearts.

She always bicycled a little faster by the Danish boys.

With every passing day Raihana found she could speak with Gunnar even more. The other day she had told him about the wedding she had attended in Viborg but didn't mention anything about Rafeeq. She hadn't seen him since the wedding. It would have been nice to confide in Gunnar about her worries for the future to ask if he thought she should get married and stop clambering to hope that Aamir was alive? But they weren't that close yet.

A part of her wanted to not marry, to have a job and live alone, like so many Danish women did. Another part of her knew that wasn't possible—Afghan women had husbands and children. And she did want to marry and have children, didn't she?

None of the Afghans would understand her dilemma; they would just say that she should get married and get on with her life. Who could she talk to besides Afghans? She couldn't talk to Christina. They only talked about Danish, the bees and Anna's leather-bound black book, and verbs and tenses. They didn't talk about personal things.

"Can I work as a beekeeper?" Raihana asked Gunnar as they sat outside in the backyard one afternoon. It was a sunny day and like most Danes, Gunnar wanted to soak in as much of it as he could.

"Most beekeepers are like me, hobby beekeepers," he said. "But there are professional beekeepers as well. Do you want to work with bees?"

"That is what I know."

"What did you do in Afghanistan?" Gunnar asked.

"Nothing," Raihana said quietly. Nothing at all. She stayed home and she had liked it. Now she couldn't imagine staying at home and just taking care of a house and a husband. Even Layla couldn't imagine it anymore. In the beginning Layla had complained that she had to work in this country, now she appreciated it. Raihana liked leaving the house. She looked forward to getting a real job and earning a real living. She looked forward to that very much.

"Did you have an okay life there?" Gunnar asked.

Raihana didn't know what to say. "Okay," she replied after a moment.

It had been an okay life. Maybe at times it was not so okay, especially at the end, but others had gone through much worse. She had met a woman at the refugee camp who was raped by several men and now her family refused to accept her. She had met little children with missing limbs and men dying of gangrene. She had seen humanity stripped away by soulless men. She had seen families abandon their so-called loved ones in the name of the Koran. Compared with those people, her life had turned out okay.

"Was it difficult to live under the Taliban?"

Raihana rose from her chair. "More for my husband than me."

Gunnar didn't ask any more questions about Afghanistan, which Raihana liked. She didn't like talking about those days. She didn't even like to think about them. When Kabir talked about Afghanistan, he invariably talked only about the good times. He had erased his memories of the Taliban, the executions in the football stadiums, the relentless fear. He didn't talk about friends who had been taken to prison and released months later with a part of their spirit missing if not parts of their body. He didn't talk about loved ones who were killed.

But Raihana's memory didn't work like that. Raihana remembered and remembered well. Kabir could talk about the good times back home, but Raihana knew that now the good times would have to be here, in this white country with its strange language and people.

Though not everyone was strange. She had started to like Gunnar, understand him. He was not Afghan and he didn't seem to be interested in prying into her personal matters.

"The first harvest will be next week," Gunnar said. "We will make honey next week."

"Will we use machine in room to get honey?" Raihana asked, glad that he had stopped talking about the Taliban.

"Yes," Gunnar said. "You should take some home with you for the family you live with."

"Do bees get angry when we take honey?" Raihana asked.

"Yes," Gunnar said.

They were silent for a while and then Gunnar asked her something he had been thinking about. "What do you do when you are not in language school or here?"

Raihana gave him a blank look, which meant that she had not quite understood him.

"*Hvad laver du når du ikke er her eller I sprogskolen?*" Gunnar tried again, slowly this time.

She got it the second time. It was a strange question. "I see movies with Layla," she said off the top of her head.

"What movies?"

"Hindi movies from India," Raihana said and then grinned. "Songs and dancing is in the movies."

"How do you get them here in Denmark?" Gunnar asked.

She told him that Kabir got the movies for them from Hamburg and even from the Skive library.

"*Bibliotek?*" Gunnar asked, surprised.

"Yes, the library," Raihana said. "The movies . . . they come with Danish words . . . Danish translation."

"Danish subtitles," Gunnar said.

"*Ja, Dansk undertekst,*" Raihana repeated.

"I would like to see a movie with song and dance in it," Gunnar said.

Raihana smiled. "You will?"

When Gunnar nodded she seemed excited. "I bring a video . . . for movie?"

They agreed that the next week she would bring one of her favorite Hindi movies. Gunnar wasn't sure if they were going to watch the movie together or if she intended for him to watch it alone but it was too much trouble to get his confusion across in Danish, so he decided to just wait and see.

Layla didn't think that the Danish man would like a Hindi movie. Not everyone could appreciate the dialogue, the nuances, the acting, the songs, and the dancing. Whenever they tried to watch an English movie, Layla didn't particularly like it and believed if the Danish man watched those kinds of movies he wouldn't like a good Hindi film.

Kabir didn't think Raihana should be getting so friendly with the Danish man, and didn't care much if he liked Hindi movies or not. "Are you going to watch the movie with him?" he asked.

Raihana didn't know. Gunnar hadn't said anything and she wondered if maybe he wanted to watch the movie alone.

"Do you think Rafeeq will mind?" Layla asked suddenly.

"What has any of this got to do with Rafeeq?" Raihana asked. Rafeeq wasn't her husband yet. He wasn't her fiancé yet. Rafeeq had no demands upon her. She had only met him once.

"He is a prospect and . . . don't get all upset," Layla said.

Since the wedding in Viborg, both Kabir and Layla had made veiled insinuations that Rafeeq was somehow part of her life. The man seemed nice enough. He was almost a Danish citizen and made a decent salary. She would be financially comfortable with him. And if this was Afghanistan, Raihana knew she wouldn't even have a choice. She would have to marry the man placed in front of her. But she was not in Afghanistan, she was in Denmark, and here she could say no to the man placed in front of her, if she wished.

Thankfully, Kabir was not like other Afghan men. He had not asked Raihana to do as he wished. Instead he had told her that she could stay in his house for as long as she wanted and should marry

Rafeeq or anyone else only if she wanted to. He always treated her with respect.

"Marriage is the next step," Kabir said quietly. "I have talked to people . . . my cousin in Lahore. Everyone is sure that Aamir was killed in prison, Raihana."

At the mention of Aamir's name, Raihana's heart started to beat fast.

"He was writing anti-Taliban pamphlets. They wouldn't let him get out of there alive," Kabir continued, though Raihana had paled and tears had started falling down her cheeks.

Layla put an arm around Raihana.

"Why is Raihana Auntie sad?" Shahrukh asked as he toddled into the kitchen from the living room where he was playing with LEGO blocks.

"Nothing," Layla said. "Go and play, Shahrukh, I will come with you." She patted Raihana gently on the shoulder and followed her son into the living room.

"You know Aamir is dead," Kabir said and then seemed unsure of himself. "You do, don't you?"

Raihana nodded. "Yes, I was told in Pakistan. And I knew for certain after I heard about Ismat and Assia. Aamir made sure I left for Pakistan. He sold the house and his truck and sent me with our neighbor's family. He was going to follow . . . I should never have left like that, I should have insisted we leave together."

"It was good you left," Kabir said. "Otherwise you would be dead."

Raihana wondered if that would have been a bad thing. The urge to survive was strong and the urge to make something of her life; she also resented that she had to do any of this, that she had not died like Aamir and Assia and Ismat and so many others.

"Rafeeq is a good man," Kabir said. "A really good man."

"He has a wife in Pakistan?" Raihana asked.

Kabir nodded. "But she doesn't want to come here. She has family there and she is staying with them. Not everyone has the courage to leave the familiar and come to a strange land."

"Is this courage or desperation?" Raihana asked him. "When they told me you were in Denmark and that you wanted me to stay with you . . . I thought that maybe you wanted a maid . . . I never thanked you for . . ."

"You are like my sister," Kabir said, lifting his hand. "Don't thank Layla or me for this. You are welcome to live with us, but you have to think about the future."

"And what is my future? Marriage and children and . . . what?"

Kabir looked puzzled. "Your future is what you will make out of it. You will get married and Allah wishing you will have children. Raihana, you think too much. What is it that you want?"

"I don't know," she said. "I think once I pass *Prøve i Dansk* 3, I will get a job in a beekeeping place. I can get a job, be independent."

"And then what?" Kabir asked. "You can't live alone, Raihana."

Raihana nodded. That much she understood. No matter how women lived in Denmark and how much she fantasized herself about living alone, she couldn't imagine living alone without someone to watch over her.

"You can get a job and still be married," Kabir said. "I know Rafeeq; he would not have a problem with that."

It was inevitable, wasn't it, Raihana thought, that she would get married. There really was no other way. Not one she could conceive of. In her fantasies she was one of those women on television reading the news. They probably didn't have to get married or live with someone. They didn't have to cook and clean and take care of the children. They could probably do whatever they wanted.

Christina had said that it was important to watch the Danish news as it would help the whole class understand Danish better and also improve her knowledge of Danish life, culture, and politics. But the news anchors read the news fast and Raihana had to concentrate very hard to understand the women.

She could never be like them, she knew that. She would never be that confident, that sure of herself or—could she?

"Maybe Rafeeq can come for lunch sometime," Raihana said, biting her lip. Layla had come into the living room, leaving Shahrukh busy with his LEGO blocks in the dining room.

Kabir and Layla both smiled. "You will not regret this," Kabir said.

They were so nice. Kabir could have put pressure on her in a hundred different ways but he hadn't. She knew she had to get married. The women reading news on television were so far removed from her that they could be living on another planet.

"How about lunch next Saturday?" Layla suggested. "You can make *biriyani* and *samboosa* and *kheer*. We will have to clean the house and the bathroom and . . . Kabir, let's go ahead and buy that new TV now."

Kabir nodded. "Yes, yes, we'll make sure everything is ready."

The television was old. Kabir had bought it used three years ago, when they first came to Denmark, and it was now time to get a new one.

Raihana wanted to be excited about having Rafeeq over for lunch. By inviting him for lunch she had all but said yes to marrying him. There was no going back.

That night as she lay in bed she tried to remember Rafeeq's face but couldn't.

For Raihana the fear that came with going into uncharted territory, of going to language school and to Gunnar's house, had abated.

Her Danish was slowly getting better but it was still a struggle. There were times in class when Raihana felt like dozing off while Christina droned on and on about the tenses. There were times she didn't want to learn Danish anymore.

Afghans were going back home, they said on the Afghan news websites. Refugee camps in Pakistan were emptying slowly as thousands of Afghans went back home to war rubble and post-Taliban horror.

"I wouldn't go back," Layla always said. "I miss home, I miss my life there but I don't miss the fear, the futureless living. Here I don't worry about Shahrukh when he goes to kindergarten. He is safe, he will always be safe."

And Denmark was safe. Safe, white, and foreign. Raihana had been here ten months now and she was forgetting her life in Kabul, like it happened to someone else, like it never happened. But the terror of her life in Afghanistan crept up on her from time to time and found its way into her mind, scaring her once again, even in safe Denmark.

Raihana and Layla decided that Gunnar should see a twenty-year-old movie, *Qayamat Se Qayamat Tak*, which meant from the day of doom to the day of doom. Since he had said he would like to watch a Hindi movie, Layla and Raihana had debated about what would be the best first Hindi movie for him to watch.

Qayamat Se Qayamat Tak was the superstar Aamir Khan's first movie and one of the biggest hits of its time.

The story was about two feuding Rajput families from Rajasthan and how the daughter from one family and a son from another fell in love and were killed in the end. It was a tragic story but one of Raihana's favorites. She hoped Gunnar would enjoy it.

Raihana had learned a lot about the Danish man in the past few months. They communicated adequately in Danish and when they worked with the bees they did so in harmony. Raihana put the tools exactly where Gunnar would find them and he did the same for her. There was an intimacy in working together like this and now whenever Raihana heard the buzzing of a bee she thought of Gunnar.

He didn't drink during the day anymore, at least not during the days she was there. And he didn't hide inside the house while she pretended to work in the garage. He came out and they went to the backyard together. Taking care of forty colonies of bees was not easy and since Raihana suspected that Gunnar did no work on the days she didn't come, there was all the more to do when she was there.

Raihana was eagerly waiting for the first honey harvest. Also, at the end of June the language school would close for summer vacation until late August. The students could continue their *praktiks* if they wished and Raihana decided to do so.

She had read about the harvest in the black book Gunnar's wife had written. She read the book now with less joy than before the scene with Maria. Every time she looked at it now she was reminded of being accused of stealing and of Maria yelling at her and the Danish man. But the notebook was still her best source of bee information and she continued to read it.

According to Gunnar's wife, during harvesttime, the frames would be so laden with honey that they would be very heavy to lift. The frames would be removed from the hives, loaded up into a small wheelbarrow, and taken to the honey extractor.

The frames would be put inside the extractor machine and honey would slowly start pouring out of the machine. This honey would be stored in buckets and stirred often for a few days before being poured into jars, ready to eat.

Gunnar had told Raihana they didn't really sell that much honey, not commercially. Most of their sales were from the back door to neighbors and friends. They gave a lot of it away to relatives as well, but during a really good honey season they would set up a sign outside their house indicating there was honey for sale.

Since she had started working for Gunnar, Raihana paid more attention to the honey available in the supermarket. Usually Layla and Raihana and most Afghans shopped at Netto because it was the cheapest supermarket, but Netto had a limited selection of honey. If they wanted to buy different types, Layla and Raihana went to Kvickly, which was more expensive but offered a wide variety of honey. There was the soft-flowing acacia honey that Shahrukh ate in great quantities with and without bread. There was the creamy Danish honey. There was heather honey, which had a very strong flavor and which Raihana liked best.

As reluctant as Layla had been about Raihana's *praktik*, she had also become a big fan of honey.

"Will you be making acacia honey too?" Layla asked as they browsed the honey shelf at Kvickly one afternoon.

"No," Raihana said. "We don't make acacia honey in Denmark. It is mostly made in America and France."

Layla looked at Raihana in admiration. "You know so much about honey."

Raihana grinned. "Well, I'm showing off a little for you."

Layla laughed. "You don't have to show off; I'm already very impressed. So how about we try this chile honey?"

Raihana examined the label on the bottle. "It's from New Mexico. I wonder how they make it," she said.

"You should ask the Danish man," Layla suggested and put the chile honey in their shopping basket.

Layla thought that if the Danish man was to watch a Hindi movie, then he should also eat Afghan food. So she helped Raihana make *samboosas* with mint chutney. Her help was, however, limited to peeling potatoes and grinding spices.

Then Layla watched while Raihana made *kheer* with cream, milk, almonds, rice, and sugar. Kabir always tried to buy silver foil when he went to Hamburg, and since it was quite difficult to replace, Layla and Raihana used it very sparingly. But for this occasion, Raihana put a thin layer of the shiny foil on top of the *kheer* and it looked like something out of a cookbook.

Now that it was obvious that Raihana's safety was no issue, it annoyed Layla that she had to go clean a supermarket while Raihana was going to watch a Hindi movie with her boss.

But Layla couldn't really complain about Raihana's *praktik* because it seemed to make her so happy. When Raihana first came to their house she had been a ghost, hiding in her room, stiffening at sharp sounds, and not talking much to either Layla or Kabir. She played with Shahrukh and took care of him when Layla wasn't at home. Those first three months she just lay there most of the time. She helped with the household chores but she did it quietly and rarely spoke until spoken to.

Once Raihana began language classes she became more talkative, less of a ghost. Now Raihana even had a marriage proposal in hand. It would be a pity if Rafeeq didn't let her work for the Danish man, but if he didn't, Raihana would just have to accept that. A wife didn't argue with her husband, not about important things such as these.

To his surprise, Gunnar liked the movie. He liked the splashes of color, the singing and dancing and the love story. The Danish subtitles probably did not convey the entire message because Raihana was crying at the end and he couldn't dredge up much emotion, but nevertheless, he liked the film.

The story was a lot like *Romeo and Juliet*. A young couple in love caught between their feuding parents, finally dying tragically for their love. The girl was pretty but Gunnar wasn't sure what to make of the actor who played the boy. He was a little fellow and didn't look much more than eighteen. Raihana said he was a big film star in India. He seemed like a good enough actor, Gunnar thought, but what did he know and it didn't really matter; he had enjoyed the movie and he had enjoyed the food Raihana had brought.

"The family I live with and I think this be a good movie for you," Raihana told him when he said the movie had been fun.

"Is the family you live with okay with you working here?" Gunnar asked.

"*Jeg kan ikke forstår,*" she replied and Gunnar smiled. She rarely admitted that she didn't understand what he said in Danish.

"Do they like it that you work here?" he repeated.

Raihana paused for a moment, thinking about how she could phrase what she wanted to say in Danish. "Layla is little jealous, maybe. Kabir think it is not right, but he does not say no to me come here."

Her tenses were still mixed up. Christina always said that the hardest thing to learn about Danish was how to use the verbs.

"Why does Kabir think it is not right?" Gunnar asked as he picked up another of the pastries stuffed with potatoes.

"He is Afghan man," she said as if that explained it all.

"And the other Afghans, what do they say?"

"Not nice things."

Gunnar thought it was interesting that the Afghans thought just like so many Danes about their *praktik* setup.

"It is sad," she said. "I want to learn new thing and they say bad things."

"It is sad," Gunnar agreed.

He had never thought about the courage it must have taken for Raihana to work in a house alone with a strange man. He knew enough about Eastern cultures to know that they were very conservative. Anna would have been proud of Raihana. She would have helped her. Regardless of what Maria remembered Anna to be, he knew that Anna would never turn away a helpless woman who wanted to learn something new.

"Do you like working with the bees?" Gunnar asked then.

"A lot," Raihana said. "I never work this way with bees before."

"I know," Gunnar said.

"I didn't lie to Christina, she think I work a lot with bees," Raihana said.

"You know a lot about beekeeping now," Gunnar said.

"Yes," Raihana said.

It was the longest conversation they'd ever had.

As Raihana bicycled home she felt intensely proud of herself. She'd had a conversation in Danish. A real conversation, not something in the language school designed to improve language skills.

But as she got closer to home she realized that she had asked him nothing. He had asked all the questions. She promised herself that next time she would ask him questions. What would she ask? What did she want to know?

She wanted to know more about his wife. The woman named Anna who had written in that black leather notebook and had taught her about bees and Danish. Yes, she thought, she would ask about his wife. But would it be rude to ask him about his dead wife?

She rehearsed her questions in Danish.

How did she die?

How old was she?

What did she do?

Would she have said yes to me working with your bees?

But even as she repeated the questions in broken Danish in her mind and imagined his answers, she knew when the time came she would be too shy to ask him about his wife. Just as she would be tongue-tied if he asked her about Aamir.

THIRTEEN

12 JULY 1980

Only the queen bee produces queen substances, which are pheromones. I heard from a friend who visited the United States last year, and went to a county fair there, that some beekeepers tie caged queen bees under their chins to attract males into a "bee beard." Gunnar and I wondered if they get stung and how badly.

The queen substance is a powerful love potion. It is the love potion's allure that makes worker bees flock to their queen and tend to her every need. Young queens produce great amounts of queen substance but as the queen ages, the power of her pheromones fades. The decrease in the production may spark a revolt by the worker bees who replace the old queen with a younger one.

He was taller than Aamir. He had a very short and well-kept beard. He was darker than Aamir. He smelled of cigarettes.

She had been Aamir's first wife. She wouldn't be Rafeeq's, though it didn't really matter. His wife was in Pakistan, his children were there, but his life and he himself were here, in Denmark. Many Muslims had wives in their home countries that Danish authorities didn't know about and so getting married again in Denmark was not considered to be polygamy.

Layla had planned the menu and Raihana had cooked. Shahrukh had been told to behave himself and Layla crossed her fingers that he would take a nap right after lunch so the adults could sit and talk.

This marriage proposal was very different from her first one. When she and Aamir married, Aamir's uncle had come to Raihana's father with the marriage proposal and her father and his uncle had bargained about money. Aamir had given a small sum of money to marry Raihana; her father had quibbled, but not much.

But now they had no elders talking about the marriage, it was just them. It somehow seemed wrong to Raihana, and somehow it also felt liberating, like she could make the decisions of her life.

Rafeeq had a stern voice, and even when he laughed it was a little harsh. Raihana knew she was looking for flaws on purpose. If this were Afghanistan, no one would ask her anything and she would have to do what she was asked. But now she had a choice. She could say no.

"Mors is a small island," Rafeeq told her while they were eating lunch. "Not too many Afghans. There are some Iranian families but that is about it. And there are some families from Somalia, I think, but I don't know them."

Conversation didn't flow easily at the table. Raihana wanted to ask Rafeeq questions, but she felt shy and stayed silent. Layla, like Raihana, was quiet, shoving a piece of chicken in Shahrukh's mouth and holding his glass to him when he wanted to drink water.

"Tell us about the factory you work in," Kabir suggested when the silence dragged too long.

"They make cast-iron stoves," Rafeeq said. "I work in the production line. I assemble the top plate and baffle—they're the top part of the stove. It's a good company and a good job. If someone falls sick on the line, the manager does not hassle about sick days. But these Danes, they take too many sick days. Not like us, they don't have pride in their work."

Raihana licked her lips then and cleared her throat. "I have met a few Danes and they have a lot of pride in their work. Christina does, doesn't she, Layla?"

"Yes, yes," Layla said.

"No, no, not all Danes are like that," Rafeeq said. "I know a lot of Danes who are proud of their work and are a hardworking people."

"Yes, yes," Kabir agreed. "Danes are supposed to be good workers." Silence fell again and this time no one picked up the conversation.

"You work for a man who keeps bees," Rafeeq said after they had eaten lunch and Layla and Raihana had cleared the plates. They were drinking tea in Layla's finest cups. Layla had also served dried fruits and nuts, bought for special occasions from Hamburg by Kabir.

"Yes," Raihana said and braced herself.

"I have a colleague who keeps bees. He says it's a lot of work," Rafeeq said. "Maybe you can find a job in Thisted. They have professional beekeepers there."

Thisted was about thirty minutes north of Mors, on the other side of the island. Christina had told Raihana about the city and said she might be able to find a job there. The fact that Rafeeq had bothered to find out about beekeeping and where she could get a job put her mind at ease.

"You don't mind I work for this man?" she asked boldly.

"It isn't our way . . . but this is not our land, the ways will change," Rafeeq said.

"So you don't approve of it," Raihana said.

"It's not about approval. We're in a different country; here women work and that is okay. If the wife works there is more money at home for nicer things," Rafeeq said.

"And after children?" Raihana asked.

"Would you want to work if you had children?"

"I don't know," she said.

"The children will need their mother," Rafeeq said.

Layla snorted but didn't say anything. She worked and she went to school and after she finished language school she planned on finding a job and working. She had a child and she thought she was an excellent mother to him without sitting at home all the time. Rafeeq was right, when the wife worked there was money for the nicer things. She and Kabir wanted nicer things, for their son and themselves.

Would these Afghan men have been so liberal in Afghanistan? Did being in a different country really change them? Or would they always be this liberal, regardless of country? Would they change if they moved back to Afghanistan? Raihana realized she would never know. Whatever change happened to people like them when they had to leave their own homes and make their way in strange and alien lands could not be reversed.

The lunch had gone very well, Kabir said gleefully after Rafeeq left. He then told Raihana that Rafeeq wanted to marry her. He would give five thousand kroner as the bride money, which Kabir said was a very good amount of money. It would be *her* money. In Afghanistan the money went to the bride's father; here the money should by rights go to Kabir, but he didn't want it and was giving it to Raihana.

"My money?" Raihana asked.

Kabir nodded. "Yes."

The idea that she would have five thousand kroner all for herself was almost unbelievable.

"So?" Layla said. "Should we start planning a wedding?" Her voice was filled with unconcealed joy.

"Can I tell you next week?" Raihana asked.

Kabir didn't seem surprised. "But no later than a week. Rafeeq is going to Pakistan for three weeks in June-July and he would like to know before he leaves. He needs to tell his family in Pakistan."

That night Raihana dreamed that she was back in Kabul in the one-room flat where she and Aamir had lived. The room had a small kitchen area and Aamir had found old car seats, which they sat on to eat. Their bed was an old mattress and the one window, which had no panes, was covered with translucent plastic. It was a cold room, but Raihana had liked living there with Aamir.

There was nothing to love about that dingy one-room flat but Raihana remembered it fondly. Life was so difficult in Kabul—the struggle to put food on the table, to go on the street, to take a bath, to buy clothes, all of it had been hard. The day-to-day business of living was like climbing tall mountains with jagged edges. Still, when Raihana remembered that flat, she remembered Aamir and along with the sadness of losing Aamir was the joy of having shared a part of her life with him.

When Raihana woke up the next day she had a strange fear in her belly. She knew she more or less had said yes to marry Rafeeq. It didn't really matter that she had a week to give her answer; everyone knew she would say yes.

What else could she do? If something was wrong with him, she could refuse the match. She had the right to refuse the match even if nothing was wrong with Rafeeq. But what if she did refuse him, then what? She had to get married, didn't she? She had to say yes, didn't she?

Christina was focusing on compound sentences that month and Raihana was struggling with them.

There was a new girl in class that week, Olena. She was from Ukraine and wore a black skirt with tall black boots and a bright red sweater. Her hair was bright red and short. She spoke German, English, Russian, and Ukrainian and seemed to be able to figure out compound sentences very easily. It was her first week in Danish class.

"I talk in Danish with my husband," she told Suzi, who commended her on her good Danish. "He is Danish and we work for a Danish company. So I already knew some when I started."

"She is one of those women . . . you know, the ones who marry Danes to live here," Wahida whispered to Raihana.

"When did you come to Denmark?" Raihana asked Olena, ignoring Wahida.

"Just last week," she said. "But we're here for six months and then we'll move back to Kiev. We have an apartment there."

Raihana envied Olena. She spoke Danish well, she understood Christina easily, and she had lived in Denmark for only a week. When she told Suzi, Suzi laughed. "And we envy you," she said. "I have been coming to class for two years to get this far and you have gotten this far in five months."

Raihana liked hearing that. She was doing okay, she thought. That changed quickly, though, when Christina made them do an in-class assignment and Raihana got eight of the ten sentences wrong.

Gunnar had thought he would never feel this excitement again. It was June—it was the first harvest. This had been his favorite time with Anna. But now, even though Anna wasn't there, he was eager and glad that Christina had brought Raihana to him so many months ago.

When he and Raihana went to pull out the hives filled with honey, both of them wore protective suits.

"Now you're scared they sting?" Raihana teased.

"They sting when we take their food away," he said.

They brought along newly wired frames with foundation wax to replace the ones they would remove and boxes to carry the heavy, honey-filled frames back to the garage.

Gunnar had shown Raihana the honey extractor he and Anna had saved for and bought almost ten years ago. Once the honey was stored in buckets, he used an electrical stirring machine to stir the honey every two to three days; then when the honey was creamy, it was ready.

The honey was poured into honey jars with a special honey-filling machine. The official Danish Beekeepers Association labels on the jars indicated where the honey was made, by whom, and what kind it was.

The previous year the harvest had not been so good. Anna had been disappointed but they had lost three colonies to rats and another five to starvation, so it wasn't surprising. Spring had started late and summer was short, so there had just not been enough honey. They were left with empty jars but Anna had said that they could use the leftover jars the next year. Anna had been so sure that there would be a next year. She had never suspected that without warning life would fail her. He had never suspected it. But now he was well aware of how fragile life was.

The bees buzzed angrily, even though Raihana used her smoker to quiet them. She and Gunnar put a large gunnysack by the colony they were removing honey from and jerked the frames filled with honey hives so the bees would fall on the gunnysack. The bees did not seem happy.

"I would never do this without mask and gloves," Raihana said as they worked.

"Neither would I," Gunnar said as he piled heavy frames into the box.

They did not take the frames that had brood in them and since they had used a queen bee excluder, they could safely take the frames above the separator without disturbing the brood or the queen. However, Gunnar insisted Raihana check each frame. "Some beekeepers don't use excluders," he told her. "You should be prepared for everything and learn how to harvest properly."

Raihana was glad that Gunnar wanted her to learn to do things the right way. But she worried she might never have the opportunity to do them again. She would marry Rafeeq, she would have five thousand kroner in her bank account, and then what? She couldn't help but feel that the money would not really be hers. It would not be money she could take and buy gold bangles or a new bed with. She would have to talk to Rafeeq and together they would decide what to do with it. Rai-hana suspected that Rafeeq would decide and she would have to agree.

But if she had a job, then the money she earned would be hers. Or would it belong to Rafeeq, just like the five thousand kroner would?

The boxes were heavy, so heavy that Gunnar loaded them on a trolley and wheeled them into the garage. It had taken Gunnar and Raihana the entire day to get the hives from half the colonies.

"I have to go," Raihana said, looking at her wristwatch. "Can the rest be do tomorrow?"

Gunnar nodded. "I'll leave the frames here and tomorrow we can put them into the honey extractor."

"No, no, you should finish. You can do without mine help, right?" Raihana asked.

"It can wait until tomorrow," Gunnar assured her.

Raihana was a little puzzled. It seemed that he only worked with the colonies when she was there. Raihana wanted to ask him why, but she didn't have the words in Danish.

As she bicycled home, Raihana made plans for her future. Maybe she could start her own colony. Then the little labels on the jars of honey would say HONEY BY RAIHANA SAIF KHAN.

She was so deep in thought that she didn't notice the boys. Didn't notice them staring at her. Didn't notice that one of them was playing with a stone. And she definitely didn't see the stone as it came toward her.

The stone was large with sharp edges and caught her left temple. The pain was searing and sudden. She lost control of her bicycle and fell into the ditch next to the road.

It had rained the previous day and her brown pants were soaked with dirt and water, as was her pink blouse. But that didn't worry her; but what almost made her hysterical was the pain in her right elbow and arm. She held her arm close to her body, a chill running through her from the pain. She saw the boys standing cockily. She knew they had thrown the stone at her. It hadn't been an accident.

Their posture and their gaze were challenging. One boy played with another stone, throwing it up in the air and then catching it. They made no move to help her.

What should she do? Raihana was suddenly scared.

Nothing. There was nothing she could do. There were three boys, stronger and meaner than she. And they had only thrown a stone; it wasn't a bullet.

She pushed her bicycle out of the ditch and then climbed out herself. The bicycle handle was twisted; she could not ride home. Tears pricked her eyes but she didn't shed them; she wouldn't give those hooligans the satisfaction.

Raihana went back to Gunnar's house, which was a few minutes away, with as much dignity as she could. Her palm was bruised and mixed with the mud and water on her clothes was her blood.

Gunnar was standing in his front yard pruning a rosebush when she got there.

"What happened?" he called, running toward her.

And the tears rolled down her cheeks, quick and fast. She stood there, sobbing loudly, holding on to the twisted handle of her bicycle.

Gunnar's hands shook as he removed her stiff hands from the bicycle handle and took her inside. He wasn't sure what to do so he went out to the backyard and hollered for fat Ulla. He had seen her earlier and knew she was home.

Ulla came running. Gunnar told her Raihana had been in an accident and she needed help getting cleaned up. He was afraid to clean her wounds because he didn't know how. He had kissed Julie's and Lars's hurts but he had never cleaned them. Anna had.

"Oh poor girl," Ulla said and got a wet towel and started wiping Raihana's face and hands.

Raihana continued to cry, unable to stop now that she was safe again.

"We need bandages, salve, and water," Ulla said. "Do you have any of Julie's clothes at home?" she asked Gunnar.

It took awhile for Raihana to stop crying. The damage wasn't so bad. The pink blouse would have to be thrown out along with her brown pants. Skin had peeled off her elbow and upper arm. Ulla cleaned the wounds the best she could and gently applied a salve on them.

Raihana had more cuts and bruises on her feet and her sandals were a lost cause. The straps on both shoes had torn off.

"Where did you fall down?" Ulla asked. Raihana was sitting at the dining table, her eyes red, wearing a black pair of pants and white shirt that belonged to Julie.

"By Frederiksvej," Raihana said. "The boys threw a stone at me." She pointed to her temple where there was a small but deep gash Ulla had also administered to.

"What boys?" Gunnar asked, though he had a sick suspicion he knew which boys she was talking about.

"The boys with no hair," Raihana said.

Ulla sighed. "Anders and his friends."

"Why they do this?" Raihana asked.

"Because they are bad boys," Ulla said. "Hurting a girl like that. Gunnar, you need to talk with Marianne and Mogens. Those boys can't go around throwing stones at people."

Gunnar nodded. "No they cannot."

"My bicycle be okay? I have no money for making it better," Raihana said. The tears she had managed to stem threatened to roll back again.

"It's okay," Gunnar said. "You can use Julie's old bicycle. It's in the back room. And I'll take care of your bicycle."

Raihana stared at him. She couldn't understand him, could barely hear him over the tears that were threatening to flow again.

"Okay," she said uneasily.

Ulla patted her shoulder. "Don't ride back today. Gunnar can drive you in the car."

The woman's behavior confused Raihana. Just a few weeks ago she had been hostile and now she was cleaning her wounds and being nice to her.

Once Raihana had had a cup of tea and was not crying anymore, Gunnar strapped Julie's bicycle to the back of his car and then walked up to Ulla.

"*Tak*," he said to Ulla.

"You think they hit her with a stone because she's a foreigner?" Ulla whispered.

Gunnar didn't respond.

"It isn't right that we have so many foreigners in Denmark but that doesn't mean you throw stones at them," she said. "Poor girl, she's so frightened."

"Yes," Gunnar said. "She deserves better."

Kabir was waiting for Raihana outside. She had called his cell phone, before leaving Gunnar's house, to let him know she would be home late and that she had fallen off her bicycle. She didn't tell him about the boys with no hair or the stone.

Kabir had asked if she wanted him to come and pick her up but by then Gunnar had told her he would take her and Raihana didn't want to insult him by refusing his help. She was also scared of telling him about the boys. If he knew, he might not let her go back to Gunnar's house and work with the bees.

"Don't tell about boys to Kabir," Raihana said to Gunnar as soon as she saw Kabir waiting outside, his face tense.

"Why not?" Gunnar asked.

"Then he will say no to me to come back to your house," Raihana said. "And I want to learn harvest."

Gunnar didn't want to lie, but neither did he want Raihana to miss the harvest.

As they walked toward him, Kabir smiled tightly at Gunnar and asked Raihana if she was okay. "Go in, Layla has tea waiting for you," he said in Dari.

"The bicycle," Raihana said, pointing to Gunnar's daughter's bicycle in the back.

"I will get it," Kabir said.

Raihana thanked Gunnar and went inside, relieved not to have to answer Kabir's questions in front of Gunnar.

"What happened?" Kabir asked once Raihana was inside the house.

For a moment Gunnar thought he would lie but he couldn't. Wouldn't her family be even more upset if they found out later that he had lied? Wouldn't they think he was protecting these boys because they were Danish?

"There are some boys in the neighborhood. They threw a stone at her and she fell into a ditch," Gunnar said. "My neighbor, a woman, cleaned her up and gave her clothes. They are my daughter's."

"Boys?" Kabir asked. "What kind of boys?"

Kabir had some fine Danish, Gunnar thought. Of course, there was an accent, but he was fluent in the language.

"They are . . . they are just boys," Gunnar said uncomfortably. What could he say? That they were racist teenagers?

"Are they boys who shave their hair?" Kabir asked. He saw the look of surprise on Gunnar's face and added, "We used to have a few who came by and screamed at us, piss-faced drunk."

"These boys are young, foolish. We have known the family for years. I'll talk to them and we will settle this."

"We'll talk to the police," Kabir said.

Gunnar put his hand on Kabir's arm. "You have every right to be angry but please, let me talk to the family first."

Kabir jerked Gunnar's hand away. "I'm not interested in protecting Danish boys for their foolishness. I want to make sure they don't hurt another Muslim woman again."

"What they did was very wrong," Gunnar said. "I promise, I'll make sure—"

"Raihana will not be back to your house. She will find another *praktik*," Kabir said firmly.

"It is harvesttime," he said. "Please, just for this week. I will drop her off and pick her up if you feel it isn't safe for her to bicycle."

"Why do you care? If you need someone to help you, I'm sure you can find—"

"No, no," Gunnar said. "She wants to learn about the harvest. She has worked so hard all season, it would be . . . sad if she couldn't enjoy the fruit of her labors."

Kabir turned to see Layla and Raihana staring down from the upstairs bedroom window.

"Just this week," Kabir said tightly. "No more than this week."

Gunnar nodded. "Let me talk to the parents and then I'll come with you to the police if they don't do anything. Okay? Can you give me your phone number? I'll call you as soon as I know more." Gunnar pulled out a notepad and from the glove compartment of his car and gave it to Kabir.

Kabir didn't say anything, just wrote a number on the notepad and returned it to Gunnar. He didn't trust Gunnar.

It was an unfamiliar reaction for Gunnar. He had always been a good guy, trusted and liked. No one had ever looked at him with the distrust in this man's eyes.

FOURTEEN

---

20 JULY 1980

I can hardly wait for harvest.

I love to watch the frames spin in the extractor and see the honey pour out of them. I love to stir the honey in buckets. Nothing is more exciting than harvesttime.

We don't sell our honey. We eat it ourselves and give it away as gifts. We feel it would be wrong to sell the honey and make money off the hard work of the bees.

Gunnar didn't know how to broach the subject with Marianne and Mogens, so he called Julie for advice.

"You mean you haven't talked to them yet?" Julie said in exasperation. "I'd have gone over right away and kicked that boy's butt."

The impulse had been there, but Gunnar had spent a lifetime curbing impulses. He wasn't a man who did things impulsively. It wasn't his age; even when he was young he was careful.

"What do I say?" Gunnar asked.

"Tell them they have a monster impersonating as their son," Julie snapped and then sighed. "I babysat for Anders. He used to tell me he would marry me."

"We gave them your crib," Gunnar said sadly. "Kabir said he wanted to go to the police."

"That would be the best, *Far*," Julie said. "It looks like this is out of Mogens and Marianne's control."

Gunnar didn't say anything and Julie continued.

"Stuff like this happened here too after 9/11. A colleague told me that an Indian friend with a beard got beaten up in the United States. He's not even Muslim but they thought he was. And in London they burned down a store owned by Iranians."

"But that's London and the United States. In Skive things like this aren't supposed to happen," Gunnar said. "Skive is safe."

"Nowhere is safe anymore," Julie said.

"You're right. If children of decent people are throwing stones at immigrants, no one is safe."

"You should tell Mogens and Marianne that if they won't talk to him and if Anders does not apologize to Raihana, then Kabir will go to the police and you'll go with him," Julie said.

"That was what I was thinking," Gunnar said.

They spoke some more about Maria and Lars, and Julie told him about a man she was dating. Gunnar got the sense that he was probably much older than she was and she was embarrassed. Anna would have demanded Julie tell them everything, but Gunnar couldn't do that. He respected Julie's privacy and he would wait until she was ready.

That night Gunnar talked to Anna for the first time since she died. He had heard of people speaking to their dead spouses and had always thought they were prime candidates for the mental hospital, but that night as he lay in bed, his mind full of confusion, he did what came naturally.

"What should I do?" he asked the ceiling and then turned to face Anna's picture by his bedside table.

Anna was wearing a dark chiffon dress and she was smiling; the picture had been taken at Lars's wedding.

"That man, Kabir, he distrusts me, he thinks I am out to get him," he said. "I don't know what to do about that. I don't know what to do about Anders."

He closed his eyes for a moment and then opened them again.

"You don't know what to do either?" he said and then sighed.

Mogens and Marianne surprised Gunnar.

"Yes," Mogens said, "you should go to the police."

Gunnar gaped at him for a moment and then looked at Marianne. They were in Marianne and Mogens's living room, which Marianne had painted pink last year. The curtains were pink lace and the furniture was dark wood and pink fabric. It was a terrible room, made for dolls not grown-ups.

"Yes, you should," Marianne said, confirming that both she and her husband had gone mad. "Maybe that'll straighten him out. He stole beer from the kiosk by the train station, the one Johnny runs. He came and told us and we gave him the money. When we told Anders we'd given Johnny money, he said we should increase his allowance so he doesn't have to steal."

"Those friends of his," Mogens said. "This started with them. Before that Anders was a good boy. These boys come from nowhere, they're going nowhere, and they're taking Anders with them."

"What do their parents say?" Gunnar asked, wondering how any parents would allow such behavior.

Mogens looked disgusted. "Karsten's father left when he was a baby and his mother is on welfare . . . Drinks beer, smokes cigarettes, and watches television all day. Totally useless! Henrik's parents say nothing is wrong and that if he wants to voice his opinion against the people corrupting our country that is his right."

"So they're no help," Gunnar said, almost to himself.

"Henrik's father is against immigrants. Very Dansk Folkeparti, you know what I mean?" Mogens said.

Marianne started to cry. "How is the girl?" she asked, wiping her eyes.

"Like I said, just scraped up a little, but she is scared. I would be too. I don't know if she'll come next week," Gunnar said.

"File a complaint," Mogens said. "We'll just have to deal . . ."

"We can't file a police complaint and ruin Anders's life," Gunnar said, growing annoyed at how helpless they seemed. This was their son, they needed to pull their socks up and get to work fixing his life.

"What should we do?" Marianne asked him desperately.

"I don't know," Gunnar said in exasperation. How come he was supposed to have the answers? He was no parenting expert.

"We're so lost," Mogens said wearily.

"Maybe we can talk to the police and see if we can find a way for them to talk to the boys without it being official," Gunnar suggested, though he had no idea if this was possible.

Mogens brightened. "Let me call Inspector Jon, he's an acquaintance, maybe he can talk some sense into these kids. Scare them a little?"

"You should be there, Gunnar," Marianne said. "You should be there when the police talk to him. He will be even more scared if he thinks you have filed a complaint."

"No, no," Gunnar said. "Look . . ."

"Please," Marianne pleaded. "It'll be a great help."

"Yes, please," Mogens said desperately.

Gunnar reluctantly consented.

He phoned Kabir as soon as he got home and told him what Mogens and Marianne and he himself had agreed to do. Kabir thanked Gunnar for calling and asked him to make sure Raihana was safe when she came to work in his house.

. . .

The familiar taste of fear filled her mouth again. Since she had left Afghanistan the fear had been disappearing. The refugee camp was worlds better than Kabul but had been no picnic and being a single woman with no male protection had left her open to innuendo, marriage proposals, and men who wished to have sex with her. Once she came to Denmark she had felt safe. There were no men with guns on the street, and no screaming at people like they were cattle. Most important she was free to live the life she wanted. And now a stone against her forehead had changed everything. If someone had thrown a stone at her in Kabul, she would have thought nothing of it. She would have considered herself lucky that it had been just a stone. But here, in pristine Denmark, the wound seemed uglier than it would have in Kabul.

"You don't have to go," Kabir said. They were sitting in the living room after a very quiet dinner.

"Actually, I'd prefer it if you didn't go to the Danish man's house anymore," Kabir added.

She'd only gotten hurt that afternoon and by nighttime her wounds were throbbing and Raihana was exhausted by thinking about the incident again and again. She kept running it through her mind. What if the stone had been bigger? What if there had been a car coming and had hit her? What if . . . ?

"Just go to school and back home, there's no need to go to that man's house in between," Kabir said.

"But if she doesn't go back to the bees, Kabir, they win," Layla said suddenly. "She should go and show that she isn't scared. You should take her to show that she has protection and that we're not scared. This is our home too, Kabir, we can't let some stupid boys run us out."

Raihana looked up at Layla in surprise, just as Kabir did.

"We don't have to show anyone anything," Kabir snapped.

"Yes we do," Layla said. She looked at Shahrukh, who was sleeping on Kabir's lap. "For his sake we need to show them that we're not scared. You want your son to be attacked like this too? We fight this now."

"And how do we fight it?"

"By not changing our lives," Layla said. "Raihana?"

"I agree with Layla," Raihana said. "I'm scared and I don't want to bicycle to Gunnar's house, but Layla is right, I need to go because I can't be scared, not here too."

Kabir looked at the women in disbelief. "This is why I want to go home."

"In Afghanistan that could have been a bullet and she would be dead," Layla said. "And remember, Kabir, not all Danes are like these boys."

"Yes they are," Kabir said.

"No, Kabir," Raihana said immediately. "Gunnar is not. You saw him."

"He said he would take those boys to the police, if he does, we'll see," Kabir said.

"Gunnar's taking them to the police?" Raihana asked.

"He called my mobile while I was out for a smoke," Kabir said. "One of the boys' parents asked him to talk to the police. It won't be an official complaint, but he hopes that it'll scare them to be taken to the police station and questioned. I'm not sure what will come of it."

"So it's settled then," Layla said, sighing in relief. "But what about tomorrow? How will she get to the Danish man's house?"

"I will drive her," Kabir said.

That night, as Raihana lay awake, fear clutching her belly, she knew she was a coward. She was not ready, she thought, not ready at all to face those boys again. What would they do this time?

Raihana went to class the next day, even though Layla had told her it would be okay if she didn't. Wahida looked at her bruises with aversion, clearly thinking, I told you, didn't I.

Of course news like this spread like wildfire in the small immigrant community in Skive. There was a certain amount of panic among the Muslims, but most of them were also aware that the mischief was perpetrated by three teenage boys. This was most likely a random incident, not a deep conspiracy to hurt them.

That first class after the attack, Raihana sat next to Tatjana, a very quiet girl. Tatjana rarely spoke to anyone and during breaks rushed outside to smoke cigarettes she carried in a blue leather purse. She wore tight jeans, equally tight blouses, and big boots. In the summer she replaced the big boots with leather sandals and the tight blouses had shorter sleeves. She spoke Danish with a strange accent and her voice was heavy, almost like a man's, and she seemed very sure of herself.

Tatjana was from Bosnia; Raihana had learned that in her first class when Christina made everyone tell their names, where they came from, where they lived, and how long they had been in Denmark.

"*Jeg hedder Tatjana.*" My name is Tatjana.

"*Jeg kommer fra Bosnia.*" I come from Bosnia.

"*Jeg bor i Skive.*" I live in Skive.

"*Jeg har været i Danmark i to år.*" I have been in Denmark for two years.

Raihana didn't know much about Bosnia, except that there had been a war there and there were refugees from Bosnia in Denmark.

Raihana was a little intimidated by Tatjana and usually sat with Suzi. But Suzi was sick at home as was Christina. Casper, another teacher, was teaching them today and he had joined his class with Raihana's. Raihana was painfully aware that all eyes were watching her bruises.

"A big stone, eh? How big? This big?" Sohaila had asked, measuring the imagined stone with her hands.

"Not that big," Raihana said. She didn't want to think about the stone. Sohaila had cornered her outside the bathroom before the classes began.

"Horrible things are happening here," Sohaila continued. "You know, they think all Muslims are terrorists."

Raihana looked forlornly at the bathroom.

"So, you're not going back there for your ridiculous *praktik* are you? It always sounded like a bad idea and now we know, eh?" Sohaila said, her eyes glittering.

"Why shouldn't I continue my *praktik*? I get paid for my work and if I want to get a job with a beekeeper, I need to go there," Raihana said defiantly.

Sohaila's eyes all but popped out.

"I heard Rafeeq has made a proposal. Then why are you talking about working, you stupid girl," Sohaila said angrily. "You don't wear a *hijab*, okay, I don't either and that's fine. But not marry? And work? What's going on with you?"

Raihana felt the bile rise in her throat. "I just want to do something."

"Then get married, plenty to do," Sohaila advised. "You think we go to class because we want to learn Danish and get jobs? We come here because if we don't they will cut off our welfare checks."

"Well that may be true for you, but I want to learn the language," Raihana said. "Now if you'll move a little, I need to use the bathroom."

The class was devoted to verbs again and Raihana didn't feel any better about how the day was turning out. Verbs were hard.

"I heard some boys threw a stone at you," Tatjana said at the start of the first break.

Raihana nearly jumped out of her chair.

"Is that how you got hurt?" she asked.

Raihana nodded.

"*For pokker!*" Tatjana cursed in Danish. "Are you scared?" she went on, looking Raihana in the eye.

"Yes," Raihana admitted.

"My husband was killed in Bosnia," she said, turning her head toward the window. "Died in the war. Never saw the body."

How could two women from different parts of the world have gone through the same thing?

Raihana's eyes filled with tears. "They took my husband away and . . . killed him in prison," she said. It was the first time she had told anyone what had happened to Aamir.

"Children?"

"I lost baby in belly when I ran from Kabul to Pakistan." The words slipped out so easily. She could not explain how she could tell Tatjana, a perfect stranger, something she had not even told Layla. Maybe it was because Tatjana had also lost a husband, maybe it was because Tatjana had posed the question so matter-of-factly—maybe it was time for her to accept what had happened and that was why the truth had finally found a way out of her heart.

"That is sad," Tatjana said. "Can you have more children?"

"I don't know . . . maybe," Raihana said.

Tatjana was silent for a while and then said softly, "We, you and I, women like us have been through hell. Stones shouldn't scare us."

"I just didn't think it would happen here," Raihana said.

"I ran with my two-year-old son and I was also pregnant," she said. "My younger son was born here, in an asylum center. I was there for five months with my boys before they gave me asylum."

"Because I have relatives in Denmark, I was there for just a week," Raihana said.

"I want to go back to Bosnia. It looks like things are better," Tatjana said, and then laughed softly. "But I don't want that for my children. Stones here are better than what is at home, ruins and bad memories."

They fell silent after that. The break ended and students started to come back and fill the chairs. Right before Casper started to speak again Raihana leaned over to Tatjana and whispered, "I won't be scared anymore."

Gunnar was just getting into his car when Kabir's car drove into his driveway. Kabir looked angry and Raihana seemed apologetic.

"*Hej,*" Gunnar said to both Raihana and Kabir as he closed the door of his car shut.

"*Hej,*" Raihana said, but her head was bowed.

"Please let her phone me when she is ready, so I can come and pick her up. You can keep your bicycle," Kabir said. He started to un-clamp the bicycle Gunnar had loaned to Raihana from his car.

"No, no, I can bicycle back," Raihana protested.

"I will drop her home," Gunnar said. "And please, she can keep the bicycle." He had looked at Raihana's bicycle in the morning and it was a lost cause.

Kabir looked at both of them sternly.

"You don't have to worry about those boys," Gunnar said to Rai-hana. "I told Kabir yesterday what we plan to do. The boy who lives here, his parents have agreed that the police should talk to him. They will pick him up after school today. I will go to the police station as well. That will straighten him out."

Kabir looked as if he wanted to say something, but he decided against it and drove away.

The fragile friendship that Raihana and Gunnar had established in the past few months seemed to have dissipated. Gunnar was acutely aware of being white, a Dane, like the boys who had hurt Raihana.

They went inside the house and Raihana put her lunch box in the fridge before going to the garage.

Gunnar followed her and pointed toward the honey extractor. "This is what brings the honey out of the honeycombs," he said.

He showed her how to put the frames filled with honey into the honey extractor. He then pressed a button, which started the extractor; the frames rotated within the machine and honey oozed out, coming out of a nozzle at the bottom of the machine.

They made five buckets of honey from the frames they had col-lected from the colonies the day before.

"We stir the honey, that makes it creamy and light," he explained. He wasn't sure if she understood. Usually she asked questions, but for the first time she was completely silent.

Christina came to visit while Raihana was at Gunnar's house. She had just found out about what had happened.

Gunnar was relieved to see Christina. He was having a difficult time speaking with Raihana. She seemed to have lost her exuberance and it was such a shame. After all that she had seen in her home country, she had lost her laughter here, in his country where she was supposed to be safe.

"I am scared," Raihana confessed to Christina when they sat alone on Gunnar's veranda. "This not happen here."

"No," Christina nodded. "But things like this happen everywhere."

Christina always spoke slowly and clearly; Raihana liked that about her.

"I can't tell you how I feel," Raihana said suddenly. "I don't have enough Danish."

Christina smiled. "You will."

"Kabir wants me to stop coming here," Raihana told Christina.

"I know," she said. "He talked to me today at the school. I told him that this could happen anywhere—it didn't happen to you because you come to Gunnar's house."

"It happened because I'm Afghan," Raihana said.

"No, it happened because those boys are foolish," Christina said.

Gunnar set coffee cups and a pot of coffee on the table in the veranda. Their outdoor furniture was beautiful, made of teak, in traditional Danish style. Gunnar had not wanted to spend a lot of money but Anna was adamant they buy Trip Trap, the most expensive outdoor furniture. They had lived with white plastic chairs and tables for many, many years, saving up to buy the teak wooden ones. They finally had bought a set three years before Anna died.

It was nice wooden furniture but Gunnar had seen similar ones in Bilka that cost a quarter of what these had. But Anna had been stubborn. Every time Gunnar sat on the chairs now, he smiled, a part of him less wounded by Anna's loss.

Gunnar joined them for coffee at Christina's insistence.

"When the honey is ready, you should take some jars home with you," Gunnar said because he didn't know what else to say. Honey was safe. "The honey is really yours too."

Raihana smiled shyly.

She looked so forlorn that Gunnar said, "Don't worry about those boys anymore," even though he had promised himself that he would try and keep her mind off the incident. But as they sat under Anna's green parasol, on her Trip Trap furniture where Gunnar could clearly see Raihana's bruises and the fear in her eyes, he realized how ridiculous it was. Of course he would have to talk about the incident. He couldn't just wish it away.

"Are Maria and the kids coming for the heather honey week?" Christina asked.

"Yes," Gunnar said, "I think so. She hasn't said they aren't."

Christina looked at Raihana. "Every year Gunnar and his wife took some of the colonies to the west coast and left them there to make heather honey."

Raihana seemed to take some time to understand what Christina said.

Gunnar cleared his throat. "We go to the beach where heather grows, and we leave some colonies there, so the bees can make honey from the heather."

"I read it in your wife's book," she said. "Put bees near bushes and they only take heather nectar. I read it."

"Yes, yes," Christina said. "Gunnar's daughter-in-law, Maria?"

"Yes," Raihana said and then added, "I meet her." She didn't add that she didn't like Maria, and Maria didn't like her.

"She comes with her children and they go to the beach for a day to leave the bees," Christina said.

"How long you bees leave there?" Raihana asked.

"About four to six weeks and we have made very good honey," Gunnar said.

"Maybe you, Kabir, and Layla would like to join Gunnar and his family," Christina said, smiling at Gunnar.

If Gunnar was surprised it didn't show. "Yes, yes," he said. "Fine idea, Christina."

Raihana understood what Christina had said but wondered if she had been mistaken.

"It'll be after the school closes," Christina said. "You should go; Layla and Kabir will like it very much. Their son can play with Maria's kids."

No, Raihana thought, she had not misunderstood. Christina wanted Raihana, Layla, Kabir, and Shahrukh to meet with Gunnar and his family. Like they were friends?

Raihana's first instinct was to refuse. Kabir would never agree and neither would Layla.

"It'll be fun," Gunnar said. "I can meet your family and you can meet my son, Lars."

Raihana bit her tongue. Gunnar seemed so excited about the prospect that she didn't have the heart to say no, not right away. She would later on, she thought. She would not ask Layla and Kabir, there was no point—she knew their answer.

"No rush," Gunnar said. "We go in two weeks."

At around four o'clock Kabir came and picked up Raihana. He didn't wait for her to call but just drove up to Gunnar's house. He spoke to Christina for a few minutes, said a quick hello to Gunnar, and then hustled Raihana into the car.

"I think you shouldn't come here during the summer holidays. We'll find you another *praktik*," Kabir said. "I don't like that man."

"Why?" Raihana asked.

"He seems like one of those frauds. One thing on the outside and another on the inside," Kabir said.

"What does that mean?" Raihana asked, feeling defensive.

"He says he'll take those boys to the police but he really won't; it's all talk," Kabir said.

"No, it isn't," Raihana protested. "He's going to the police."

"Whatever," Kabir said. "These people, they think we should only clean their houses and supermarkets, that we aren't good for anything else."

"That's not true," Raihana said.

"Why do you defend him? He makes you clean things in his house, doesn't he? Don't you wash his clothes and dishes and clean floors?" Kabir demanded, driving faster.

"I do it because I want to," Raihana said. "And he doesn't think I'm a servant."

"Why? Because he saw a movie with you? And ate *samboosas* with you?" Kabir asked.

Raihana sighed. "No, because he is kind and talks to me with respect. Because he invites you and Layla and Shahrukh and me to come with him and his family to his summer house by the beach in July."

Kabir didn't say anything for a moment. "He was just being polite; he is the type who will say anything to sound like a nice—"

"No," Raihana interrupted. "How can you be so bitter about these people? You live here, Kabir, in this country and—"

"What? You think they want us here? They hate us. See what they did to you? Why don't you get it? They don't want us here." Kabir was all but yelling as he pulled into the narrow driveway between the house and the garden hedge.

"Then why do you want to live here? Why do you want to stay here?" Raihana asked.

"Because I can't go back home, because I am a refugee and no one wants me," Kabir said, his eyes bright with tears.

Raihana took a deep breath. "We are creatures of desperate times; you feel you have nowhere to go and I feel I have no future, no further life. I have to marry or . . . there is no option for me. And now this. I don't know what to do. But, Kabir, that is not the fault of all the people here. This country has been good to us."

"But what about the people who don't want us here? What about those boys who threw stones at you? What about them?"

Raihana put her hand on Kabir's. "Not all of them are like those boys. Not all of them want to hurt us. You keep saying that the people here judge you because you are Muslim; because of the acts of a few terrorists, the entire following of Islam is now suspect, isn't that what you say? And you're doing the same thing, judging all Danes by the acts of those three boys."

Kabir let go of the steering wheel. "I know, I know, not all Danes want us dead . . ."

"Gunnar is a decent man," Raihana said.

"He really invited us to go to the beach with his family?"

"Yes," Raihana said and smiled. "They make heather honey there."

"Heather honey?"

"I'll tell you and Layla all about it," Raihana said. "I read about it in that leather notebook that Gunnar's wife wrote in. Her name was Anna."

The last day of language school was sunny. Just the day before it had rained with thunder and lightning, but as it was with summer rain, the clouds vanished into thin air and the sky looked like it had never seen a dark cloud before.

Christina was taking the class to Mønsted to celebrate the last day of school. The Mønsted limestone caves were supposed to be beautiful and the temperature inside was quite low, so everyone was advised to dress for winter.

It was a half-hour drive from the school, and after the trip to Mønsted, Christina was taking all of them to her house for lunch.

As soon as they walked inside the large entrance the chill seeped through.

"Very beautiful," Suzi said as they leaned over a small pool of water and saw the reflection of the limestone formations on the other side lit up with hidden lightbulbs.

"I've come here four times before," Olena complained. "Every time my relatives come to visit us from Kiev we bring them here. I know that show by heart."

They walked into crevices and on strange paths, got stuck at one place because one of the girls, Noor from Iran, was six months' pregnant and couldn't go up and down as easily as the others.

Raihana found a quiet place by the theater and stared at the still waters in front of her. The limestone caves were hundreds of years old and had in the past been used to mine limestone to build churches. Raihana could smell the faint odor of cheese.

"It smells funny here," Raihana said to Olena, who came and sat next to her.

"They make cheese here; the temperature and moisture is supposed to be good for the cheese," Olena said. "And it stinks because of it."

Raihana didn't like Danish cheese. She had tasted blue cheese once when they had samples on top of rye bread at the supermarket. Layla had warned her against it but she was so curious she couldn't stop herself.

"The blue part is fungus," Layla told her afterward and Raihana had felt like throwing up.

But Raihana liked the soft feta she and Layla often used in salads. It didn't smell like the inside of the limestone caves and wasn't bitter.

Raihana's and Olena's reflection were still in the water and Raihana could see the bruises on her face. The bruises might have been uncomfortable but they saved her from giving an answer to Rafeeq before he left for Pakistan. No one would press her into saying yes or no to marriage while she was recovering from the attack. But he would be back in three weeks and she would have to give an answer then.

"Pretty, isn't it?" Olena said, looking at their reflection.

"Yes," Raihana said.

"Do your wounds still hurt?" Olena asked.

"No," Raihana said. "But I know they are there."

"Yes," Olena said and nodded. "That's the scary part, isn't it?"

They didn't say anything for a while.

"Sometimes I wish I had stayed back in Afghanistan. I don't feel

safer here anymore—and at least in Kabul I was prepared for the violence," Raihana said.

"My parents live in fear all the time," Olena said. "They had safety
and security during the terrible communism days. They knew they
would always have a job. But since democracy has come to Ukraine,
nothing is for sure."

Olena's Danish was at about the same level as Raihana's and they
managed to communicate quite well.

"They want things to go back to the way they were, so that they can
be safe again," Olena continued. "But those were horrible times. We
had no freedom to do what we wanted. We couldn't get the education
we wanted. We couldn't go on vacation where we felt like. But they
want those days back—because they don't want change. No matter the
insecurities, I don't want to go back."

"You're right, in Denmark things will never be as bad as Afghanistan," Raihana said.

Olena nodded. "No, never that bad."

They all agreed Christina's house, a refurbished farmhouse, was
gorgeous, but the large garden was truly stunning. There was even
a fountain and flowers of all kinds, roses in all colors. The vegetable garden was rich with peas, lettuce, sunflowers, and pumpkins.
There was a greenhouse where chiles, tomatoes, and other vines grew.
Two metal chairs and a table, painted in white, were in the greenhouse and Raihana imagined it would be nice to sit there on a sunny
winter day, soaking in the warmth without being stung by the bitter
cold.

Christina also had a huge herb garden with several types of mint,
coriander, sage, rosemary, citron melisse, and some other herbs that
Raihana had never heard of.

"It isn't easy but it's very satisfying," Christina said when Olena
asked how they managed to do all the work in the garden. "We work
together but he is the botanist, not me."

A husband did help. Raihana wondered what Rafeeq would say if she told him that she wanted to travel and have a pretty house, that these things were important to her. Would he care? Was he even supposed to? Shouldn't she just be happy someone wanted to marry her? The house was decorated with things from all over the world. Christina and her husband liked to travel and they had masks from Africa, dolls from Russia, carpets from Turkey. Raihana wished she could have Christina's life. She wished she could travel and have a house like this. She wished she could have a garden so bright and beautiful.

They had lunch on the terrace. Christina served bread with roast beef, chicken, and smoked salmon, as well as some cheese she'd picked up from Mønsted. They drank strawberry juice and talked about their plans for the summer holidays. Olena was going to Venice in Italy. She told them that she had always wanted to go there and since she and her husband had not had a real honeymoon when they married last year, this was their honeymoon. Christina was going to France, some place called Provence, where she and her husband had rented a villa with some friends.

It sounded very strange and very exotic. Raihana knew no one in France and she had no idea what Provence was. She didn't know how to garden. She knew nothing about the life Christina had. If she married Rafeeq would she get a chance to go to places like Provence and buy masks from China? She didn't know a single Afghan in Denmark who went on vacation to a strange place just to see it. Afghans only visited family on vacation, and usually ended up going to Pakistan.

As they drove back to the language school, Raihana felt like a complete failure. She couldn't even drive a car, like Olena and Christina. She would never travel like Olena and Christina, go on vacations to exotic places. Once she married Rafeeq and had children, what would their lives be like? They would probably go to Pakistan for vacation and then come right back to Denmark.

What kind of life would that be for her children? Would they have the opportunity to go to France and Venice?

Maybe she should ask Rafeeq a few more questions before she said yes. She could find out what he liked to do when he wasn't working and how he wanted to raise their children. No, that wouldn't be right, she told herself. Rafeeq would think it was an insult that she was asking so many questions before saying yes. If he was a Danish man, maybe the questions wouldn't bother him, but an Afghan man, he just wanted a quick answer. Already, she was trying his patience by waiting so long to say yes.

She'd just say no then. She'd tell him she couldn't marry him. And then next time someone was interested, she could ask all the right questions in the beginning.

Even as she made that decision, fear bloomed inside her. What if no one ever asked to marry her again?

FIFTEEN

22 JULY 1980

Mite infestation is rampant in the wild and in apiaries. Beekeepers are always looking for advanced medical means to protect their bees from mites, but wild bees may be facing extinction because of the mites.

Mites move from one bee to another when the bees touch each other. Bees are very social creatures, and not just within their colonies. They meet up with strange bees on flowers and touch in greeting for a split second, just enough time for a pregnant female parasitic mite to change mounts and ride to a new destination.

A politi betjent, police officer, picked Anders up at school and drove him to the police station in a Ford Mondeo, nearly a week after the stone-throwing incident.

Mogens, Marianne, Gunnar, and Jon Vittrup, the police inspector, were waiting for them in Jon's office. The sun poured straight through the windows and the white curtains didn't do much to curtail the heat. Jon had a small table fan creaking away on his desk, but it didn't actually help with the heat either.

Gunnar had been to the police station to get his driver's license, the kids' driver's licenses, their passports—for so many things. But he had always stood outside the main offices, at the counter, right by the glass door leading into the building. He had never been in the inner sanctum on the first floor. The police station also had a jail in the back that could accommodate fifteen to twenty prisoners at one time. Right now it was empty, Jon said, but he joked they usually got some action on Friday nights.

"People get drunk and cause a ruckus. The Crazy Daisy gets a lot of high-profile people in," Jon said, leaning over the desk. "Prince Joachim is there quite often, and not with the princess."

No one said anything and there was silence for a while until Marianne suddenly started to speak.

"My father says it's because we're too easy on the boys, we don't punish them enough," Marianne said. "But they're my boys and I love them. I love Anders and I know he did a bad thing but I can't be really angry with him."

"I'm angry," Mogens said. "I am angry enough to wring his neck, the little bastard. Hurting someone like that. At this rate he's going to end up in jail."

"He isn't going to become a criminal," Marianne said firmly. Gunnar could see she had convinced herself that her son hadn't really done anything wrong and this whole police station scene was unnecessary.

"Yes, yes he is," Mogens said. "He threw a stone at that Afghan girl. What if he throws something else?"

"Oh, Mogens, he's just being—"

"Stop," Mogens thundered. "This is why we're unable to discipline either of them, because you keep letting things go. But enough is enough. It stops now."

Marianne's face flashed with rage. "Well, why shouldn't he be angry with immigrants? I am. They're all criminals anyway and my son is being punished—"

Jon raised his hand. "If you two want to fight, please do it in your house, not in my station. And Marianne, if this is the kind of nonsense you're telling your son, it's no surprise he's throwing stones at innocent women."

Marianne gasped. "I'm telling him no such thing."

Jon's phone rang then and he spoke for a moment and put the receiver into the cradle.

"They are here," he said and stood up, rubbing his hands together.

Marianne fell silent and Mogens looked as if he were being led to the guillotine.

Anders came into the office and the officer who brought him in stood by the door, his hands locked behind him, his legs slightly apart.

Anders looked up at his parents in confusion and then at Jon. "What's going on?" he asked. "Why am I here? *Mor, Far?*"

Marianne was about to say something but Mogens put a hand on her shoulder to silence her. He cleared his throat. "You threw a stone at a girl and—"

"Whoever said that is lying," Anders said, cutting his father off.

"Really?" Jon said, smiling slowly. His bald head glistened with heat and his eyes were menacing. Gunnar thought that when he was sixteen, a policeman like Jon would've scared the life out of him, but Anders was nonchalant.

"I didn't do anything," Anders said and walked back to lean against the wall.

"Stand up straight," Jon said coolly and banged his fist on the table.

Marianne flinched, Mogens seemed pleased, and Anders, well, Gunnar thought happily, the boy did as he was told.

"I shave my head because I don't have much hair left," Jon said. "I hear you do it because you think you're a neo-Nazi, are you?"

Anders's Adam's apple bobbed for a moment. "I believe that Denmark is for Aryans, for us, not"—he seemed to pick up his courage to look at Gunnar and say—"the scum some people are bringing into this country."

Jon stood up and Anders took a step back. "It isn't for you to decide, you little punk. Raihana Saif Khan has lodged a complaint against you. We take complaints of assault seriously and racially motivated ones, we take especially seriously."

"She's lying," Anders said and turned to his mother. "I didn't do anything. She . . . her type . . . they always lie. I didn't do anything . . . *Mor?*"

Marianne stared at her shoes, her lips quivering.

"Don't lie, son," Mogens pleaded.

"What the hell do you know about anything," Anders said. "You never believe anything I say anyway."

"Watch the way you talk to your father," Jon said. "Mogens, Marianne, thanks for coming in. Please step outside. I need to speak with Gunnar and Anders alone now. Palle, please take them outside and give them a cup of coffee, maybe some cake?"

The police officer who had brought Anders to the station walked Mogens and a very reluctant Marianne out of Jon's office.

"Look here, you shit-faced liar," Jon said just as the door closed behind the police officer. "You think I will believe some spoiled teenager over a respectable woman who is working hard to become a productive member of the community."

"That bitch is a Muslim," Anders said.

Jon turned to Gunnar. "Could you please wait outside?" he said.

Gunnar stood up, unsure, and then quietly walked out of the office. Jon shut the door behind Gunnar.

There was a sound of something crashing and then Gunnar heard Jon say, "She's a respectable woman and we don't go around calling a respectable women names."

Gunnar heard Anders cry out, a tremor in his voice. "I will report you, you asshole, you can't do this."

"Report what?" Jon demanded and then there was another crashing sound.

Gunnar got nervous but stood outside, waiting to hear Jon or Anders say something.

Oh God, had Jon just slapped the boy? This was Denmark, cops didn't slap young boys—slapping of any kind was not acceptable. Even in a riot situation, cops could get into trouble for hitting someone unnecessarily. In Denmark, spanking your own child was against the law.

"Report what you want, no one cares. You think they'll believe you over a respected police inspector?" Jon asked.

The door opened then and Jon gestured to Gunnar to come back inside. Anders's face was red and he looked frightened.

"We were just getting a few things straight," Jon said and sat down. Anders was shaking slightly now.

"Now, your friends will be picked up as well and they'll be informed that you told us that they threw the stone. That you're escaping punishment for ratting them out," Jon said.

"I didn't say their names. They had nothing to do with this," Anders said.

"Yes you did," Jon said, looking at some papers. "Karsten Rasmussen and Henrik Jensen. What do you think your friends will say about this?"

Anders just stared at Jon.

"Right," Jon said. "Now, I'm going to let you go because I know your father and I owe him some favors. But the other boys will be punished."

"No," Anders said, now scared. "You can't do that. They didn't do anything."

Jon nodded. "I know, but what do you want me to do? One of you threw the stone and the girl got badly hurt."

"I threw the stone. It was just me," Anders said, panic now lacing his voice.

"So you threw the stone? Why should I believe you? No, no, I need to speak with Karsten and Henrik," Jon said implacably.

Anders turned to Gunnar. "Look, I'm sorry, okay Gunnar? I'm really sorry. It was an accident. I didn't mean . . . look . . . they had . . . the stone . . . I threw it. Can't you do fingerprints or something? You will see, I threw it."

"The boy sees too much American television. I don't need finger-prints to put you away; I have Raihana Saif Khan, who will identify you. I can put you all away, but for now I'll be happy to put those two away," Jon said.

The fight visibly drained out of Anders.

"What can I do? Whatever . . . ," he began helplessly, his hands held up in submission.

Jon raised his hand. "Stay away from that woman. Actually, stay away from all women. Give Gunnar five hundred kroner for fixing Ms. Saif Khan's bicycle and another five hundred kroner to replace the clothes you tore. I'm hoping you jokers can find this money by the end of the month without committing a crime?"

"We can't get a thousand kroner just like that," Anders protested.

"Yes, you can. It's summer, go get a summer job," Jon said. "And I want a written apology. The woman's name is Raihana Saif Khan. Here, let me write it down for you. Write a note to her apologizing for what you did and give it to me. I will read it and then I will give it to her. You can give me the money at the end of the month, but the note comes next week. On Monday. Am I clear?"

Anders picked up the yellow sticky note with Raihana's name and looked at Gunnar. There was anger in his eyes, not remorse.

Once a month, Kabir drove to Bazaar Vest near the immigrant area in Århus, an hour and a half away from Skive. The bazaar was in a huge building with stores everywhere. There was a vegetable market and row after row of stores run by Iranians, Iraqis, Indians, Afghans, and Turks.

The smell of Turkish coffee, freshly baked baklava, and cigarette smoke permeated the air of the crowded bazaar.

Raihana had been surprised to see quite few Danes at the bazaar on her first visit. Even Christina had talked about the bazaar and how she went there at least once a month to buy meat.

Kabir didn't go to the bazaar to shop, but to meet other immigrants like himself. He always spent time with Faisal, who had the best meat shop in the bazaar; Qadir, whose café served oily pizza and Turkish coffee; and Khaled, whose clothes, DVD, and video store was thriving.

Layla, Shahrukh, and Raihana would start at the vegetable market where the vegetables were always fresh, in abundant varieties, and cheap. After vegetable shopping they would eat at the small Indian place at the other end of the bazaar. A couple, Azhar and Tasnim from Hyderabad in India, ran the restaurant. Tasnim spoke fluent Dari because she had Afghan relatives who migrated to India from Afghanistan when she was young and she had picked up the language from them.

Tasnim chatted with Layla and Raihana as they ate lamb curry or chicken *tikka masala* with freshly made *rotis*.

"What happened to your face?" Tasnim asked as Raihana had expected she would.

Before she could explain, Layla launched into a tirade about the incident, explaining how Raihana had gotten hurt.

"So did they take the boys to the police?" Tasnim asked, sliding a plate of *samosas* in front of the women and handing a *laddoo* to the irritable Shahrukh, who didn't like being strapped in his pram.

"Well, the man she works for told Kabir they would take the boys to the police," Layla said with a sneer.

"And he will," Raihana said in Gunnar's defense.

"Terrible," Tasnim said and sighed when Shahrukh let out a wail. "Layla, get him out of that pram and let him walk around."

Layla looked at Shahrukh, whose face was scrunched up. She unstrapped him and pulled him out.

"*Arrey*, Azhar, take him into the kitchen," Tasnim called out in Hindi and pushed Shahrukh toward the kitchen, where her husband would keep him fed and entertained.

"So what else is going on?" Tasnim asked.

Layla looked at Raihana. "Rafeeq, you know that Afghan who lives on Mors, he made a marriage proposal for our Raihana."

"*Arrey wah!* What good news!" Tasnim said. "So, when is the wedding?"

Raihana shifted uncomfortably.

"Well, she hasn't said yes yet," Layla said.

"What's to say, *arrey*, Raihana? Rafeeq comes here every month, handsome man and well mannered," Tasnim said. "I know he's looking for a wife and he makes good money. He's almost a Danish citizen."

Raihana nodded politely. "Yes, he seems like a good man."

"So will you marry him?" Layla asked.

"I just got hit by a stone," Raihana pleaded.

Layla put her hand on Raihana's. "Is that a no?"

"No, no," Raihana said, shaking her head.

Tasnim grinned. "Then it's a yes, isn't it."

"Maybe," Raihana said. A part of her wanted to just say yes and be done with it.

"Have children, be happy," Tasnim said. "You deserve it."

"Yes, she does," Layla said.

"This is all very strange," Raihana said. "The first time I got married . . . it was different and now . . ."

"The first time was in Kabul, this time is here," Layla said. "You are lucky to have come here, now make something of your life."

"I really want to work," Raihana said and then looked at Tasnim. "You like it don't you, running your own business."

"Oh yes," Tasnim said. "Without this . . . I don't know. I don't abide by those career women, always away at work and whatnot. But here, I raised my children and worked and helped the family."

"I want to do the same," Raihana said. "I am learning to be a bee-keeper."

"She knows a lot about beekeeping," Layla said proudly.

"I would like to become a beekeeper," Raihana said.

Tasnim nodded appreciatively. "You can have your own bees, make your own honey," she said.

"But won't that be expensive?" Layla asked, peering into the kitchen as she heard Shahrukh's laughter. He ran past the open door-way with a sweet in his hand.

"The Danish government will pay," Tasnim said. "You need a small-business loan, it's quite simple."

"A loan? You mean borrow money?" Raihana asked. "That doesn't sound right."

"You're not in Kabul anymore. Here everyone borrows money to make their life better," Tasnim said.

Azhar brought their food out and went back into the kitchen to play with Shahrukh. As the women ate, the topic swiftly changed to the latest Hindi movies and what Azhar had brought back with him from his most recent trip to India.

After they left, they found Kabir at the Qadir's café smoking a ciga-rette and drinking Turkish coffee. While Layla talked with Qadir, Rai-hana stood in front of a clothes store, window-shopping.

Clothes hung on the glass wall of the store and at the center was a green Afghan wedding dress. Could she be ready to wear a wedding dress again? She was getting used to the idea of getting married, espe-cially after the incident with the boys. A part of her wanted the secu-rity that marriage and a man by her side offered. That was a good reason to get married.

There were beautiful *salwar-kameezes* hanging by the wedding dress. Raihana wished she had the money to buy pretty clothes. She had been saving up ever since she came to Denmark, wanting to go back to Afghanistan. There was nothing to go back to, she knew that now, and she knew she couldn't go back. This was her home; it had become her home. She had made friends, Afghan, Indian, and Danish; she had become someone here.

And what was there to go back to? Aamir was dead. She had always known, but she had hoped so desperately. Kabir had called his friends in Pakistan just a few days ago and confirmed that Aamir was dead. He had done that for her.

A small hand pulled at her *kameez* and she smiled when she saw it was Shahrukh, licking a lollipop. "Raihana Chachi," he said and then grinned. "Catch me," he cried out and ran from her. Raihana ran behind him. When she caught him he shrieked with laughter and then laughed even harder when she tickled him. His lollipop fell from his mouth, but he didn't care.

"Tickle me again, Raihana Chachi," he insisted, giggling.

Raihana was breathless with happiness as the vibrant body of a child wrapped up against hers, warming her all the way to her soul.

Right then, Raihana decided she would marry Rafeeq. He had proposed and she would say yes and she would have children, a family, and a life.

She hugged Shahrukh close to her as he caught his breath.

She kissed him on his hair and left Afghanistan behind.

SIXTEEN

23 JULY 1980

My daughter gave me this beautiful poem about bees by Emily Dickinson. She read it on a trip to Istanbul and she sent me a torn page from a book of poems, along with a postcard.

THERE IS A FLOWER THAT BEES PREFER

There is a flower that Bees prefer—
And Butterflies—desire—
To gain the Purple Democrat
The Humming Bird—aspire—

And Whatsoever Insect pass—
A Honey bear away

Proportioned to his several dearth
And her—capacity—

Her face be rounder than the Moon
And ruddier than the Gown
Or Orchis in the Pasture—
Or Rhododendron—worn—

She doth not wait for June—
Before the World be Green—
Her sturdy little Countenance
Against the Wind—be seen—

Contending with the Grass—
Near Kinsman to Herself—
For Privilege of Sod and Sun—
Sweet Litigants for Life—

And when the Hills be full—
And newer fashions blow—
Doth not retract a single spice
For pang of jealousy—

Her Public—be the Noon—
Her Providence—the Sun—
Her Progress—by the Bee—proclaimed—
In sovereign—Swerveless Tune—

The Bravest—of the Host—
Surrendering—the last—
Nor even of Defeat—aware—
What cancelled by the Frost—

Julie always came to Denmark for a week in July. Gunnar and Anna would rent a summer house and stay there for two to three weeks. With the bee season in full swing in the summer, it was hard to get away. So it was nice when Julie came to visit, because when she came, Lars, Maria, and the grandchildren came — and that one week in summer became a family affair with the kids running around the house and Lars and Julie arguing over everything under the sun.

Without Anna, Gunnar hadn't wanted to rent a summer house, but both Julie and Maria insisted. Lars didn't care one way or the other but his wife had convinced him that it would be good for Gunnar.

Julie flew to the Århus airport, which was an hour-and-a-half drive from Skive. Gunnar liked going to pick her up alone because then they got time together before Anna monopolized every conversation.

"So, I have a boyfriend . . . I'm telling you because it could be serious," Julie said as they drove out of Århus.

She was such a delight, his little girl, all grown up now. He remembered her blond pigtails and shining blue eyes. Now she was tall, almost as tall as Lars, who was six feet two inches. Julie complained it was hard to find men to date because of her height. "Men are intimidated by tall women. They want a petite woman, not a Viking," she would say to Anna, who would tell Julie she got Anna's grandmother's genes and she should be proud of them.

Julie had the prettiest face. Gunnar knew that he would think that even if Julie were not his daughter. Everyone said she was beautiful, that she could be a model with her looks and height. Julie sneered at the idea.

After studying journalism in Copenhagen she had taken a job with *Jyllands Posten* in London and then several years later she started working for *The Times*.

Gunnar was very proud of his daughter. "Learned English without any extra help and now she writes articles for newspapers in English in England," he told anyone who would listen.

Anna, of course, couldn't understand why Julie wouldn't live in

Denmark. "We want you to be close; you can come and visit us often, we can come and visit you," she would say and Julie would respond, "But that's what I want to avoid."

Gunnar didn't know why Anna and Julie had a tough time getting along. He and Lars got along just fine; hell, he and Maria got along better than Julie and Anna had.

"So how are things with your Afghan girl?" Julie asked as they neared Skive.

"Good," Gunnar said. "I invited her and the family she stays with to come to the summer house."

"Will they come?" Julie asked.

Gunnar remembered how Kabir had looked at him. "The man doesn't trust me. Not me specifically; he doesn't trust Danes."

"It happens," Julie said. "Refugees often feel resentful of their host country."

"Why? They get money, a place to stay, why should they be resentful?" Gunnar asked.

"Because we give it grudgingly," Julie said. "No one makes their life easy. They are shunted from refugee camps to asylum centers and then when they think, ah I'm out, we ask them to learn Danish before they can go and find a job. No, no, we say spend three years learning Danish and then after that you can start looking for a job."

"Learning Danish in Denmark is necessary," Gunnar said.

"Sure it is," Julie agreed. "But can't they learn the language as they work, make real money? An electrician, does he really need to know how to speak in Danish to fix wires? Does a construction worker?"

"Yes," Gunnar said. "How will they understand what needs to be done?"

Julie was flustered. "Well, yes, they need to learn some Danish; why do they need to be fluent?"

"I think it's important. For example, I don't want someone who doesn't speak Danish to work on the construction of my house," Gunnar said. "Danish is vital in Denmark, Julie. No way around that one."

"Oh like all the Poles we've been hiring to do odd jobs in Denmark speak fluent Danish," Julie said.

"Poland is part of the EU," Gunnar said and then added, "I wouldn't want the Poles to work on my house either."

Julie sighed. "But after they learn Danish do they really become Danish?"

Gunnar looked at her, puzzled.

"Do people accept a brown-skinned Muslim as Danish if he speaks fluent Danish?" she said.

"But they're not Danish," Gunnar said. "They're from wherever they are from."

"My point exactly, no matter what they do, they are never perceived as Danish," she said vehemently.

"How can you be so anti-Danish? Danes believe that immigrants should have a job when they live here, not live off welfare."

"Are you okay with a Dane living off welfare?"

Gunnar nodded. "Sure, he's a Dane, that's his right. But people who come from the outside have to find a job. That's why Christina sent Raihana to me, to learn something and get a job afterward."

Julie smiled. "And has working with you been a real job for her?"

"Yes, it has," Gunnar said. "She is competent with the bees. But she won't go out without protective gear."

"She's scared of getting stung?"

"Another two or three years and that fear will be gone," Gunnar said.

"Their summer house?" Kabir asked for the hundredth time.

"Yes," Layla snapped. "But like Raihana said it isn't theirs, they are renting it."

"You want us to go all the way to Vorupør? And what will we do there?" Kabir asked.

"We don't have to go," Raihana said wearily.

"I want to go and so should you. Once you finish school you will need a job. It is good to have Danish contacts," Layla said.

"And he said we all could come?" Kabir asked once more.

"Yes," Raihana said. "Look, they are nice people. They have children Shahrukh can play with."

Kabir shook his head again.

Layla glared at him. "Fine, we'll go alone. I'll ask Walid to drive us or maybe we can ask the Danish man to drive us."

"They don't want us there," Kabir said. "I can't see how this will be a good thing."

"If you don't try, what will you find out? Nothing," Layla said. "It will be good for Shahrukh. It's good for us to know some Danes."

"I don't know—," Kabir began.

"Okay, I will phone Walid and . . . ," Layla said.

Shahrukh came into the room looking at his parents with impish eyes. Raihana picked him up and took him into the dining room so that he didn't have to hear his parents arguing.

"*Sulten*," Shahrukh said to Raihana. He was hungry. He spoke more Danish than Dari. Poor Kabir!

"How about a banana?" Raihana asked in Dari, pointing to the banana in the fruit bowl on the table.

He nodded eagerly and Raihana peeled the banana and tore off half for him. He walked around the dining room and kitchen as he ate, peeking into the living room once in a while.

When Layla came into the dining room ten minutes later, the banana was all but a sticky memory on Shahrukh's hand and Raihana was wiping it with a wet cloth.

"I didn't mean for it to cause a fight," Raihana said.

Layla waved a hand. "He's just being pigheaded. We'll go; he said he'll drive us. He can get directions from the Internet for the address the Danish man . . . ah . . . Gunnar gave you."

Raihana smiled. "His daughter will be there. She lives in London; she's a journalist."

Layla nodded, impressed. "So she's a smart girl."

"I think so," Raihana said. "Gunnar is very proud of her."

"And how about the daughter-in-law; you think she'll like that we come there for a day?" Layla asked.

"That's her problem," Raihana said and kissed Shahrukh on the nose.

Kabir had finally agreed to visit with the Danish man and his family so that Layla would stop nagging. Allah, but that woman knew how to nag. At least there was peace in the house now after the fireworks in the afternoon.

"I spoke with Rafeeq on the telephone yesterday," he told Raihana after dinner as they sat to watch a new Hindi movie.

"He's very concerned about your accident," Kabir continued. "He worries about you going to Gunnar's house."

Raihana's resolve to accept Rafeeq's proposal weakened slightly. "Gunnar didn't throw the stone at me."

Kabir raised his hand. "He doesn't want you to stop working. He's just concerned. He even talked about you starting your own beekeeping business."

"Tasnim said the same thing," Layla said. "She said the Danish government gives loans."

"First become a citizen," Kabir said. "First pass *Prøve i Dansk 3* and then dream big dreams."

"She's learning so fast, she'll be speaking fluent Danish in another year," Layla said.

"Yes, it must be our good influence," Kabir said.

"Must be," Raihana said and laughed.

"So have you decided what to do about Rafeeq?" Layla asked.

"Yes," Raihana said. "It's yes."

"Well then," Kabir said, clapping his hands together. "What made you decide?"

"I don't know," Raihana said. "I see Shahrukh and I wish for my own children. I lost my baby and . . ."

Layla gasped. She had never heard about a baby. A dead husband, yes, but a dead baby? That was news. "When? When did you lose the baby? How old was the baby?"

"It wasn't born yet. It was all that traveling across the mountains, coming into Pakistan," Raihana said. "I saved my life from the Taliban but I couldn't save the baby."

Sensing the conversation was of a feminine nature, Kabir snuck out for a cigarette.

"How far along were you?" Layla asked.

"Four months," Raihana said. "Aamir was so scared. He kept saying what a bad world to bring a child into, so he sent me away first, so that I would be safe. He was going to come along as soon as he could. I wish I had stayed in Kabul. I wish I hadn't left him alone like that."

"And how would that have helped? They would still have killed him and you might have lost your life too," Layla said.

"And would that have been so bad?" Raihana asked.

"Yes," Layla said. "That would have been horrible. We would not have met. You would not have learned about beekeeping, seen a new country, eaten rye bread, married again, done so many things. Life is precious. Don't think it's nothing."

"I know," Raihana said. "But still, somewhere inside it seems pointless. People killing each other and just when you think you are safe . . ."

"Forget about those boys; the Danish man and the police will take care of them," Layla said. "You think about your future. You think about Rafeeq and getting married. How about this September?"

Layla was one of the bravest women Raihana knew. She so easily talked about the future, about moving on—and Layla of all people knew there was nothing easy about moving on. Layla had lost Shahrukh's older brother to a stray bullet in Afghanistan and that had convinced Kabir to leave Kabul. Layla had told Raihana about it just once when Raihana had first moved to Denmark.

Nothing could be worse than losing your child, yet Layla was a positive person who was forcing change on Kabir and making a dignified life for herself in a cold and white country. Layla didn't talk about going back like so many other Afghans. She didn't hate Danes or Denmark. She wanted to get to know Danes, even though she was not entirely comfortable with them. She wanted to have Danish friends, even though the other Afghans laughed at her because they couldn't imagine Danes interested in being friends with an Afghan.

"September sounds good," Raihana said and then because she knew Layla liked to talk about clothes, she added, "I saw this wedding dress at the bazaar, it was beautiful."

Layla started to list the best places to buy clothes and what jewelry Raihana could wear. And as they made their plans, the past shed away just a little more.

"That bitch," Anders said as he paced Karsten's room. Karsten's mother had gone to Århus and they were alone in the house. Not that it mattered when she was there. She sat in front of the TV with a beer and a cigarette and didn't care what Karsten did anyway.

"You should've slapped him back," Henrik said as he rolled a joint. "You should've slapped that son of a bitch cop in his face."

Anders stood uncomfortably. He wanted to be macho, like Karsten and Henrik. He wanted to talk to his parents the way they did. Karsten barely noticed his mother and when she said something to him he told her to shut up. He actually said, *"Hold kæft."* And the magic of it was, she did.

Henrik's father talked to them about Hitler and how Nazism was rising again. It was time, he would say, for the white people of the world to take back what was theirs. Henrik's mother sat in the kitchen cooking or was cleaning or doing the dishes. She was always doing things around the house.

Their parents were so cool while his had handed him over to the cops.

"What did you do when the cop called you in?" Anders asked Henrik.

"No one called me in," Henrik said, proudly lighting a joint. "No one calls Henrik in."

"How about you, Karsten?" Anders asked.

"Not me either," Karsten said.

"That bastard was lying then," Anders said bitterly.

"Man, your parents sold you to the devil," Karsten said, and then took a long drag from Henrik's joint. "They just hung you out to dry."

Anders plucked the joint from Karsten and took a drag himself. "Son of a bitch, I can't believe this. My parents betrayed me for that brown bitch."

"That's what they do, this filth that we let come into our country, they turn white man against white man," Karsten said. "That's how they beat us. We should stand united against them."

"We should do something," Anders said.

Karsten nodded. "Yeah, you have any ideas?"

"Does anyone know where that bitch lives?" Anders asked.

Henrik grinned. "No, but we can find out."

"I read something online that will be just perfect for this," Anders said.

He walked up to Karsten's computer and pulled up a website. The text was in English but the boys, raised on American movies with Danish subtitles, had no trouble understanding it.

SEVENTEEN

---

25 JULY 1980

I love heather honey! It has a unique and strong taste. Every year we rent a summer house for a week and find a nice place laden with heather to leave two of our colonies.

This year we rented a summer house right by the beach. Gunnar and I used to joke that when we made a lot of money from the selling honey we could buy our own summerhouse. Of course, we have always known that you don't keep bees to make money; you keep bees because you love it.

We took our colonies, picnic baskets, and the children to the west coast near a beach where we have been leaving our bees for two bee seasons now.

We place the colonies next to each other in a clearing amid the heather and watch them for a while. Julie reads a book while Lars goes to sleep.

The bees buzz around, landing on the heather. For me, these are the perfect moments.

To Kabir's chagrin even the weather was good on Saturday. The sun shone brightly, the sky was blue, and there was no wind. It was a beautiful summer day.

Layla was packing for a picnic, food in a wicker basket, tea in a thermos, packets of juice for Shahrukh, and blankets to sit on.

"They probably have something for us to eat," Kabir grunted when he saw the amount of food Layla was putting inside plastic containers. "And maybe they don't want to eat mutton *biriyani*."

"Then they don't have to," Layla said.

"Raihana got friendly and look what she got for her troubles," Kabir said.

Layla sighed. "Go out, do something, clean the car or whatever and stop picking a fight with me. Make sure Shahrukh puts on his new shoes."

"You want him to wear nice white shoes at the beach? They'll get ruined," Kabir said.

"I don't care," Layla said. "They're new and the best he has."

"I don't know who you're trying to impress," Kabir muttered as he walked out of the kitchen.

Layla was determined this was going to be a good day. She would make a Danish friend if it killed her. Her Danish was steadily improving. Her pronunciation was often terrible, but she was able to communicate. Her Danish wasn't as good as Kabir's, but it was good enough to apply for a job at the local kindergarten.

If Raihana could even think about starting her own business, Layla could at least make a Danish friend.

It was not an impressive summer house, Kabir said when they got there. Raihana and Layla thought it was very charming with its white fence and blooming flowers. The house was right by the beach and already Brian and Johanna were making a sand castle with a man Raihana had not seen before.

"Those are the kids," Raihana said. "And that man is probably the son, Lars."

Lars came up to them as they got out of the car, which Kabir parked behind Gunnar's in the driveway.

"*Go' morgen*," Lars said.

All three of them said "Good morning," and Shahrukh openly gazed up at their host.

"Do you want to make a sand castle?" he asked Shahrukh, bending down to the boy's height.

Shahrukh nodded and then looked at Layla for permission.

"He can't speak much," Layla said, suddenly uneasy. "He's only twenty-three months old."

"That's okay," Lars said. "We just want to get him dirty."

"We have plenty of clothes," Layla said nervously. She was frantic, unsure about her Danish, anxious that she was sounding like a fool.

Maria came out then with a very tall woman whom Raihana suspected was Gunnar's daughter.

"*Hej.*" Maria waved and came toward them. They all shook hands and introductions were made.

"I brought some food," Layla said.

"Afghan food?" Julie asked. "I love Indian and Pakistani food."

"Then you'll like Afghan food," Kabir said.

As they walked inside the house Maria leaned toward Raihana. "She wears a scarf," she whispered.

"She does," Raihana said.

"Why does she and not you?"

Raihana was learning that Danes looked at the *hijab* as a symbol of Islam and of oppression.

"She was raised that way," Raihana said.

"And you were not?" Maria asked.

"I was too . . . but I don't like *hijab*. I am not worried that my you can see my hair," Raihana said. "Would you like to try a *samboosa*? I made fresh in morning."

Lars was more comfortable with having Afghans in his company than Maria, and Gunnar was proud of his son's acceptance of Raihana and her family. He was also relieved that they had agreed to visit as he now had a chance to show Kabir that not all Danes were untrustworthy.

They started the day at the porch, drinking coffee and eating cookies, and then went for a stroll down to the beach. Lars and the children started making a sand castle, while the adults got their feet wet in the waters of the North Sea.

"We should drive down to where we left the colonies yesterday," Gunnar said when there was a lull in the conversation. "Have you seen bee colonies before?" he asked Kabir and Layla. They shook their heads.

"Oh, this is going to be quite an experience for you then," Gunnar said.

"My father thinks everyone is as obsessed with those bees as he is," Julie said drily and Kabir smiled for the first time.

Gunnar had to hand it to Maria. She was behaving herself. She had not said one untoward thing, even though he knew she was uneasy about this whole inviting-Afghans-to-the-summer-house nonsense, as she called it. Lars on the other hand didn't care about Shahrukh's skin color or that his parents were immigrants, and neither did his children.

Raihana hung close to the other Afghan woman. What was her name? Layla. If he was honest he would admit that these names were difficult for him. It had taken him awhile to get the hang of Raihana's name, and that boy's . . . he wasn't even going to try. It started with an S, and that was all he remembered.

"Shahrukh," Lars called out to the Afghan boy as they walked together to the beach. "Look, look, a seagull."

Kabir immediately sidled up to his son and said something in Dari.

It was obvious that the boy responded better to Danish than to Dari. When Julie had mentioned that, Layla had proudly said that it was the *vuggestue*, the day care's influence.

"The day care is almost next door, just a five-minute walk," Layla said. "And they're so careful about not giving him any pork, but accidents do happen. We don't care so much."

Her husband didn't seem that complacent. "No, no, they should be more careful, more thoughtful of our culture and traditions. Shahrukh is a Muslim and we don't eat pork."

Maria didn't agree. "But he lives here now, don't you think he should try to be more Danish?"

"My son isn't Danish, he'll never be Danish, no matter how good his Danish is and how much pork he learns to eat," Kabir said firmly.

"Your son is being raised here," Julie said. "Don't you think he's going to be more Danish than Afghan?"

"I don't think Danes will accept him as Danish," Kabir said softly. "I don't think they ever will."

"You're right, you're absolutely right. But an old country like Denmark can only change slowly," Julie said.

"Do you understand what everyone is saying?" Gunnar asked Raihana as they walked toward the bee colonies.

"Not so much at some times. Language school closed, so I not speak in Danish . . . so I forget, I think," Raihana said.

Gunnar had heard this from Christina, that her students went home on vacation and it took a few weeks for them to get used to Danish after they were back.

"But you come and take care of the bees and we'll speak in Danish. You won't forget then," Gunnar said.

"I don't know," she said in a small voice.

"Those boys will not hurt you," Gunnar promised.

"I know, I know," Raihana said, and turned to look at Layla speaking with Julie and Kabir holding his son's hand while Lars held the hands of Brian and Johanna in each of his own.

"Is everything okay?"

Raihana smiled at him uneasily. "I will marry," she said.

Gunnar was shocked but broke into a polite smile. "Congratulations! Congratulations!"

"*Tak*," Raihana said, blushing.

"Who is your future husband?" Gunnar asked.

"*Han hedder Rafeeq*," she said. "He works in a factory on Mors."

"When will you marry?"

"Rafeeq is in Pakistan now, when he come back we know when wedding," Raihana said. "Layla says September, but he will have to say final when."

Raihana and Gunnar went to work as they always did. Raihana put on Anna's protective suit, which Gunnar had brought along, this time with no comment from Maria, and helped Gunnar as he sorted through the colonies. For Raihana this was a special moment, when she could show Kabir and Layla what she had learned about bees.

Lars, who found bees truly uninteresting, took the kids to stroll farther down the beach to the water. Kabir didn't like the idea of Shahrukh going away with some strange white man, and he meant to follow, but Layla grasped his hand.

"It's okay, we can see him from here," she said.

As they moved box after box and added frames, checked on the brood, and stuck in queen bee excluders, Raihana explained to Layla and Kabir what she did.

"This"—Raihana held up the queen bee excluder—"makes sure that the queen bee stays in the bottom box so that we can get honey from the top box."

"What's wrong with the queen being in the top boxes?" Kabir asked.

"Then there will be brood in the top cells from where we'll get honey and that is not good," Raihana said. She wasn't sure why that was not good but she was not about to ask Gunnar and taint her know-it-all image. She would ask Gunnar the next time they were alone.

Raihana wished she didn't have to wear the protective suit, so that she could impress Layla and Kabir some more by being as confident as Gunnar, but she wasn't ready. This was her first bee season, maybe after she'd had five or six she'd be that confident.

She offered Layla and Kabir a taste of honey from a honeycomb as Gunnar had done for her. They both said it was the best honey they had tasted.

As all of them walked back to the summer house, Layla hugged Raihana close. "You know so much," she said. "I can't believe how much you have learned."

"I do know quite a lot about this, don't I?" she gushed.

"I am glad we came," Layla said to Raihana, swinging her slippers in one hand. They had all abandoned their shoes and were letting their feet curl into the warm sand. "They're good people," she added.

"You think Kabir is still angry?" Raihana asked.

"No, he is not. He thinks he should be, so he's pretending," Layla said.

Next year she would come here with Rafeeq, Raihana decided. Gunnar would invite her again, wouldn't he? And she would bring Rafeeq along.

Kabir had already told Rafeeq about Raihana's decision. September sounded promising to Rafeeq for the wedding. Rafeeq had spoken to Raihana as well. A short conversation in which Rafeeq asked if there was anything she would like and Raihana had asked him to bring back some good tea, which she missed. Raihana had felt an excitement before the call and after she was disappointed because it was a very short conversation.

Raihana wondered what Rafeeq would think of this outing. He worked in a factory with Danes, so obviously he must be comfortable with them. Would they have a nice house? A house of her own, she thought in excitement. She could have a garden and decorate as she wished.

How life had changed. Just a few years ago all she wanted out of life was to live. She and Aamir had lived in a shabby one-room apartment with bullet-ridden walls and sheets of plastic for windows. She was caked with dirt almost all the time, her body smelly, covered with a *burkha,* her belly empty, and her heart constantly drumming with fear.

Now she was eating good food, sitting outside a charming summer house imagining her future. Her past seemed like something on television, not real, someone else's life.

They ate lunch outside. Maria and Layla had spread out blankets on the grass for them. Lars seemed uncomfortable until Kabir picked up a beer from a bucket.

"You drink?" Lars asked surprised.

Kabir nodded. "I also smoke."

"That's not a good habit," Lars said.

"I know," Kabir replied. "But I can't quit."

"I used to smoke," Lars told him. "But haven't in ten years, not one cigarette."

Kabir started asking questions about how much Lars used to smoke, how he quit, and what he thought about those nicotine patches, did they really work?

Layla nudged Raihana. "See, he's already getting friendly," she whispered.

Maria did not eat any of the Afghan food, nor did Johanna, who made faces at all the dishes. She stuck with Danish rye bread with liverwurst and a cucumber on the side. Brian happily ate the *korma* and *pilau* his aunt fed him. Gunnar ate a little of everything, Raihana noticed. Julie, like her father, tried everything but seemed partial to Danish food.

Lars ignored the Danish food and ate the food Layla had brought. He took two helpings of the *korma* and *pilau,* one helping of the mutton *biriyani,* and two helpings of the rice pudding, *firni.* Layla was pleased at how much Lars seemed to like Afghan food and dug her elbow into Raihana's waist each time he took another helping.

"*Far* says you're getting married," Julie said to Raihana.

"Yes," Raihana said.

"Congratulations," she said and the others joined in.

"She's marrying a very good man," Kabir said. "He works for a factory on Mors."

"That's great," Lars said. "Why didn't you bring him along today?"

"He's in Pakistan on holiday," Layla said.

"He has family in Pakistan," Kabir added. "They left Kabul ten years ago."

"When did you come to Denmark?" Julie asked Kabir.

"Four years ago," Kabir said. "A few years after the Taliban came to power."

"What was it like with the Taliban?" Julie asked.

Silence fell outside the quaint summer house.

"It was hard," Kabir said.

"It was harder for the men than the women at times," Layla said. "I was already wearing a *burkha*, I was already at home . . . but Kabir had to work with them. He had a garage, he repaired cars, and he had to work on the cars of the Taliban."

Raihana knew talk of the Taliban made Kabir very uncomfortable.

"I'm sorry," Julie said. "We have reporters who have been to Afghanistan and they tell us horrible stories."

"It was a violent time," Kabir said slowly. "Violence everywhere. No safety, no peace. Only fear. People were taken away to prison, beaten, tortured, thrown back out, then taken back in. They were killed in the stadium, executed in front of everybody. Everyone's life was affected."

"I'm glad you got away," Lars said. "And I'm glad you're here to build a new life."

"Not everyone is," Kabir said wearily. "Not all Danes, but I am thankful that you are."

Silence fell again.

"Is there any more of that?" Brian asked Layla, pointing to the *firni*. "It tastes very good."

Conversation started to flow again.

The rest of the day slipped through their fingers like sand.

Raihana and her family stayed until dinner. They had eaten leftovers, with the little boy eating *fiskefrikadeller*, fish cakes, and drinking *safte-vand*, juice made with homemade strawberry concentrate. Maria was pleased that the Afghan boy was eating food she had cooked, consider-ing how Lars and Brian had betrayed her and eaten that spicy Afghan food.

Julie looked at her father with pride, as if he, single-handedly, had managed to bring together two cultures. Gunnar's only concern was Raihana's impending marriage. From tidbits he had picked up, the man she was marrying already had a wife and two children in Pak-istan. Raihana would be a second wife.

"They have second and third and fourth wives," Maria said. They sat on the patio with glasses of port and some chocolate Julie had brought. The sun was still bright, the day warm. Not all Danish sum-mers were good, most were cold and rainy, but this one was a summer that would be talked about for years to come.

Johanna and Brian had fallen asleep as soon as they started watch-ing television and were lying on pillows in the living room.

"All Muslim men don't have four wives," Julie retorted. "And this man's first wife isn't here."

"It's still sad that she has to be a second wife," Gunnar said.

"But he'll be her second husband too," Lars pointed out.

"Her first husband is dead," Maria said. "His first wife is still alive. What a strange culture."

"At least Muslims want their widows to get remarried; Hindus don't believe in that," Julie said. "It's changed now but in the good old days, Indian women died with their husbands."

"Totally barbaric," Maria said. "All that talk about the Taliban and what they did. I mean what kind of people do such things?"

"The same kind that followed Hitler," Julie said. "It isn't a cultural or national thing, Maria, people are good and bad, regardless of where they are from."

"I thought that Kabir seemed very solid, very capable," Lars said.

"You know, he's going to *handelsskole*. He has a high school degree from Afghanistan but they won't validate it here, so he has to go to school again. He's going to start his apprenticeship next year and has already lined one up with Grundfos in Bjerringbro."

Gunnar sipped his port. "Sounds like a decent man, working hard to make a living."

"It's nice to hear that this man wants to work and not take welfare money. Not all immigrants work, though," Maria said. "Do you know that half of all immigrants are on welfare?"

"And how do you know that?" Julie asked.

"I read it in *Jyllands Posten*," Maria said. It was Julie's former newspaper, one she had been proud to work for.

Julie leaned back on her chair and put her feet up on the white plastic garden table. "Statistics can be twisted any way you like. Why didn't they do a story on immigrants who are working, people like Kabir who work so hard?"

"That's up to you journalists, isn't it? What we, the poor public, should know or not know?" Maria said.

"Maybe I should write a story about Kabir and Raihana. What do you think, *Far*?" Julie said. "I'm sure I can sell it to *Jyllands Posten*, Allan is still there, he would buy it."

"A good project for your vacation here," Gunnar said, toasting her with his glass of port.

"Working during your holiday?" Lars teased. "Not much has changed, has it! You always found some work to do during holidays and you never spent any of the money you earned, always hoarded it."

"Well, you spent enough for both of us," Julie said in good humor.

Lars grinned. "So I did. I am glad you never kept track of all the money you loaned me. If I ever had to pay you back, I'd be broke."

"Who says I never kept track? I have a file with all the details on my computer," Julie said. "So, I hear your work is going very well."

"Yes it is," Lars said. He had recently become the deputy mayor of Odense, which was an administrative position, not a political one. "I have a very cushy job."

"Cushy?" Maria said reproachfully. "Working all the time. He comes home at eight at night some days. He has terrible work hours."

"Terrible but flexible work hours," Lars put in. "I can go in when I like and leave when I like. There's just been a lot of work lately with the whole H. C. Andersen anniversary, but the hours are getting better. I'm home by six most days."

"How about you, *Far*? You must be glad to be retired," Julie said.

"Your *mor* was," Gunnar said. "And so was I. But it's been tough without her." He looked around as if Anna would step out of the darkness and share a glass of port with them. "I really miss her."

"We all do," Julie said and put her hand on his.

"Until Raihana showed up I was drinking, sleeping, and watching some television in between drinking and sleeping," he said. "But then once she started coming . . . my bees would have died if it weren't for her."

"You sound lovesick, Gunnar," Maria said almost affectionately.

"Maria," Lars said in embarrassment.

"What?" Maria asked.

Gunnar laughed. "No, not lovesick, just fortunate to have found someone to help during a time when I had no idea how to get up in the morning and get on with my day. She gave me purpose. And I have taught her. She could work for a beekeeper once her Danish is good enough, or she could have her own colonies."

"You did a good thing here, *Far*," Julie said. "*Mor* would have been proud. If she were around, she would have helped Raihana . . . and you know what, Raihana's Danish would be far better than it is now. *Mor* would have made sure of that."

"Yes, yes," Gunnar said, smiling at the thought. "Anna was one hell of a teacher. She taught me everything I know . . . about almost everything in life."

What Raihana liked best about the Danish summer was how it was light almost until midnight. The sun stayed up and up and up and set so late and rose so early. When she had commented about it in class,

Christina had said that in Norway, there were places where the sun never set in the summer and never rose in the winter.

Raihana wanted to visit Norway. She wished she could go to these places and see how darkness engulfed the land or sunshine lit it all through the day, for months.

Shahrukh had fallen asleep in the backseat of the car and Layla was dozing in the front.

"So, was it too bad?" Raihana asked Kabir from the back.

"No, not at all. They are good people," Kabir said. "Lars seemed to be okay with all of us, like he really liked having us over. He works for the mayor's office in Odense. He has so much self-confidence, did you see?"

Raihana had been thrilled to see him eat the food she had cooked, and even more thrilled to see that little boy, Brian, eat *firni* like there was no tomorrow.

"I liked him very much," Kabir said. "Gunnar was very nice, very friendly. Good people."

"Yes, they are," Raihana said, giddy with relief.

When they got home, Layla and Shahrukh were still sleeping. "Why don't you take Shahrukh inside? I'll take Layla and go to the kiosk to buy some cigarettes," Kabir suggested.

He hadn't smoked the whole time they were at the summer house and Raihana knew he was itching to do so.

"Okay," she said and started to unstrap Shahrukh.

His head nestled on her left shoulder as she carried him to the front door. She heard Kabir reverse the car and drive away.

Raihana opened the door with her right hand and laid the house keys on the table Layla had set by the front door. She toed off her shoes so that she wouldn't make too much noise on the wooden stairs and wake up Shahrukh.

She was halfway inside when she saw the open window in the living room. Layla liked to keep the windows open in the summer and she had probably forgotten to shut this one before they had left in the morning. Raihana was thinking about closing the windows to keep the mosquitoes out when her eyes snapped wide open. The boy with no hair was standing outside on the street. He held a glass bottle in his hand, which looked bright with fire.

He was looking around stealthily. When he held up the bottle that was on fire and threw it inside the house, Raihana crushed Shahrukh to her chest and ran to get through the front door.

She didn't hear the crash the bottle made when it landed on the carpeted floor because Shahrukh cried out at the force with which she was holding him. She was outside the house, in the driveway, when she saw the fire blazing inside.

It wasn't until she saw Kabir and Layla running toward her that she started screaming. Her voice was caught in a high pitch, waking Shahrukh up fully and drawing the attention of almost everyone on the street.

EIGHTEEN

ENTRY FROM ANNA'S DIARY
A Year of Keeping Bees

1 AUGUST 1980

Today was a bad day! One of our colonies is anemic and the bees have deformed wings, two signs that varroa mites, which can devastate a colony, could be present.

We called our friend, Ole, a beekeeping expert, and he confirmed our fears. Varroa mites had taken residence in one our colonies. To get rid of varroa mites, we need to spray the frames with oils of wintergreen, thyme, eucalyptus, and rosemary—as we don't want to use any chemicals. We hope we will not lose our colony.

The fire was almost out before the fire truck arrived. A neighbor across the street was a fireman and he got everyone filling buckets of water and throwing them inside the house. The fireman used his long garden hose to douse the fire as well.

Raihana sat on the curb shaking. Layla sat next to her huddled with Shahrukh, who thought it was great fun that people were throwing water into their home. He wanted to be set free but Layla held him in a tight grasp.

Two of their neighbors had brought over water and juice but only Shahrukh drank. He was pointing to their house and saying, "*Ild, ild,*" fire, fire.

The police arrived soon after the fire truck. Helle, who lived across the street from Layla and Kabir, sat on the curb with Raihana and Layla, her arm around Raihana. She had seen a boy throw a bottle inside the house and the fire. She had called emergency services and alerted her husband, who was gardening in the backyard.

"It's a small fire, see how quickly it was put out," she said. "Don't worry, everything is fine. No one got hurt."

"But my son could have been," Layla said, breaking into tears. "Raihana, thank Allah you ran, thank Allah."

Raihana couldn't respond. Her hands were cold, her breath caught in her chest, and her heart was pounding. How could this have happened? How could it happen here? And what if she hadn't run? What if Shahrukh had gotten hurt?

A paramedic came and spoke with Kabir. He kneeled in front of Raihana. "Are you okay?" he asked.

When Raihana didn't respond, Helle helped her up. "Maybe we should go inside my house. Please, come in," she said to Layla.

Kabir nodded at Layla and walked over to the policeman, who was speaking to some of the neighbors.

Helle's house was just like theirs, only bigger. But there were no Afghan rugs or paintings; it was a Danish home, like Gunnar's. There were tea lamps everywhere and there were fresh flowers on the dining table. The paintings on the walls were Danish, of the west coast and Skagen. They had pictures of their children on the mantel over the open fireplace. They had carpets over the hardwood floors . . . Oh, Layla's mother's rug, Raihana thought sadly, it was right beneath the window—it must have burned.

And Kabir's new computer? Her heart twisted. He had saved and saved to buy it. He had been so excited about it and now it was gone. But what if she hadn't moved? What if she hadn't run? What if she had stayed in the living room with Shahrukh?

Shahrukh was aware that something was wrong but butter cookies and a huge box of LEGO toys took his mind off the fire in his house. Helle had two girls who played with Shahrukh even as they kept peering out of the window to see what was happening. The sirens had stopped, but the flashing lights were still on. The fire was completely out and smoke was rising up from the house.

Helle made tea and served it to Layla and Raihana as the paramedic checked first Shahrukh's vital signs and then Raihana's.

"Can you breathe?" the paramedic asked.

Raihana started to cry.

Layla put a hand on her shoulder. "No, she ran . . . ran with my son."

The paramedic nodded. "It's okay then. No one got hurt."

They kept saying that, Raihana thought. But what about the hurt inside her body? The pain of knowing that she was not going to be safe ever again, not here, not in Kabul, nowhere. What about that hurt?

A policeman came in with Kabir and Helle's husband. He sat across from Raihana and Layla and introduced himself. "I'm Inspector Vittrup."

"Coffee, Jon?" Helle asked, and he shook his head.

"You called us?" He looked at Helle.

Helle looked at her children before answering him. "Maj, Stine, take Shahrukh and go into your rooms."

"But *Mor*—" the older one began and then stopped short when her mother glared at her. They took Shahrukh to their room, promising him more toys.

Layla wanted to keep Shahrukh with her but she curbed the impulse. There were two little girls playing with her son; nothing bad was going to happen to him.

"It was a boy with his head shaved," Helle said. "He came with two others on bicycles; their heads were shaved too. I saw this one boy light something and I thought it was a cigarette. I was thinking that boys start young these days."

"Then what happened?" Jon asked.

Helle sighed. "I was cleaning the windows, Stine ate cake and put her fingers all over and . . . anyway, I saw one of the boys take a lit bottle and throw it inside the house. I knew it was a firebomb. I'm married to a fireman, I know that much. So I called 112."

Jon looked at Raihana. "Gunnar came to me when you got hurt last week. I spoke to all the boys, I warned them . . . I had hoped that was the end of it."

When Raihana didn't respond he continued, "Did you see anything?"

Raihana rubbed her face with both hands. "And now what? You will threaten again? And then what will they do? Shoot us? This is all my fault . . . my fault." She started to speak in Dari then. "These good people give me a home and what happens? Their home is burned down."

"No, it wasn't your fault," Kabir said in Danish. "You are not to blame. We don't blame you, do we, Layla?"

"Of course not," Layla said quickly. "You saved my boy."

"I put him in danger," Raihana continued in Dari. "I put all of you in danger. Maybe I should go back to Kabul . . . what would the difference be? Maybe it'll be better there. At least I'll expect the violence."

Jon looked at Helle. "A cup of coffee *will* help."

"Did you see anything?" he asked Raihana again.

"I saw the boy," she said to Layla in Dari. "I . . . I can't speak in Danish right now." Kabir translated what she said into Danish.

"Who was this boy? Have you seen him before?" Jon asked and took the coffee Helle had brought.

"It was the same boy who threw the stone at me," Raihana said to Kabir and then turned to Jon. "*Samme dreng. Jeg har set.*"

"This is very serious," Jon said gravely. "This time I will have to arrest them. If I show you pictures, could you pick out the one who threw the bottle?"

"*Jeg kan aldrig glemte hans ansigt,*" Raihana said to Jon. She would never forget that face. She had forgotten the faces of the people who had arrested Aamir. The people she had seen dead on the streets, the soldiers whom she feared, but this boy, she would always remember his face. He was the boy who had brought Kabul into Denmark.

"Good," Jon said. "Then we will arrange for you to see a lineup tomorrow."

Kabir was about to translate but Raihana spoke in Danish. "I understand," she told him.

"Where will you stay tonight?" Jon asked Kabir.

"At our home," Layla responded.

"There is a lot of damage," Jon said.

"It's our home, no one will scare us away," Layla said.

Jon arranged for Kabir and Raihana to visit the police station the next day. Raihana would identify the boy who had thrown the firebomb and give an official statement regarding what had happened.

Raihana wasn't sure if it would help. First they had been throwing stones, now they were throwing firebombs. The police in Denmark could do nothing to stop them—they didn't even want to. Who cared if a few Afghans got hurt or killed?

"It's my fault," Raihana said, crying again. "I'm so sorry for putting your son in danger."

"What is she saying?" Helle asked Layla.

"She blames herself," Layla said.

"Why?" Helle asked. "Bad people do bad things to good people. That is the law of nature, it isn't your fault."

.   .   .

Gunnar and Lars heard about the firebombing from a friend of a friend while they were in the summer house. They reached Kabir's house a few minutes after Jon left.

Lars was furious. "You should've had him arrested when he threw that damn stone," he said.

Gunnar nodded. This was his fault, he thought. He was pretending to be a hero by inviting Raihana and her family to his home, but had done nothing to keep Raihana safe from those boys. He should have let Kabir file a complaint. A real complaint would have meant a real punishment for those boys and then this wouldn't have happened.

Lars and Kabir walked through Kabir and Layla's house and Gunnar invited them to stay at his house for as long as it took to fix the damage. But Layla was adamant. This was their home and they would not be pushed out because of some crazy teenagers.

Gunnar admired their courage and their conviction and had to agree that the damage was only downstairs; their bedrooms were untouched.

She and Layla were standing in the damaged living room. Shahrukh was still in Helle's house at her insistence. "Just let him stay here. We'll feed him and put him to sleep; you can take him when you're settled," Helle had told them.

Raihana was trying not to panic at how much work they'd have to do fix the place up.

"We'll take care of this," Gunnar said to Raihana.

How was he going to do that, Raihana wondered.

"I'm not coming back for the bees," she told Gunnar. "Thank you for your help, but I can't come back."

Gunnar knew it was futile to speak with her now. She had just been through a shock; she needed time to process the incident and find her way. But he promised himself that he would make this right, somehow.

.   .   .

Kabir closed the window through which the firebomb had been thrown. It was amazingly untouched. There were some burn marks on the windowpanes and the wood and it didn't close as tightly as it did before, but it did close.

Layla's mother's carpet was nothing but sodden burned cloth and Kabir's computer, a dark shell of what it used to be. The sofa was completely soaked but only a little burned on the arms. Layla thought it could be salvaged; Raihana was doubtful. The desk on which the computer sat was ruined as was the chair that went with it. But the worst was the floor. The carpet was burned and so had the wood beneath.

It was almost two in the morning when they got to bed. Shahrukh had fallen asleep in Helle's house and Layla and Kabir carried him into their own bed.

Raihana couldn't sleep. She paced her room and her mind wandered. She had to move out of Kabir and Layla's house, no discussion there. And she had to stop working for Gunnar, no discussion there either. She would ask Christina what women like her did. Was there someplace for women like her, who had nowhere else to go? She stopped to think about Rafeeq . . . what about him? She couldn't think about that right now. When he came back from Pakistan, then she would think about him.

She had no illusions that those boys would be arrested. Danes would not arrest Danes for hurting immigrants. She could simply not see it happening.

Raihana was going downstairs to get water and see the living room again when she overheard Kabir and Layla.

"Will we have to pay for all the repairs?" Layla was asking.

"Yes, we don't have renter's insurance, remember, it was too expensive," Kabir said. "The owner will want the room repaired. The walls have to be painted and there is all that water damage."

"We have some money, the house money," Layla said. They had been saving up to buy their own house; they would soon have enough for a down payment.

"We can buy a house later," Kabir said.

"You're right . . ." Layla trailed off. Then Shahrukh started to cry and they stopped talking.

If guilt was already making Raihana's stomach churn this conversation made her feel worse. Why did she have to be so stubborn and keep going to work with those bees? Why? If she hadn't gone to the bees, the boys would never have seen her, they would have left her alone.

She sat in her room up in the attic and finally fell asleep a few hours later, convinced she had to leave Kabir and Layla's house as soon as possible.

Raihana was shown six pictures in the policeman's office. She easily picked the boy whom she had seen outside the window. She told Jon Vittrup that she knew his face, had seen it before when he had thrown a stone at her.

Jon slid two more sets of pictures and she picked out the other two boys who had been there when the first boy threw the stone. She had not seen them by Layla and Kabir's house, though, and she said as much to the policeman.

"They were all arrested last night," Jon said. "Your neighbor, Helle, she also identified all three, including the one who threw the fire-bomb into your house."

Raihana understood bits and pieces of what the policeman said. Her nerves had started to fray almost as soon as they arrived at the police station. And she when she was under stress Danish was harder for her.

"What happens now?" Kabir asked.

"The other two boys probably won't go to jail for too long, if at all," Jon said. "But the boy who threw the firebomb will get four to six years. Of course, if he knew that someone was inside the house when he threw the bomb in, then it becomes eight to ten years."

"I don't know if he saw me or not. When I looked at him he was looking around, not looking inside the house," she told Kabir in Dari.

Kabir translated for Jon.

"The boy says he didn't know you were inside the house," Jon said. "He says he saw the car drive up and leave; that's why he threw the bomb then."

"What do you think? Did they know she was inside with my son?" Kabir asked Jon.

"I don't think he has the guts to kill someone, but I think he's stupid enough and malicious enough to want to damage your house," Jon said.

"What happens now?" Raihana asked.

"There'll be a trial. You'll be called in to tell the court what happened. Don't worry, there will be a translator and you can testify in Dari if you like," Jon said when he saw the panic in Raihana's eyes.

"By the time you have a trial, her Danish will be better," Kabir said confidently. "How long will it take, a year or so?"

"I expect we'll get a court date within a month at the latest."

"Court? Will they say it my fault?" Raihana asked.

"How is it your fault?" Jon asked, confused.

"I work with bees, with Gunnar, that wrong people think . . . court also think that wrong and . . ."

"No matter what you do, Raihana, no one has the right to hurt you," Jon said.

As they drove back, Kabir seemed pleased with the meeting at the police station. "That was a good policeman," he said. "In the past few days I have met many good Danes."

"And some bad ones tried to burn your house down," Raihana said.

"Yes," Kabir agreed. "But no one thinks it's okay for them to do that. All the Danes I have spoken to say it was wrong. That makes me happy. It makes me feel safe."

"I don't know when I will start feeling safe again in this country," Raihana said bitterly.

"It will happen slowly," Kabir said. "After nothing bad happens for a while you'll stop feeling afraid."

"I know this is going to cost you a lot of money," Raihana said. "I have some saved up and . . . don't say no, Kabir, that money is yours to fix the house."

"I wasn't going to say no," Kabir said. "We need the money. But it'll be a loan. Once I have a job we'll pay you back . . . and you don't say no to that."

When they got back Layla was standing outside their house on the street, talking with Helle. Two trucks were parked outside the house and workmen were going in and out.

The burned computer, the sofa, and almost everything from the living room was in the driveway. Kabir parked behind one of the trucks, then he and Raihana walked up to Layla.

"They showed up right after you left," Layla said, half laughing, half crying. "They just came, seven or eight of them, and started to move things out. Told me I shouldn't clean and one of them asked me to get out."

"But what are they doing?" Raihana asked.

Kabir started toward the house. He smiled when he understood what was going on.

Gunnar peered out of the window through which the boy had thrown the firebomb and waved at Raihana.

"What is he doing here?" Raihana asked.

Helle smiled. "Gunnar, Lars, and their friends are fixing your house. Gunnar used to teach carpentry at the technical school—he's a really good carpenter."

Gunnar's friends, like him, were in their sixties. A raucous bunch, they talked loudly and drank beer while they cleaned up the debris and laid down a new wall-to-wall carpet in the living room.

"We thought we'd help," Gunnar said and when Raihana was about to say something, he added, "We'd do it for any friend."

"What are you standing there for? Come here and hold this," one silver-haired man called out to Kabir. He handed him a hammer.

Kabir took the hammer and stared at it. "We're building a new desk for your new computer. The computer won't come until next week."

"At least Mogens shelled out the money," Lars said. "Come on, Kabir, get to work. Maria and Julie are going to show up with lunch. God knows what crap they'll bring."

"Your wife shouldn't be allowed to cook," another man said.

"You shouldn't talk," Lars said and whispered to Kabir, "His wife makes bread you can play football with."

Raihana and Layla slipped their arms through each other's. "You have good friends," Helle said to Raihana and Layla.

"Yes, yes we do," Raihana said.

EPILOGUE

21 SEPTEMBER 1980

The bee season is almost over. We will be harvesting heather honey soon and after that it's time to put the bees away. There are so many things to do to prepare for winter. This is the part that inspires me least but it needs to be done because we want our bees to come out of winter alive and healthy.

We check to make sure there is a queen in each colony, painted in the right color. We make sure there are enough frames in all the boxes. We check on the brood and the larvae. We make sure the hives have enough food for the winter and start feeding the bees thick sugar syrup.

The hives must be properly ventilated and if there are any cracks they must be sealed with propolis. Mouseproofing is very important and not fool-proof but we do it every year.

And as I watch the skies get dark more quickly with every passing day and feel the chill in the air, I feel a pang that it all ends so soon.

Next bee season we will have ten colonies. We plan to buy four or five to add the four or five we have now, depending upon how the winter goes. Gunnar worries that ten colonies might be too much but I know it will work out fine. There will be five colonies for Gunnar and five for me. It is going to be a great bee season. I can just feel it.

People stared at him and his family, Gunnar knew, but he ignored the stares.

He fidgeted with his tie again. Maria was very uncomfortable in her black knee-length dress and had asked Lars at least five times if they could go back to Gunnar's house so she could change into something more appropriate. Lars said that she looked beautiful and she shouldn't worry about the dress.

Julie was surprisingly comfortable in the traditional Afghan clothes Layla had loaned her. The *salwar-kameez*, a kind of pantsuit, was pink and golden and the silk scarf was printed with the same pattern as the dress. Layla draped the scarf around Julie's head, holding it in place with hairpins.

This was the strangest and most interesting wedding Gunnar had ever been to. The ceremony was rich with color, food, drink, and music.

The official part of the wedding had taken place in city hall the day before, with Gunnar and Kabir as witnesses. Gunnar had been honored when Raihana asked him to be a witness.

"Are you okay with being his second wife?" Gunnar asked her.

"He'll be my second husband," Raihana had said. "And his wife lives in Pakistan. She isn't really part of his life."

He wasn't sure if Rafeeq was a good man or even the right man.

Anna would have had a wonderful time at this wedding, he thought as he looked around the room.

"How is Raihana's Danish?" Gunnar asked Christina.

"It slipped a little in the summer, but it always does," Christina said. "Raihana's one of the fastest in her group. She'll be finished with language school by next December."

"Good, good," Gunnar said. "But what do you think about her husband having two wives?"

"Many Muslim men have two wives," Christina said. "We can't judge them by our cultural standards."

"I know," Gunnar said, but he couldn't help feel it was strange to be married to two women at the same time. Raihana obviously didn't seem to care that he had a wife and two children in Pakistan.

"She looks beautiful, different, and so settled . . . I'm so happy to see her get married," Christina said watching Raihana sit in her green dress next to her husband.

"And I'm glad you brought her to my house," Gunnar said, thanking Christina for the first time.

Kabir was hovering around, as was Layla, making sure everyone was being taken care of. Rafeeq had no family in Denmark so Kabir and Layla acted as the relatives for both the bride and the groom. A few of Rafeeq's friends were helping with the food and the drinks, ensuring the guests were comfortable.

"Hello, Gunnar," Walid said. Gunnar had met Walid when they worked on fixing up Gunnar's house.

Within just two days, the house was in better shape than before the fire and water damage. Layla's mother's rug had been irreplaceable but one of Lars's friends had a contact in Århus who had found an Afghan rug. It was a different color, a different size, and a different design, but it was from Afghanistan and Layla had seemed happy enough to get it.

Walid had just gotten Danish citizenship and was planning on getting a loan to open an ethnic store in Skive, he told Gunnar at the wedding. He said it would do well because the Afghans and Pakistanis he knew had to go to Randers or Fredericia to buy spices, clothes, magazines, movies, and other ethnic wares. He would not be short of customers.

Gunnar knew nothing about retail so he listened to Walid speak in his imperfect Danish. Walid might have passed the exams at language school, but his Danish was so accented Gunnar sometimes had to guess what he was saying.

The food was wonderful, Gunnar and Lars agreed, though Maria had a tough time eating. Brian cleaned his plate and asked for more, just like he had at the beach.

For a wedding gift, Gunnar gave Raihana five colonies of bees, the ones she had taken care of, the ones that had belonged to Anna. Her husband hadn't objected and Gunnar hoped that meant that Raihana would actually be able to start her own business. Since she would not live in Skive, she would have to take the bus to the language school. To make it easier for Raihana, Gunnar had found a beekeeper on Mors who would continue her *praktik*.

The music at the wedding was fairly jarring, very different from what Danes were used to, but some of the melodies were quite catchy. Gunnar felt like a foreigner in his own country. He was the odd one here, he and his family. The Afghans had carved a piece of Afghanistan in Denmark. Julie said there was a group of Danes in London that did the same. They got together and ate Danish food, drank Danish beer and liquor, and talked in Danish. Maybe when you were an immigrant you gathered people from your own country close to feel like you were at home.

These immigrants, most of them refugees, hadn't had a choice about living in a foreign country. So many of them had run for their lives. Raihana definitely had. Her husband had been killed. If she had stayed, she would have died too.

For a moment, Gunnar mourned the other Raihanas who had not been able to get out of Afghanistan, who had died without getting a chance to live a normal life. But this Raihana, she had done well, and he was proud to know her.

"They are all looking at us," Maria said to Gunnar.

"No," Gunnar said, though Maria was right, most of the Afghans were surprised that so many Danes had come for this wedding. They were welcomed by most, shyly and sometimes with a little suspicion, but Raihana had promised Gunnar that everyone would treat them with respect.

"They all know how you fixed up Kabir's house and bought him a new computer," she said.

"I didn't buy the computer. Mogens and Marianne did," he told her.

"You made it happen. I know. I just know," Raihana said.

Gunnar shrugged. He had gotten his friends from the carpentry school together and told Mogens what he needed to do to make things up, in monetary terms, but they had all pitched in of their own free will.

"Admit it," Julie said to Maria as they prepared to leave late in the night. "You had a good time."

Maria laughed. "It was quite an experience; something to talk about at my book club next week."

"The food was great," Lars said, patting his belly.

"Can you think beyond food?" Julie asked.

"Sure, I can, I thought that *sherbet* thing was great too . . . too bad they don't serve alcohol; a beer would have really worked well with all that spicy food," Lars said.

"*Bedstefar*, why was this wedding not in a church? When Tina got married, she got married in a church," Brian wanted to know.

"Let's get into the car and I'll tell you why Raihana didn't get married in a church," Gunnar said.

He waved to Raihana as they all left and she held her hand up and waved back. They were meeting the next week at his friend's apiary on Mors. There was to be no honeymoon, but she and her husband would go to Pakistan next summer. Raihana had said she was looking forward to meeting her husband's family.

"Thank you for coming," Kabir said as he shook hands with everyone. "It means a lot to all of us that you came."

"It means a lot to us that we were invited," Gunnar said and Kabir flushed with embarrassment.

They got into Lars's car, saying *farvel*, good-bye, and *vi ses*, see you again.

Kabir stood in the lit doorway of the *forsamlinghus* until Lars's car disappeared into the night.

ACKNOWLEDGMENTS
AND AUTHOR'S NOTE

This is my first book that isn't about Indians and/or India. It's about an Afghan refugee and a Danish beekeeper and their unusual friendship. Since I'm not a Dane, an Afghan, or a beekeeper, I needed the help of many people to research and write this book.

Abdullah and Shaima Saghar made this book come alive and I couldn't have written it without their help. They opened their hearts and their home to me, answered my persistent questions, and shared Hindi movies with me.

Flemming and Dorthe Vejsnæs taught me almost everything I know about beekeeping. They never hung up on me even though I called very frequently, answered all my questions, and keep us well supplied with honey.

Linda Mølgaard, the finest Danish-language teacher I have ever had, shared her experiences with me and offered me a glimpse into the life of a teacher who has to be intensely sensitive to the circumstances of her students. I wish I had found her earlier because my Danish would be a lot better.

Masha Hamilton, an excellent writer and reporter, told me what she saw in Afghanistan. I thank her for the story about the nail paint; I couldn't use it but it still warms my heart. Another excellent journalist, Eva Arnvig, read my manuscript in record time and shared her intimate knowledge of Afghanistan (and Denmark).

Politiassistant Martin Bjørnskov Jensen helped me understand the Danish law-and-order system and answered several questions that began with "What happens when . . ."

Two books and one blog helped me with my book: A *Book of Bees* by Sue Hubbell, *Letters from the Hive: An Intimate History of Bees, Honey, and Humankind* by Stephen Buchmann, and the blog "Diary of a Bee Keeper" by Oriondog from Western Massachusetts.

There are, of course, the usual suspects: my editors, Allison Dickens and Anika Streitfeld, who kept me on the straight and narrow; my agent, Matt Bialer, whose faith in me keeps me going; my husband, Søren Rasmussen, without whom not much writing would take place; my children, Isaiah and Tobias, who bring great joy to my life; and last but not least, my mother, Lakshmi Malladi, who listens to me complain (many, many, many times) and is always supportive.

If there are any factual errors in this book, I take full responsibility. I apologize and promise to do better next time.

Happy reading!

Amulya Malladi
14 June 2007

THE SOUND OF
LANGUAGE

AMULYA MALLADI

a reader's guide

A CONVERSATION WITH
AMULYA MALLADI

I moved to Denmark from the United States in 2002 and was immediately struck by how refugees and immigrants in general are treated
in this country. We moved to Denmark in large part because my
husband is Danish and we wanted our boys to get a dose of Europe.
Since I had already been an immigrant in the United States, I didn't
think Denmark would be much different; needless to say, I was
wrong.

The Sound of Language almost didn't get written. I had this idea
about writing a story about the friendship between an Afghan
refugee and an old Danish beekeeper—but I didn't know where to
start. One Christmas, while I was doing the dishes with Dorthe
Vejsnæs (my husband's aunt), I told her my idea about this story.
She suggested I speak with her husband, Flemming, a beekeeping
expert. Flemming was kind enough to help me with my story by
telling me stories about beekeepers and beekeeping. We recently
spoke about the origins of the novel.

Flemming Vejsnæs: Why did you choose the title *The Sound of Language*?

Amulya Malladi: Well, when I first came to Denmark, Danish sounded like the buzzing of bees. I never ever thought I'd learn the language. And that's when I first started to think about the sound each language has and when I thought about an Afghan refugee in Denmark, I was sure she'd also think about the buzzing of bees when she heard Danish. The title of the book was pretty obvious; I always thought of this story as *The Sound of Language*.

FV: You wrote this story during a very turbulent period. 9/11 certainly changed the world, but the small kingdom of Denmark came into focus because of the Mohammed cartoons that a Danish newspaper, *Jyllands Posten*, published in September 2005. Did this unpleasant situation influence your book?

AM: I can't say it did. The controversy went into full swing in January 2006 with people burning down Danish (and sometimes even Swedish) embassies in Middle Eastern countries. The base of the book was already in place and the timeline wouldn't allow me to mention these incidents in the book. But it would have been interesting to see how Layla, Raihana, and Kabir reacted to the Mohammed cartoons. Would they have been offended? Or would they have been like many other moderate Muslims in Denmark who thought that *Jyllands Posten*'s bad taste didn't mean that there should be death threats against Danes and Denmark.

FV: You came from an enormous country—the United States—to a small country, Denmark. Now you have been here for almost five years. What is your opinion about Denmark?

AM: That is a loaded question coming from a Dane and I really want to be able to say that Denmark is wonderful—but that wouldn't be the truth. To be honest, I miss the United States very, very much. I miss the friendly people, I miss the wide-open spaces, I miss the online shopping, the excellent customer service, Barnes & Noble with Starbucks, Denny's for breakfast. . . .

What's interesting is that I rarely meet immigrants who say they love living in Denmark. It's a difficult country to immigrate to and I can only imagine how hard it is for people who don't have my advantages—who are not educated and don't have the familial support system I do.

The hardest part about living in Denmark is that as an immigrant you are expected to leave where you come from behind, completely, and become Danish. But there are good things about Denmark too. My husband and I love the Danish kindergarten and day-care system. First, it's top-notch child care; second, it's subsidized, so you can actually afford it. The companies in Denmark don't expect you to work insane hours, and coming from Silicon Valley, that was a surprise. Companies constantly talk about reducing work pressure, and don't expect employees to work long hours or on weekends—they want you to go home and be with your family.

AND—and this is a big *and*—we get thirty vacation days a year. The first year we had this luxury, my husband and I couldn't quite figure out what to do. We'd never taken three weeks vacation in a row and we had to actually work at finding out what kind of vacation we liked to go on.

FV: In the book you describe the horrors Raihana goes through before coming to Denmark and I believe that her story is true. Are the stories you tell about refugees in these books real?

AM: The stories are not real in their entirety. I did speak to refugees and I also read a lot of refugee reports online. So I mixed and matched, I think, to come up with Raihana, Layla, and Kabir's stories.

FV: Layla, Kabir's wife, says, "We are here, Raihana, and we live here. If you keep one foot in Afghanistan, you will be neither here nor there." She is right, but it seems like a very difficult situation. Do you think a lot of refugees feel this way?

AM: The refugees I spoke with all said that they wanted to go home. One man said to me, "You always want to go home. That's how it is. I'm sure you want to go home too." I realized then that I was different because I left my country by choice and I could always go back, so I didn't have this burning desire to go back. I wondered if it would be different if I'd had to run for my life away from my country. I think it would be.

FV: One of the main themes in your book is language barriers. Confusion and misunderstandings are the results. Why is language so important?

AM: When I was young I read a *Reader's Digest* story about a couple living on a boat. They spoke different languages and had been together for nearly fifteen years. They had showed up in front of a judge, asking for a divorce. I don't remember the rest of the story, but the idea of people being unable to communicate and still having a relationship really stuck to me.

I still think it's interesting that people get together even though they can't communicate very well. When my husband and I first started dating, we'd end up getting into fights because I thought he was rude. Danes are in general a little sarcastic and straightforward, which translates into English as being rude. We had to learn to talk to each other without hurting my finer feelings—we've been together now for nearly twelve years, so I guess we figured the language part out.

For Gunnar and Raihana, the communication gap is more extreme.

FV: I am a beekeeper, so a novel about beekeeping makes me very happy. I read Anna's diary with pleasure. The book actually offers lessons on beekeeping. But why beekeeping?

AM: Since the language sounded to me like the buzzing of bees, I had decided that Gunnar would be a beekeeper. It was a great help that you are a beekeeping expert; otherwise, getting information would have been very difficult.

FV: When you first told me about this idea I told you about a couple similar to Anna and Gunnar. But that woman is fortunately alive. You describe them perfectly. The man you based Gunnar on is also a skilled carpenter and the couple is passionate about beekeeping. Just like in the book, the husband loves his wife, who's smarter than he is, which also annoys him. For me these characters are very real; and their story is beautiful.

AM: Thanks, Flemming. I was quite enchanted by this couple that loved beekeeping—and it fit perfectly with who I wanted my characters to be. I already knew who Gunnar was, but your story about this beekeeping couple helped me flesh out Anna's character.

FV: Does Raihana save Gunnar from becoming an alcoholic or does Gunnar save Raihana from being caught up in her past?

AM: I think they both help each other. Raihana gives Gunnar a purpose to live because she needs him. Gunnar gives Raihana a future by teaching her a skill that could help her financially in the future. They also became friends—which is precious to both of them.

FV: Is the relationship between Gunnar and Raihana realistic or do you use it to provoke the reader?

AM: I think it is realistic. Someone like my father-in-law, Ejgil, would happily become friends with an Afghan woman without thinking anything of it. Do you think this is a provocative book? How do you feel about how immigrants are treated in Denmark?

FV: I think this is a provocative book and it brings to light an important point, as Christina, the Danish teacher, says, that the homogenous Danish society needs different skills, cultures, and perspective to grow. I think someone like Christina, who is committed to her job, will bring change and that people like Maria will realize that immigrants are just like regular Danes in what they want out of life.

But I do have a problem with one thing in the book. People like Anders and his friends are a minority; why did you feel they needed to be in your story?

AM: I meet many young people who say things like, "I'm afraid of colored men." Racism is rampant among Danish youth and I'm not sure that boys like Anders and his friends are going to remain a minority in the not-so-distant future.

I think we need to be careful about what we say to our children and how we speak with them. The other day I was in my son's kindergarten and this little girl came and asked me, "Where do you come from?" I said that I came from home and asked her where she came from. She said she comes from "Danish land" and that I did not. It freaked me out. She was all of five. I thought, where is she picking this stuff up and what's she going to be like when she grows up?

Just a couple of years ago, seven neo-Nazi teenagers attacked a Somali family in the town of Langeskove on the island of Fyn. The family was in the house when the young men started to break the windows with bats. The family had to run with their children to a neighbor's house to avoid getting beaten up. This attack caused quite an outrage in Langeskove. I modified this incident and used it in the book.

FV: Amulya, I think this is a very good and timely book. It's interesting for me as a Dane to read about an immigrant's point of view of what's happening in Denmark.

AM: Thanks, Flemming, for all your help and support; and of course, the honey.

READING GROUP
QUESTIONS AND TOPICS
FOR DISCUSSION

1. What is the significance of the title *The Sound of Language*? How does it relate to bees?

2. Is the racism in the novel worse than the racism you see or hear about elsewhere?

3. Do you know any refugees? How are refugees treated in your country? Did the novel affect your sense of the refugee experience?

4. Gunnar is a retired widower who is set in his ways, yet he makes room for Raihana in his life. How does Raihana fit into Gunnar's life?

5. How would you characterize the reactions of Gunnar's friends and family toward Raihana and the reaction of the Afghan community toward Raihana's unusual *praktik*?

6. Anna's beekeeping diary opens each chapter. How do these entries enhance the story? What struck you most about the beekeeping practices she outlines?

7. The story takes place in a small town in Denmark. Did the setting remind you of anywhere in America?

8. Why do you think Raihana holds on to the hope that her husband is alive? What allows her to let this go? Do you think she makes the right choice?

9. The incident of the firebomb is based on a real attack against an immigrant family in Denmark. Can you understand the motives of the boys who firebomb Layla and Kabir's house? How would your community react to racial violence such as this?

10. Since 9/11, discrimination against Muslims has been increasing. In Europe, several countries are even considering banning the scarf and the *burkha*. What do you think about this development?

11. Honey plays an important part in the book and is almost a character by itself. Did the book inspire you to try different types of honey? Discuss various ways that you have eaten honey and the recipes you use it in.

12. What do you think of the way Denmark is depicted in the novel? Is this how you perceived Denmark to be? Did anything surprise you?

13. Did you think Gunnar and Raihana would become romantically involved? Would that have been a good or a bad thing?

AMULYA MALLADI was born and raised in India. She lived in the United States for several years before moving to Denmark. She now lives in Copenhagen with her husband and two sons. You can contact her at www.amulyamalladi.com.